Joe Perrone Jr. -

OTHER TITLES BY JOE PERRONE JR.

Fiction

ESCAPING INNOCENCE *(A Story of Awakening)* – A humorous look at coming of age in the tumultuous '60s, the era of "sex, drugs, and rock 'n' roll" – Hilarious!
(Regular & large print paperback, Kindle Books)

Non-Fiction

A "REAL" MAN'S GUIDE TO DIVORCE *(First, you bend over and...)* – A hysterically funny look at matrimonial division from a decidedly male point of view. Chock full of good, sound advice and more than a few laughs – A must read for every man!
(Regular print paperback, Kindle Books)

GONE FISHIN' WITH KIDS *(How to Take Your Kid Fishing and Still be Friends)* **by Joe Perrone Jr., and Manny Luftglass**
(Regular paperback)

Watch for Joe Perrone Jr.'s new novel, OPENING DAY, the second in the Matt Davis Mystery Series, coming in 2010.

As the Twig is Bent

Joe Perrone Jr.

As the Twig is Bent

By Joe Perrone Jr.

© 2008 Joseph Perrone Jr.

ALL RIGHTS RESERVED

ISBN 144049634X
EAN-139781440496349

FIRST EDITION

This is a work of fiction. Names, characters, places, and incidents either are the product of the author's imagination or are used fictitiously, and any resemblance to actual persons, living or dead, business establishments, events, or locales is entirely coincidental.

WARNING: This book contains explicit sexual content that may be inappropriate for some readers.

DEDICATION

This book is dedicated to my dear wife, Becky. Without her inspiration, everlasting patience, mammoth understanding, and undying love, it is doubtful that it ever would have been completed. This is for you, my love.

CHAPTER 1

7:48 p.m., Thursday, March 16

Wriggling impatiently in his narrow tourist class seat, George Spiros gripped the armrest fearfully and fought against an almost overpowering impulse to scream. The huge DC10 airliner was being buffeted wildly about, as if it were nothing more than a leaf in the wind. Below the plane, bright electrical flashes exploded spectacularly. An enormous line of thunderclouds had spread its ugly tentacles over the entire eastern seaboard. Consequently, the American Airlines flight had been diverted from its direct route from Los Angeles's LAX Airport to New York's JFK Airport along a more northerly path. The captain had announced that they would be coming in over Jamestown, then into the sprawling New York City airport. Despite the change of route, the airliner had still caught the edge of the storm.

The forty-seven-year old Greek immigrant had a deathly fear of flying, and the storm had come as a disconcerting addition to an already unpleasant trip. Lately, these sales trips had become a necessary part of life. He owned a small wrought-iron furniture-manufacturing firm, and as such, wore many hats. He not only designed and supervised the construction of the furniture, but was also the company's sole representative. The sales trips, though irksome, were the price he had to pay for the gains he hoped to make.

The West Coast trip had been a huge success, and he couldn't wait to get home and tell Melina the good news. A large, upscale furniture chain, with stores in Beverly Hills, San Francisco, and Palm Springs, had committed to a generous order, one that would keep the little Queens shop active for the foreseeable future. Of course, he would still have to make the usual monthly car trips to the neighboring New England states to insure that his regular business continued uninterrupted.

The man straddled Melina Spiros' naked, spread-eagled body, and began to methodically rape the thirty-four-year old housewife. Her face was battered beyond recognition. Her right cheekbone was shattered; her nose was broken, and crusted blood filled both nostrils. She had a split lip, and there were angry red welts that covered both breasts.

Occasionally, the man would raise his face upward, his lips moving in a kind of silent prayer, almost as if pleading—to whatever entity he called his god—for some sort of divine intervention. None came. Beneath him, Melina drifted in and out of consciousness. Each time she showed signs of awakening, the man pummeled her unmercifully, until she drifted off again to that state between life and death that now held her in its grip.

Outside the plane, the storm had intensified. Huge claps of thunder accentuated each flash of lightning, like the orchestral score of a gothic film. Inside the cabin, lights flickered on and off, and passengers shifted anxiously in their seats. Beads of perspiration poured down George's face. His newly acquired, three-piece Brooks Brothers suit was already stained beneath the armpits. He made a note to remember to have it cleaned. A violent mechanical shudder, accompanied by dimming lights, caused him to tremble. Packages and baggage stored in the overhead compartments shifted and bumped noisily as the craft was tossed about in the increasing turbulence. Women shrieked in alarm, and men coughed nervously. Thoughts of his wife raced through George's mind.

He began praying silently, imagining the worst. Fortunately, his imagination was not sufficient to the task.

After knocking Melina unconscious, the attacker had stuffed a sock roughly into her mouth to insure that she couldn't yell for help. Her legs were anchored to the posts of the footboard by stockings tied to her feet; and her hands were tethered to the headboard—one with her bra, and the other with her panties. When she was awake, Melina's terror was as palpable as her pulse, which beat like a trip hammer within the cavity of her heaving chest. This must be the way a mouse felt, she thought, caught between the claws of a playful, but deadly, cat.

The man she had arranged to meet this evening was someone she had met several weeks ago in an Internet chat room, called "Manhattan Singles." He had intrigued her from the start, and when he had invited her to meet him for a drink, she had been pleasantly surprised, accepting immediately. Privacy was important, so they had agreed upon a small tavern, just out of the neighborhood, where no one would know either of them, especially her. Inviting him back to her apartment had been a risk, but she never intended to do anything more than talk, so she had taken it.

They had another drink in her kitchen, where they continued to converse and laugh, genuinely enjoying each other's company. During a lull in the conversation, he had surprised her by leaning over and kissing her on the lips. She laughingly kissed him back, and then he pulled her closer, and forced his tongue between her lips. Melina had pulled away then, not wanting to offer further encouragement. Hoping not to offend him, she explained that she liked him, but wasn't interested in anything other than a platonic relationship.

Immediately, he had accused her of teasing him. She protested, but he grew more agitated, persisting with his allegations. The more she tried to placate him, the angrier he grew. Finally he grabbed her by the shoulders and shouted in her face, "You goddamn cock-teaser, I'll teach you to fuck with me." The first punch had broken her jaw. Mercifully, the next one had knocked her unconscious.

Now, awake again and helpless on the bed, she reflected upon her predicament. It was George's fault, she rationalized, for always being away on business. After all, a woman has needs too! Never mind the fact that he was killing himself working in an effort to get them out of the small apartment in the crowded Chelsea neighborhood that they called home.

At the same moment that her husband was praying to live, Melina Spiros was wishing she would die.

CHAPTER 2

Detective Lieutenant Matt Davis of the Tenth Precinct Detective Squad scratched his head, as he slouched in his leather recliner in front of the ancient little black-and-white television set perched precariously on his neat but crowded desk. The Mets were ahead of the Pirates, 2-1, in the final spring-training game of the season. Davis did not expect the lead to hold up.

He was forty-five years old, and had been a police officer for nearly twenty years, the last fifteen as a detective. His thick but graying hair was testimony to life in the homicide division. There was also a slight paunch that Matt considered an unwelcome advertisement for middle age, yet many women found curiously irresistible. He had a face with "character" that sported a nose broken on more than one occasion in countless PAL boxing matches. His gold-wire framed reading glasses gave his pale blue eyes a magnified look that prompted good-natured ridicule within the department, but his overall appearance was such that it was attractive to the opposite sex, and non-threatening to most men. He was of average height and build, and carried himself with a quiet dignity that commanded respect.

The small study in the Chelsea walk-up where he lived with his wife, Valerie, was a reflection of the preferences of its male occupant. Pictures of Bobby Jones, Gene Sarazan, Ben Hogan, Palmer, Player, and Nicklaus, adorned two of the four walls in the little room. Many of the photos were autographed, and some carried personal inscriptions. Other golfing mementos and souvenirs, including several antique golf clubs, hung carefully from shiny brass hooks.

The remaining two surfaces were covered with artistic representations of fish. Scattered among the stuffed specimens were paintings and sketches of trout and salmon. All of them were numbered prints rather than originals, more a misleading reflection of the detective's modest budget rather than any disdain for one-of-a-kind artwork.

Next to his passion for golf, there was nothing Davis loved more than to fly fish for trout. As for salmon angling, that was still a dream to be realized, a reminder of the financial constraints imposed upon him by his meager detective's salary. He often fantasized how he would someday realize his dreams of fishing on the storied Miramichi River for Atlantic salmon — after retirement, of course. It wasn't really the money, but the lack of free time that represented the obstacle. Until then, he still had his pictures and his books. Fishing publications of every size and description filled the ancient walnut bookshelves, which spanned the area beneath the large, triple window that faced the street below. He often sat until late into the night poring over their pages, imagining himself on the mystical waters of the Margaree River of Cape Breton Island, with a crusty old guide standing by his side. Occasionally, his wife, Valerie, would find him in the morning, asleep with his head in the pages of one of the treasured tomes.

The detective glanced at his wristwatch, then flipped off the television set. Although it was only nine thirty-five, it was nearly his bedtime. "Shit," he exclaimed, as he realized that he had spent the whole evening watching baseball, never eating the sandwich Valerie had made for him. He had missed dinner (as usual), and now the remains of an ice-cold grilled cheese sandwich, accompanied by a dill pickle slice and a handful of stale potato chips, lay attached to the plate by a string of congealed cheese. He reached for the pickle, took a bite, and was just fingering the cold sandwich, when the telephone rang. He picked it up on the first ring

CHAPTER 3

T he storm had subsided at last, and the plane banked lazily as it dropped into its final approach to the rain-slicked runway.   The PLEASE FASTEN SEATBELTS sign had been flashing regularly for several minutes, and George grasped the textured armrest in the traditional "white knuckle" manner and held his breath.   His stomach flip-flopped nervously as the lumbering jetliner neared its destination below.   A blond flight attendant standing nearby met his nervous glance with her eyes , and offered a reassuring smile.

Melina would be surprised to see him a day early, he thought.   He pictured her dark brown, moody eyes and her full-figured body – still relatively young, still alive with passion. He imagined himself holding her tightly, the smell of her hair, the weight of her breasts against his tired chest.   He felt himself becoming aroused at the thought and looked around nervously, half expecting to find the attendant staring at him.   To his relief, he discovered that the pretty blond was already busily arranging herself in an aisle seat in preparation for landing.   He glanced at his gold-colored Citizen watch and noted that it was seven fifty-five.   Maybe next year he'd be wearing a Rolex.

As the attacker clumsily attempted to enter the helpless woman, he babbled incoherently, and occasionally swore, as he poked and prodded between her wide-stretched legs.   Melina frantically slid her hips from side to side in a feeble effort to avoid the erect penis that pushed insistently against her. Strong hands grasped her buttocks roughly as the attacker triumphantly thrust himself inside her. She felt something inside of her tear, and thought of the children she would probably never be able to bear. Well, she would not make it easy for him, she thought.

With a mighty effort, she bucked her hips sharply against the invasion. But, she was no match for her attacker, and the more she struggled, the stronger he seemed to become, and the more aroused. She was incredulous that any man – especially this man – could be doing what he was doing. Earlier, he had seemed so kind, so gentle – not at all like the crazed person who was now violating her.

Melina's mind raced furiously in an attempt to recall what she was supposed to do. A fleeting glimpse of an Oprah episode flashed through her mind. What had the expert said? Be quiet? Make noise? She couldn't remember. It was impossible to focus her thoughts. Desperate to detach herself from the agony of the present, she tried to picture her husband's face. But the image of George's loving countenance only filled her with despair, and she began to cry, tears streaming down her face.

Her attacker was oblivious to her fear and pumped into her angrily. Perspiration dripped from his face and the moisture fell on her body like a macabre rain. He was hurting her, and she desperately wished he would stop. Maybe he would leave then. Finally, his watery blue eyes glazed over and his hips bucked in the unmistakable throes of orgasm, and she felt him spurt his pathetic seed deep inside her body. No sound came from his twisted face, as if words would tarnish the sanctity of the moment. She was filled with a sudden sense of outrage, and she screamed angrily against the sock inside her mouth. The muffled noise brought a brief, satisfied smile to the man's face.

He paused and removed his hands from beneath Melina's hips, and for an instant, she foolishly expected him to untie her.

She relaxed slightly, and he began massaging her shoulders — rhythmically, as if he were kneading dough. Melina took shallow breaths through her swollen nose. Gradually, however, the force of the pressure increased, and she felt his hands moving to her throat. Melina realized at last that there was no hope for escape. The killer's breath came in ragged gasps as his powerful fingers closed against her unprotected throat. Her eyes bulged grotesquely, growing dull and unseeing, and her arms and legs jerked ineffectively against the restraints that held them tight.

The man saw the look of fear in his victim's eyes and smiled. Melina saw her own desperate face reflected in the attacker's eyes and recognized it as the face of death.

A dull thud announced the lowering of the landing gear, followed by the familiar hydraulic sound of the wing flaps being extended. Shortly afterward, a welcome bump relayed their landing. George was assaulted by the roaring whine of the reversing engines, and the abrupt pressure of the seat belt against his hips. Gradually, the big jet decelerated, and then lumbered toward the terminal.

Things would be different now, he thought. Melina often spoke of her biological clock — teasing him with the tick, tick, tick sound of nature's timepiece. George acknowledged that a child could provide the missing ingredient in their otherwise perfect marital mix. From now on, he would pay more attention to his wife's needs. He would call her more often when he was on the road, and he would bring her gifts that would make those dark eyes sparkle with delight and — yes — passion.

The killer carefully undid the stockings and undergarments fastening the dead woman's arms and legs to the bedposts. Then he removed the sock from Melina's mouth, tossing it casually into a corner. He had already carefully cleaned the brown stain that Melina had made between her legs when her anal sphincter had relaxed and released a flood of warm feces in a deadly orgasm of death. Only a clear, wet spot now showed beneath her limp form, and even that would soon be dry. He was pleased with his efforts, stubbornly refusing to acknowledge the disfigurement of her face.

Rummaging through his pockets, he extracted a small, pearl-handled penknife. He ran his thumb over the miniature blade, biting his tongue when the edge pierced the skin, prompting a deep red drop of blood to well up on its surface. Satisfied, he quickly put the instrument to work. With the skill and dexterity of an artisan, he traced the shape of a small heart on the dead woman's left breast. Then, he delicately carved two sets of initials inside the design. He stepped back to admire his handiwork. A look of dismay crossed the killer's face, for there were small droplets of blood obscuring the clean edges of the heart. That would never do. He took several tissues from a box of Kleenex on the night table and blotted the fresh blood. Although Melina's heart had long since ceased beating, the killer maintained steady pressure on the wounds until, at last, the design was sealed forever.

The yellow taxi screeched to a halt in front of the Spiros' apartment building. George paid the young Israeli driver, tipping him generously, and moved to the rear of the vehicle to retrieve his battered suitcase. Then, like a nervous horse free of its rider, the cab lurched forward. George was alone on the empty street. A steady rain beat down on the umbrella above his head. He had been gone nearly a week and was glad to be home. The heavy suitcase grew a bit lighter when he saw the illuminated bedroom window in the apartment, bringing forth the pleasant image of his wife preparing for bed; it made him smile.

The killer closed the apartment door quietly behind him and slipped down the single flight of stairs to the small, poorly lit lobby below. He opened the scarred, metal front door at the end of the hallway and stuck his head outside into the cool evening air, glancing up and down the street before exiting. He started down the deserted sidewalk, his footsteps echoing off the walls of the surrounding buildings, and nearly collided with a man carrying two suitcases. The killer lowered his head, avoided eye contact, and continued on his way. He crossed the pavement and disappeared into the shadows.

George shrugged his shoulders against the burden of the heavy bags, and entered the apartment building. He didn't ring the bell, his usual signal that he was home, but instead climbed the stairs to the apartment. He reached for his key, but saw that the deadbolt was unfastened. How many times had he reminded Melina to fasten it? Suddenly an overpowering sense of dread washed over him. He dropped his luggage and entered the apartment, drawn by some unseen force through the living room, past the kitchen, and down the hall toward the bedroom.

The door was open and George breathed a sigh of relief when he saw Melina lying quietly asleep on the double bed in the corner of the little bedroom. *Thank God, she's all right*, he thought. He started out into the hall, stopped, and turned back to gaze upon the scene again. Something was wrong. He stared at the naked woman lying on the bed. *Naked?* His wife *never* slept in the nude. A cold sweat broke out on his forehead as he crept closer to the bed and looked down at his wife. Something was dreadfully wrong. Thick yellow bile rose in his throat, threatening to choke him. He stared at her in horror, a silent scream echoing inside his head. The room began to spin, and he retched violently, collapsing on the bed in a pool of his own vomit, next to his very beautiful and very dead wife.

CHAPTER 4

D etective Davis?" inquired the voice on the other end of the line. Matt hesitated before replying; somehow sensing a tone in the caller's voice that made him wish he hadn't answered. "Yeah," he said, "this is Lieutenant Davis. Who's this?"

"It's Patrolman Harder, sir."

"Of course, I should have recognized your voice," said Matt.

"Yes sir," said Harder.

"So, what's up, Hard On?" he joked, using the vulgar nickname that everyone substituted for the patrolman's real name. Paul Harder was a recent transfer to the Tenth Precinct's uniformed squad, and had been immediately tagged with the unflattering moniker by the detective Precinct Commander, Captain Ed Foster.

"Sir, the captain asked me to call you. He said you better get down here right away."

"What's the problem?" asked Davis.

"Looks like we've got another heart murder," said Harder.

"You're sure?" inquired Matt. A particularly brutal homicide had occurred about six weeks ago. The victim's name was Ida Simpson, a part-time social worker. They were still at square one with that one, and he definitely didn't need another. The murder had all the earmarks of a serial killing, complete with a distinct signature. A vivid mental picture of the previous murder victim flashed through his mind. The attractive twenty-five year old housewife had been bound hand and foot, raped, and strangled. Nothing particularly unusual about the crime – except for the heart carved into her left breast.

"Lieutenant? Are you still there?"

"Yeah, I'm here," answered Davis. He massaged his forehead. "Tell the captain I'll be right down." He hesitated, looking for the right words to say. "One more thing, Hard-on—"

"Yes, Lieutenant?"

"That heart stuff – keep it to yourself. Do you understand? That particular bit of information isn't supposed to be—"

"I know, I know," replied Harder quickly. "I'm sorry, Lieutenant. The captain already told us. Don't worry. You can count on me."

"Yeah, yeah," said Matt quietly, "just tell Foster I'm on my way."

If this new one was like the other, it meant bad news. Usually two homicides with strikingly alike *modus operandi* indicated a serial killer, the most difficult of all to apprehend. He gently placed the receiver in its cradle, flipped off the light in the study, and headed down the hall towards the kitchen. It would be a long evening, and he was not about to get started without something in his stomach. He dumped the remains of the grilled cheese sandwich and stale chips into the garbage. He opened the refrigerator, and bent over a cold platter of leftover turkey that monopolized the small top shelf of the well-worn appliance. He was stalling, and he knew it.

"Who was that on the phone, honey?" It was Valerie, his wife of five years, who was sitting in the living room, working on a crossword puzzle – her passion.

"Hard On," answered Matt matter-of-factly.

He heard his wife laugh at the nickname. Valerie had a wonderful sense of humor, and never flinched at the off-color stories her husband regularly brought home. She represented his second attempt at trying to achieve the perfect marriage.

His first wife had left him after fifteen years of being alone too often; the broken promise to have children had not helped. This time around was proving to be nearly as difficult; the main obstruction was still "the job." Only the combination of Valerie's devotion and Matt's determination were preventing a repeat performance.

"What did he want?" asked Valerie.

Matt either didn't hear her or pretended not to as he studied the turkey, knowing it was the healthier choice, then reaching instead for a container of leftover lasagna.

"I said what did he want, honey?" repeated Valerie, from the other room.

"Guess," replied her husband. He stabbed a fork at the cold pasta, spearing a hunk and stuffing it into his mouth.

Valerie got up from the over-stuffed flowered sofa, placed the puzzle book on the lamp table, and joined him in the kitchen. She crossed behind him to where he sat at the Formica-topped table and began tenderly massaging his neck and shoulder muscles. Val didn't need to be a genius to guess what was coming next – another night by herself. It was a part of the job, but no one said she had to like it – and she didn't. Matt closed his eyes and luxuriated in the moment. He leaned back and looked up into his wife's deep blue eyes. She leaned down, kissed him gently on the lips, then left the room, shaking her blonde head back and forth in resignation. It wasn't that she disapproved of her husband's job; he was good at it, and she respected him for his dedication. It was just that she loved him so much, and worried that some day it might drive the final wedge between them. Davis, too, wished he could just stay home with Valerie. He shrugged his shoulders and sighed. Just fifteen more months, he thought. That was how much longer he had until he would be eligible for retirement.

Another mouthful of lasagna, followed by a cold swallow of cranberry juice and a couple of red grapes, finished off the abbreviated feast, and Davis grabbed his jacket and headed for the door. He paused to plant a kiss on Valerie's forehead, and whispered, "See you later." She looked up from her book, smiled, and mouthed "I love you, Matt."

"Me too," he replied quietly. He turned and exited the apartment, the door closing silently behind him.

CHAPTER 5

D etective Second-Grade Chris Freitag was Davis's partner of nearly seven years, and also his best friend. He was waiting in an unmarked black Chevrolet Impala in front of the precinct house. In contrast to Matt, the younger Freitag stood six-three, and was built like a refrigerator, with huge shoulders, bulging biceps, and a shock of jet-black hair that revealed his one-quarter Mohawk Indian ancestry. He was forty-one, and hailed from upstate New York near Newburgh, where he had been a standout on his high school football team. Unlike his partner, he had never married, and saw no reason to change the status quo. He was quite at home in the tiny Eastside walkup he called home.

Sitting in the back seat was Captain Foster. Davis opened the front passenger door, nodded at his boss, and climbed in next to Freitag. Chris slapped the magnetic light onto the roof and pulled the car into traffic.

"It doesn't look good Matt," said Foster. "It's just like that woman we found six weeks ago over on Eighth Avenue. Feet tied with her stockings, hands bound with her underpants and bra, sock stuffed in her mouth and —," sighed Foster, "— the heart".

"Shit," said Davis. They had yet to come up with so much as a weak lead for the previous murder, and he saw no signs for optimism.

"I hear you," replied Foster, matter-of-factly.

"Who called it in?" asked Matt.

"The husband," answered Foster. "Comes home early from a business trip. Says he wants to surprise her."

"I guess the surprise was on *him*, huh?" Freitag quipped.

Foster shot him a disapproving look.

In just over three minutes, the car screeched to a stop in front of the four-story walk-up. Yellow crime scene tape was stretched between the wrought-iron railings lining each side of the concrete stoop. The rain had abated, and the wet sidewalk glistened in the night's light. Several standard-issue blue and white cruisers sat in front of the nondescript building, lights flashing, their engines running. Behind them was a red and white Emergency Services truck, its high-pitched alternator humming reliably. The call to 911 had come in at nine-thirty five, and the unit in B sector had responded to the scene. A young acne-faced patrol officer stood guard at the entrance to the building. His somber posture bespoke the seriousness of the crime.

Davis, Foster, and Freitag hustled up the few concrete steps to the landing and addressed the man in blue. "Did you see the body?" asked Matt.

The uniformed cop shook his head. "Hanley was the first one in. The asshole puked his guts out."

Davis studied the young cop's face. "Wipe that smirk off your face."

The patrolman blushed in embarrassment, and then said, "I mean, I'm glad it was *him* and not me," as if that would clear him with Davis.

Matt frowned in response.

"Sorry, sir," mumbled the cop.

CSU and the ME are on their way already, sir," said the patrolman. "I called them myself." He smiled at his efficiency, hoping Davis would approve.

Matt smiled a tight-lipped smile and acknowledged the remark. Normally it was the responsibility of the detectives to make such a call, but protocol often took a back seat to expediency.

Davis led the way up the stairs to where the second patrol officer stood maintaining a watch outside the apartment. His uniform was soiled, a souvenir of his first experience with a homicide. He grinned uneasily at the detectives. Foster and the two plainclothesmen showed their badges and filed into the apartment. The rookie patrol officer followed them inside.

"The victim's name is Melina Spiros. Her husband is in the living room," he said.

The distraught spouse sat hunched over on the couch, sobbing quietly into his damp handkerchief. He looked up as Davis approached and started to stand. Davis put a hand on his shoulder and stopped him.

"Mr. Spiros? I'm Detective Davis. I'm very sorry about your wife, sir."

The man shook his head in quiet acknowledgment.

Hanley addressed the captain and the two detectives. "The deceased is in the bedroom on the right at the end of the hall," he said quietly.

"Thanks," replied Freitag. The three men started down the corridor. Matt scanned the naked walls, noting the lack of pictures or other meaningful adornments.

The detectives entered the bedroom as young people might enter a funeral home for the first time – with respect and trepidation. Both emotions were appropriate.

"Jesus Christ," whispered Chris. The specter before them was not a pretty one, and Davis inhaled deeply through clenched teeth. Freitag tried not to breathe at all. His heart started pounding as it always did at the sight of a murder victim. Melina Spiros's right eye was black and blue, and swollen shut; the left bulged grotesquely, staring sightlessly at the ceiling. Her face was distorted by extensive swelling, a mass of bruises and abrasions. Blood matted her hair, and red welts covered most of her body.

As the two detectives stood solemnly by the bed, each was aware of the other's discomfort. Sex crimes were never easy. Freitag's present-day girlfriend had been a rape victim as a teenager. Davis's first wife had also very nearly suffered a similar misfortune while doing wash at a coin-operated laundry. Only her martial arts training and the quick-witted actions of a fellow customer had prevented her attacker from succeeding.

A noise at the front door of the apartment caught the attention of the two men. Several seconds later, two crime scene technicians padded into the room, coughing noisily to announce their presence, before positioning themselves alongside Freitag and Davis. Foster stood at the opposite side of the bed.

"I want this place gone over with a fine-toothed comb," ordered Matt. "Phones, door knobs, toilet bowl handle, everything." His orders were not necessary, but he gave them anyway, fulfilling an unspoken promise to the deceased. Routine procedure mandated that every possible effort be made to gather all physical evidence at a crime scene. Included would be the collection of any blood, hair, and fiber evidence, as well as semen, if there were any. The evidence would be placed in plastic bags, sealed, and labeled.

There would be extensive dusting for fingerprints. Every possible point of entry would be tested, in addition to telephones, counter tops, the victim's own skin (with Polaroid film used to lift any marks), and any other items or surfaces that could possibly yield fingerprints. They would take measurements, collect fingernail scrapings, and note temperature readings. In addition, the scene would be photographed from every conceivable angle.

Along with the bruises and cuts, there were extensive abrasions on her wrists and ankles, a result of her fierce struggle against her bonds. Each mark was photographed and noted. There was some swelling around the vaginal area, and also bruising and swelling on the victim's neck. Strangulation appeared to be the obvious cause of death, but only an autopsy could confirm that as fact.

While the crime scene men gathered physical evidence, detective Freitag was busying himself elsewhere in the apartment building. The tall detective canvassed neighbors, copying down anything they said that might give the slightest hint of what had happened. Then he moved outside, and wrote down license plate numbers from the cars parked on the block.

But, the most unique evidence was plainly visible for even the most casual observer to see – two clues that were so compelling and unusual that no one had even dared to mention them. It was as if by not acknowledging the clues, the horror of the crime could be denied.

Now, their presence could no longer be ignored.

The young medical examiner, Cathy Ahearn, had arrived, and was bent over the corpse, examining it from every angle. Finally, she began speaking slowly and deliberately into her small, portable tape recorder. Her words grimly and matter-of-factly described the dreaded evidence in its grotesque detail.

"There is a small heart-shaped incision on the victim's left breast," she noted. "The incision appears to have been made either by a scalpel or other similarly sharp cutting instrument." She coughed and then continued, "The heart is approximately seven and one-half centimeters long by five centimeters wide. There are located directly within the heart what appear to be two pairs of initials, one set positioned precisely above the other...."

It was impossible, of course, for words to describe the brutality of the senseless disfigurement. But, there might be added significance to what they saw. *One* set of initials was the same as one of those found on the body of Ida Simpson: J.C.

Jesus Christ? Can this be real? The medical examiner already knew the answer.

CHAPTER 6

avis and Foster looked across at one another from opposite sides of the bed. Their eyes reflected a mutual concern. Each, in his time, had investigated countless homicides, many with characteristics far more offbeat than those currently on display. What disturbed them both was the fact that while individual murder cases were solved at the surprisingly high rate of around seventy-five percent, the probability of solving serial homicides was much lower. Often, these types of crimes involved complex motives, and frequently defied the best efforts of even the most aggressive detective work. Davis addressed the ME regarding his most pressing concern.

"Listen, Cathy, about these initials," he said. "If the press gets a hold of this we're gonna be screwed. We were lucky as hell to keep it out of the papers last time."

The ME nodded. "So?"

"It's all we've got to go on right now. Other than that we don't have a clue."

"And?"

"I just don't wanna let things get out of control."

The ME was a tall, slender woman, always immaculately dressed. Her short hair was coifed in the latest style, and her make up was impeccable. She straightened her charcoal gray skirt, and regarded Davis with an icy stare. Leaks were like cancer. Once they started there was no saving the patient – or the case. It was common knowledge that most leaks to the press originated either in the DA's office or in the office of the medical examiner. Davis wanted to be at least reasonably confident of securing the latter.

The ME resented the implication. "Don't worry about *my* office, detective," said Ahearn, sarcastically. "Worry about your *own* blabbermouths."

Davis's jaw tightened in response. Only on rare occasions did a rumor escape the confines of precinct headquarters, and then only by way of a uniformed officer. Leaks from detectives were almost nonexistent. Davis let her remark pass in the interest of harmony, but Ahearn could tell by the detective's silence that she had overstepped the boundaries of propriety. After an uncomfortable pause, she broke the stalemate.

"Matt," she offered, almost in apology, "you might want to get in touch with the archdiocese. Maybe they can shed some light on any religious angle." Then, almost as an afterthought, she added, "There *does* appear to be a connection, don't you think?" Davis nodded automatically, subconsciously making a mental note of her suggestion.

Foster and Davis left the ME and returned to the living room. Freitag had returned from the canvass, and sat beside the victim's husband.

"I'm afraid I need to ask you a few questions, Mr. Spiros," said Matt, his voice trailing off. This part was never easy, no matter how often he did it and this was his thirty-third homicide investigation. It always made him feel the same – very uncomfortable, and more than a little sad.

"Sir," he began, "when did you first discover your wife's body?"

Spiros blew his nose before he answered. "Around nine-fifteen, I guess." Davis had his notebook out, and wrote down the information. "I noticed the dead bolt wasn't on," he continued. "I'm always telling Melina 'Lock the door, Melina. It isn't safe.'" He started to cry again, then tried to regain his composure.

"Yes, sir," replied Davis. "You told her the right thing." He smiled and patted the little Greek man on the shoulder. *A lot of good that did*, he thought.

"Anyway, I came home a day early. I want to surprise her, you know?" His eyes brightened at the memory of his anticipation, then dimmed at the reality of what had followed.

"I see the bedroom light from the street. I figure she's watching TV. But the door is unlocked. I know something is wrong. I just know it..." The man began weeping openly now. Davis waited patiently for him to stop.

"Were you away long, sir?" he asked.

"Five days," replied the husband.

"Business trip?"

"Yes, to California. I was at a trade show. I make furniture, and..."

The questioning continued for another five minutes, but Davis had already dismissed the man as a suspect. He concluded the routine interrogatory as quickly as possible, hoping to save the tired man any further agony. Finally, he thanked him, and turned to Freitag and Foster. "I think we're done here," he said, softly.

They left the apartment as quietly as they had entered it.

Matt took the wheel on the way back to headquarters; he hoped the driving would serve to distract him from the crime – at least for a while. Instead, dozens of questions flashed through his mind as he steered the Chevrolet in silence. When did the killer carve the initials? Were the women still alive? Was it before he raped them, or afterwards? To whom did they belong? Did the J.C. really refer to Jesus Christ? Did the killer *love* women or did he *hate* them? Maybe he couldn't *get* women – except by force.

The possibilities boggled the mind, but one thing *was* clear. There was a compelling reason for the heart *and* the initials, and the sooner he discovered what it was, the sooner he would possess the key to unlocking this mystery.

CHAPTER 7

The Tenth Precinct buzzed with excitement like a Times Square hotel ballroom minutes before midnight on New Year's Eve. A mob of reporters had gathered in the lobby beneath the raised platform occupied by the desk sergeant. The reporters were waiting for the Precinct Commander to hold a press conference. Police radio scanners had attracted them like scavengers to carrion, and they were everywhere. Foster, Freitag, and Davis brushed past them, to where a microphone had been set up. The newsmen shouted rudely at them. Davis stood alongside Foster as he prepared to speak. Freitag moved to a spot behind the two men.

"Hey, Captain. Is it true you have another Boston Strangler on your hands?" shouted one reporter.

Foster smiled and held up his hand, waiting for the noise to abate.

"Gentlemen," he began. "As you probably know, there's been a murder. The victim is a thirty-four year old housewife. The deceased was found by her husband at around nine-thirty this evening, upon his return from a business trip. The cause of death appears to be strangulation. There are no witnesses and no suspects at this time. Identification is being withheld until all relatives have been notified. That's all I can tell you at this time. Thank you."

"Is the husband a suspect?" a voice yelled from the back of the crowd.

"I repeat," said Foster, with a dirty look, "At this time we have no suspects. Thank you."

Another reporter yelled out his question. "Is there any truth to the rumor that there might be a connection between this murder and the woman who was killed last month?"

"No comment," said Foster.

"There's been talk that there were signs of some kind of ritual," said another scribe. "Any truth to that report?"

"Gentlemen, the press conference is over."

Foster turned and hurried past the reporters, making his way upstairs, and leaving Davis to face the anxious newsmen. The questions came fast and furious. Davis raised his hands and repeated the captain's response, "No comment," like a mantra. He finally recognized the last questioner as Harry Cohen of *the New York Post*.

"Sorry, Harry. I'm not saying 'boo' until I know something definite," said Matt.

"Oh, come on Davis. Give me a break. I'm just trying to make a living here. What about the ritual business?"

Davis pulled the reporter close to him and whispered, "Listen, Cohen, I can't discuss the case with you. When *I* know something, then *you'll* know something, okay?"

Cohen stared directly into the detective's eyes, decided he was being honest with him, and replied, "Okay, Davis, but don't forget, you promised!"

"Yeah, right," answered Davis, "and next week we'll pick out the furniture."

With that, he exited the lobby, quickly making his way upstairs and into the sanctuary of the wood-paneled office that Captain Foster called his second home.

Closing the door behind him, Davis headed for the ancient two-burner electric hot plate that held two Pyrex coffeepots – one filled with the appropriate brew, the other with steaming hot water. Rummaging through the enameled cabinet that supported the hot plate, he retrieved a clean paper cup and a packet of generic hot chocolate mix. He dumped its contents into the cup, slopped some hot water into it, and stirred the whole thing with the eraser end of a number two pencil. He sucked the end of the pencil dry, and then took a sip from the cup, burning his lip in the process.

Davis *never* drank coffee, seldom if ever, tea – except the Chinese kind – and rarely consumed alcohol. But chocolate was his passion. He stood with one foot propped against the green wall of the office, drinking a cup as Foster began talking.

CHAPTER 8

Baltimore, Maryland: April 3, 1942

M*arie Dameski was sixteen years old. She was poor, not particularly bright, and the only child of a widower father who drank. However, she had several things going for her – she was extraordinarily good looking and she had a great body. With it she was able to get any boy she wanted, and she wanted them all. There was a lot smoke, but no fire, none that is until Jack Curran came along and lit the flame.*

Jack was the neighborhood Errol Flynn. He was a hard-drinking Irish youth whose sexual appetite was well known. Marie's father had forbidden her from seeing the boy and even threatened to throw his daughter out if she ever so much as spoke to him.

Right now, it was the sixteen-year old girl's mind, not her body, which was working overtime as she shifted her firm buttocks against the rough, uncomfortable back seat of Jack's 1936 Ford sedan. The two of them had been seeing each other on the sly for almost a month. So far, Marie had been able to hold off Jack's advances with promises and excuses, but it was becoming more difficult. She found herself trying half-heartedly not to become another of Jack's conquests, just as her father had predicted she would be.

Jack Curran's breath reeked of cigarettes and whiskey as he pleaded in Marie's ear, "Come on, Marie. Let me do it. You know you'll like it."

"What if I get pregnant?" She knew her father would throw her out if she did. She couldn't take a chance.

"Marie, come on. You know I love you." He quickly added, "We'll even get married if we have to."

Maybe he really would marry her. Maybe at last she could get away from her crude, abusive father. She lay trapped beneath Jack's sweaty body, her skirt around her ankles. Her blouse was unbuttoned, and her head was spinning from too much whiskey. Jack rubbed her thigh with his callused hand, and she thought of her father, who often touched her like this when he returned home after drinking all night. Her cheeks flushed even further. She felt an overpowering tingling between her legs, and her resolve weakened. It would serve her father right if she got herself knocked up. She relaxed for a second and Jack took this as a sign of encouragement. Soon there was no turning back, and the awkward coupling had taken place.

Afterward, Marie popped several Sen-Sen tablets into her mouth in an effort to mask the scent of the liquor on her breath. Jack drove her home. He pulled the Ford to the curb, a half block short of the rundown tenement on Quincy Street, and reached over and pulled the girl toward him. She allowed herself to be cuddled. They sat like that until Jack broke the uneasy silence.

"Marie, I gotta tell you something."

The girl swallowed hard and felt her lips grow dry. "What is it, Jack?"

"I got my notice today."

Marie shut her eyes and covered her ears with her small, slender hands. The war was heating up and she understood the significance of what Jack had told her. She did not want to hear anymore.

" I gotta get goin'," she said.

"Marie," said Jack. "Did ya hear what I said?"

The young girl shook her head up and down, tears coursing down her cheeks.

"I'm leavin' a week from tomorrow." Then, he added, *"I want ya to marry me."*

Marie was shocked. She liked Jack a lot, was crazy about him, in fact. But marriage? That was something she really had not been ready for – not yet, anyway. Jack gripped her arms firmly and repeated his awkward proposal.

"Marie? Did ya' hear me? I said I want ya' to marry me. Please?"

Gradually, the girl regained her composure. She loosened her boyfriend's hold on her arms and turned to face him. With a deep breath, she gave him her answer. *"Do you really think I'm gonna marry you and then watch you go off and get yourself killed?"*

Jack winced. The image of himself being blown to smithereens overwhelmed him.

"I don't think so!" continued the girl. *"Thanks a lot! Thanks for nothin'!"*

Rebuffed, Jack replied, *"Hey, fine. I don't give a shit. I'm only tryin' to do the right thing, you know. I mean...Hell, I'd marry ya' ...I mean, if you really wanted me to..."*

"Look, just take me home, okay?" said Marie.

"Sure, fine, whatever you say," he answered, the relief evident in his voice.

Jack put the car into gear and advanced the remaining half block to Marie's apartment house. Before the vehicle had rolled to a complete stop, Marie was out the door and up the stairs into the hallway of the tenement. The apartment was dark as Marie closed the heavy door quietly behind her. The smell of her father's breath arrived along with the first punch, which caught her completely by surprise. She put up her hands in meek self-defense. After that, it didn't matter.

Marie and Jack were married the following day. After the brief civil ceremony, they moved into a furnished apartment. Six days later Jack went off to fight the Japanese. Marie was left to fend for herself. At first, she enjoyed the change. Living on her own was sort of fun, and, with World War II in full *bloom, work was easy to find. Marie got a menial job on an assembly line making hand grenades in a defense plant, where she earned more than enough to pay for her room and board. Her father, relieved to be free of the responsibility, never bothered her again.*

After seven weeks, Marie's worst fears were realized. She visited an outpatient clinic, and confirmed that she was pregnant. She continued to work right up until her eighth month, but was finally forced to quit when her swollen belly would no longer allow her to sit at the assembly line. On December 31, 1942, exactly two-hundred and seventy-two days after her initiation into womanhood in the back seat of Jack Curran's Ford, Marie gave birth to John Curran, Jr.

Happy New Year!

From the start, Marie hated motherhood and *her baby. He cried from morning to night, never giving her a minute's rest. Most of all, she hated feeding him. Her breasts ached continually; heavily swollen with milk, their weight was a constant reminder of her unwanted offspring and his absent father. She would tease the hungry baby by holding his mouth an inch or so away from her distended nipple. Then she would watch with fascination as his little lips sucked voraciously at thin air. His arms would wave frantically until she finally allowed him to partake of the watery milk – and only then to alleviate her own discomfort.*

In March, she received a telegram informing her of Jack's death in the South Pacific. There would be some insurance money, said the communiqué, and a monthly support check. Good riddance, she thought. Now if she could only get rid of the kid.

CHAPTER 9

9:13 a.m., Monday, March 20

Archbishop Alfonso Romero of the New York archdiocese paced nervously back and forth in his ornate office. The décor of the prelate's expansive quarters was dominated by rich mahogany wainscoting, which covered two thirds of the twelve-foot high walls. Wide, matching crown molding accented the high ceiling and complimented the wall covering. A massive silver crucifix on the south wall demanded the attention of anyone entering the room. But, it was the life-sized portrait of a young Jesus, on the opposite wall, that ultimately held their focus.

Romero was the first Hispanic to rise to the position of archbishop in the history of New York City, and, at sixty four years of age, he was not about to let a couple of murders with religious overtones tarnish his auspicious tenure. Surely, the murderer was a Baptist. Perhaps a Methodist? But, certainly not a Catholic. He would afford whatever help he could to the detective who, even now, was on his way up to see him. A buzzer on the bishop's large, mahogany desk announced the arrival of his visitor. The white-haired cleric padded toward the heavy wooden door to admit the detective.

"Detective Davis?" he asked, rhetorically.

"Good morning, your Eminence," replied the detective. "Thanks for seeing me on such short notice."

"Nonsense," he replied. "It's the *least* I can do. I only hope I can be of some help. Please, come in."

Davis's eyes darted around the spacious room, noting the contrast between his own cluttered office and the lavish – almost decadent – interior of the archbishop's quarters. Sensing Davis's silent assessment, Romero moved to dispel any apprehensions the detective might have.

"Don't be misled by my opulent office, detective. It is intended to lend an air of respectability to the title. As a rule, we try to maintain an image of austerity. "I can assure you that we are forever fighting a budget deficit."

Davis chuckled at the obvious contradiction. "No indictment here, your eminence. Innocent until proven guilty, just like anyone else." Davis laughed aloud at his own cleverness.

"Please, detective, call me Father Al. All of my friends do."

Davis found the new "worldliness" of the Catholic Church somewhat disconcerting, and for a second was at a loss for words.

"Well, Father – uh – Al," he began, deferring half-heartedly to the bishop's request for informality. "As you may or may not be aware, we've had two particularly gruesome homicides in our precinct in the last six weeks. The second one occurred last Thursday. The two women were raped and strangled."

The bishop winced at the mental image of the crimes. "And how can I help you?"

"Based on some of the evidence, we think there could be some kind of religious connection," replied Matt. "And I was hoping... *we* were hoping that the church might be able to shed some light on things."

"What makes you think there is a *Catholic* connection to these murders?" asked the bishop.

Davis was caught off guard by the bishop's defensive posture, and didn't have a ready answer. He paused to gather his thoughts. After a moment, he spoke. "We're not sure that there is one. But both victims were Catholic, and…"

"Yes?"

"What I'm about to tell you must remain absolutely confidential."

"Yes, of course."

"We found two unusual pieces of evidence on each victim."

The bishop studied Matt's face intensely. Despite being alone with the detective, he moved in closer and lowered his voice as he spoke. "And what might those two things be?" he asked.

Davis removed his coat and carefully draped it across his lap.

"A small heart cut into the left breast..." said Matt.

The bishop gasped and closed his eyes, as if doing so would eliminate the sight he pictured in his mind.

Davis continued, "...And inside each heart two sets of initials were carved into the victims' flesh."

The archbishop grimaced, drawing an exaggerated breath through his clenched teeth.

"One set matched those of the deceased individual. But, in both cases, the other initials were the letters 'J.C.' so, naturally we thought—"

"Madre de Dio," sighed the clergyman.

"—there might be some kind of religious significance," said Davis. "Since the victims were Catholic, naturally we came to you first."

The archbishop crossed himself and shook his head in disbelief. "How can I possibly help you?" he asked.

"The fact is, with the exception of *that* evidence, we've got absolutely *nothing* to go on," said Davis. "We'd like permission to speak with one of your priests down in the One-O."

"Excuse me?" asked Romero.

"I'm sorry, Father, I mean the Tenth Precinct, in Chelsea. We call it the 'One-O.' It's where both murders took place. I believe that would be St. Jude, down on Ninth Avenue. We'd like to talk to whoever is in charge down there."

"Yes, that's correct," replied the bishop. "That would be—" he scratched his head, searching for a name, "ah, yes, Father Richter, of course. A fine man. I'm sure he would be happy to work with you. I'll call him and tell him to help you in any way he can."

"Thank you," replied Davis "I'd also like a list of priests, religious students, janitors, anybody you can think of who might have had problems with that church in the past, disgruntled employees of the church, even priests who—well— you know—might have had problems. Anything at all." Davis shrugged his shoulders in a display of frustration.

"That's a tall order, detective," replied Romero.

"I assure you that everything will be kept secret."

Romero smiled. "Of course," answered the prelate. "It might take a while."

"I understand," replied Davis. "Naturally, we'd be most grateful, and of course, if we should stumble upon *anything* that might reflect poorly on the church, we would advise you immediately—before the press could find out."

Matt studied the archbishop's face, measuring the man's character. Finally, he spoke. "It's very critical that *no one* knows about these details."

"You have my word," said the archbishop.

Davis thanked him, stood up, and headed for the door. He stopped short and turned to the aging priest.

"How soon can I talk to Father Richter?" he asked.

"Right away. I'll call him immediately."

"Thank you," answered Davis. "I really appreciate it."

The two men shook hands, and Davis hurried down the stairs to the Chevy. The motor was already running, and Freitag reached across the front seat and opened the door.

"Let's go, Chris. St. Jude's, over on Ninth Avenue. We've got a lot to do."

Freitag gunned the big V-8 and the unmarked car shot away from the curb and out into traffic.

CHAPTER 10

Baltimore, Maryland

*T*he small apartment had only one bedroom. Marie and the men she brought home from the bars would have sex on the bed while John slept peacefully alongside them in his crib. In the beginning, most of the men were halfway decent and tried their best not to wake the sleeping child. Marie could not have cared less. One night she actually shook the infant awake so her lover could make believe he was being watched while they did it. The idea appealed to both of them so much that, from then on, they made sure to have sex only when little John was awake and watching.

At first, the baby would just lie quietly in his crib, too preoccupied with his bottle to pay attention to the couple on the bed. Then, when the bottle would run dry or he would become bored, he would stand up on his wobbly legs and watch as his mother allowed herself to be violated in front of him. If he dared to make a sound, Marie would explode in a rage, screaming at him to be quiet. If he continued, she would hurl a pillow or other object at him to silence his crying. But, on other occasions, she would urge him to cry, especially if it excited her male visitor. If her lover wanted to slap the baby or pull his hair, she had no objection.

By the time he was two Marie grew tired of having him watch. She began shutting him up in the narrow clothes closet outside the bedroom. Once, during a two-day drunk, she left him there, while his pathetic cries went unanswered. When she finally staggered off to work, she entirely forgot about her son. When she returned home that afternoon, sober, she found the *crib empty and went into a panic. She searched frantically throughout the apartment until, finally, she found him asleep in the closet, his pajamas soaked with urine.*

Marie was sure he had hidden there to anger her. As punishment, she dragged him out and spanked him with a wooden spoon until the handle actually broke from the force of her blows. She made certain to inflict pain on his genitals.

"That'll teach ya to wet your fuckin' pants!" she screamed hysterically.

When he tried to cover himself, she tied his hands behind his back and continued the punishment. At last, tired from the exertion, she threw the little boy into his crib. His small hands were still tied.

At two-and-a-half, when other toddlers were beginning to talk, John was still mumbling unintelligibly. At three, when he finally did begin to speak, it was with great difficulty. Marie got so tired of hearing him say, "M-m-m-m-mom-m-y" that she began covering his mouth with tape.

"Shut up, ya fuckin' idiot!" she would shout.

She began tying him up and stuffing a stocking in his little mouth. Hours would pass until, finally, she would say to him, "Ya promise not to open your mouth? Huh? DO YA?" The little three-year old would nod his head sadly up and down. Only then would his loving mother remove the saliva-covered sock from his mouth.

Eventually, little John not only stopped stuttering, but ceased talking altogether. He would only grunt when he wanted to eat or go to the bathroom. When Marie's sexual partners commented on his strange behavior, she told them he was part chimpanzee. Everyone would have a good laugh, even little John. Then, her mood suddenly darkening, Marie would beat the boy unmercifully, stopping only when she grew too weary to continue. Occasionally, the beatings left the boy unconscious.

CHAPTER 11

W hen Father Richter saw the story of Melina Spiros' murder on the evening news, it had shaken him to the core. It was only a week or so ago that she had called the church, and asked if she could speak privately with him at her apartment. He had hesitated, suggesting, instead, that she come to the rectory for the meeting. She persisted with her argument, but in the end, he had convinced her to come to the church.

She was an attractive woman. Indeed her beauty had attracted his attention on several occasions, especially when she had dressed up for holy days like Easter and Christmas. But, when she came to the rectory, he was surprised at how disheveled she appeared. It was obvious that she was a woman in conflict. They made small talk while he prepared a pot of coffee, but finally she got to the matter that had prompted the meeting.

She had a confession to make, she had said. She was weak. Her husband traveled often for his business, and when he did, she tended to become angry, even resentful. She wanted children, and so did George. The difference was that he wanted to wait until they were more secure financially, while Melina didn't concern herself with money, only her biological clock, which was ticking loudly.

Richter had counseled her to be patient. Then she had dropped the bombshell. She had been cheating on George. It had only been a couple of times, and nothing of consequence had occurred, but it was still cheating. She was having a difficult time hiding her guilt. George was from the old school, and wouldn't understand, if she told him. Father Richter advised her to stop. It was only a matter of time before something *would* happen, he had said. He even pointed out passages in *the New Testament* relating to infidelity and matters between a husband and a wife.

Before she left, Melina told Father Richter she would make an effort to stop. But he had to understand how lonely and frustrated she was. If he hadn't known better, he would have thought that she was coming on to him.

CHAPTER 12

S t. Jude's occupied an edifice that was a throwback
to the Middle Ages: four large spires towered into
the air, gargoyles and detailed busts of saints,
devils, and angels were on every surface, and stained glass
windows threw off broken reflections of the passing traffic and
surrounding buildings. Davis was familiar with the church, but
only from the outside. He was a Catholic, but in name only,
and not at all like Valerie, who was an Episcopalian,
worshipping regularly and participating in fundraisers, bazaars,
and support groups.

Father Peter Richter was tall and athletic looking, with a
touch of gray in his well-groomed hair. He greeted the two
detectives with a smile and a firm handshake. Davis liked him
instantly. He wished they were meeting under more pleasant
circumstances.

"I'd appreciate it if you'd call me Father Pete," said the
priest. "It's what my parishioners call me, and I really prefer
it."

Davis thought back to the archbishop and his similar call
for familiarity. "No problem," he answered. "Call me Matt,
okay?"

Father Pete nodded.

Davis said, "This is Chris Freitag."

"You can call me Detective Freitag," joked Chris. All
three men laughed, breaking the awkwardness of the moment.

"Well, can I get you fellows a cup of coffee...or perhaps
some tea?"

"No thanks, Father Pete," answered Freitag. "We're running kind of behind." Then, he looked anxiously at Davis, aware that he may have stepped on his partner's toes.

"Maybe some other time, okay?" said Davis.

Father Richter smiled. "Right. How can I help you?"

Davis got right to the point, sparing no detail in describing the most recent murder. Reluctantly, he also revealed that this was the second such murder to occur in the same parish.

"How well did you know them?" asked Matt.

Richter reflected on the question. "Not particularly well. Neither woman was a regular at mass – mostly on holidays, that sort of thing."

"Of course," replied Davis. "If you knew anything more, you'd tell us though, wouldn't you?"

"If you're referring to something they might have confided to me about, like a confession or something—" here Richter hesitated. "I'd have to think about it. It's a very delicate subject with the church. In fact, once I...well, you understand."

"Absolutely," replied Matt. "Anyway, it looks as if the killer has some kind of obsession with religion, or at least that's how it looks right now. We were figuring he might possibly be...well...a member of your church. What do *you* think?"

Father Richter rubbed his hands together. "I guess anything's possible. But, I really can't think of anyone. I mean, I'm certainly willing to try, but—"

"Well," replied Davis, "if you think of anyone at all in the parish who might be—let's say, you know—behaving a little odd, please call me right away." He handed the priest his card. "I've asked the archbishop to get me a list of anybody connected with the church who might have had a gripe or a problem."

"Is there anybody who comes to mind?" asked Chris, "somebody you can think of who might be capable of doing something like this?"

A deep sigh escaped the priest's lips, and he closed his eyes. Then, he opened them and looked hard into the eyes of both detectives. "There is the basic problem, of course, that we've already alluded to."

Davis had been dreading this subject.

"You mean the confidentiality issue?"

"Yes," answered the priest.

Davis was prepared with an answer.

"I'm not asking for anything specific necessarily. Just a name – a place to start."

"Yes, I know" replied Father Richter. But, his voice appeared to betray his true feelings.

"I can do my own snooping around after that, okay?" said Davis. He and Freitag glanced nervously back and forth at one another. Working with clergy always presented problems. In this case, however, it was imperative that any objections be overcome.

"Okay, what do you say we try it something like this," began Davis. "Let's suppose we just talk in generalities. You know, suppose a Mr. X comes in to Confession, and *just* happens to mention that he had impure thoughts about Sister Margaret... or... *whatever*. You get the picture, *right*?"

Father Richter smiled and nodded. "In other words, you want to know if I've had any unusual confessions lately. Is that it?"

"Yeah," answered Davis. "Something like that."

"At least we'd know if we're in the right pew," joked Freitag, making no effort to hide his amusement at the humor he had created.

Davis flinched and flashed his partner a look that said, *not now, asshole!*

"I'm sorry, Matt. I only hear confessions when one of the other priests is out sick, and I'm afraid I haven't heard *anything* unusual lately, except for the man who admitted he hated Mick Jagger."

Matt looked puzzled, not quite sure what the reference to the rock star was all about.

He wanted to know if *that* was a sin," said Father Richter. "You know, *hating* Mr. Jagger."

"And?" queried Davis.

"I told him that he probably didn't really hate *him* – just his music."

Everybody laughed, and just like that the tension was broken.

"Listen, Father Pete, if I come up with any theories, I'd like to stop by and pick your brain, okay? You know—sort of run the whole religious thing by you."

"Absolutely," replied the priest. "Perhaps then you'll join me in a cup of coffee, and we'll see what we can accomplish."

"Good," answered Matt. "I'll look forward to it."

He genuinely liked the man and anticipated their next meeting.

"Oh, Father Pete," he said. "There is one other thing."

"Yes?" asked the priest. "What's that?"

Matt smiled sheepishly. "If it's not too much trouble— well—I'm kind of a hot chocolate guy. You know," he blushed. "I mean—instead of coffee."

The priest smiled warmly. "No problem at all, Matt. I'll make sure I have some on hand."

The two detectives said their good byes and headed out of the rectory. They had to make a stop at the ME's office, and Davis wasn't thrilled at the prospect.

CHAPTER 13

C athy Ahearn shrugged as she handed the autopsy report to Davis. "I'm afraid there's not much there, Matt," she said. "Death by asphyxiation, and of course she was raped. Pretty much the same as the first one, *except* the initials were different— at least the other set."

Matt acknowledged the news with a nod. "I took your advice and got in touch with the archbishop."

"Any luck?"

"Not yet," he said. "I met with Romero, and he's got his people checking on unhappy ex-employees within the archdiocese. Also, Father Richter down at St. Jude's is going to see what he can come up with inside his church. Both murders occurred within the same parish, and—"

"Oh, Matt, there is something else," interrupted Ahearn.

"Yeah, what's that?"

"Well, it looks as if the same 'perp' did both of them."

"How do you figure?"

"Same blood type. We ran an acid phosphate test on some of the stains on the sheets and turned up semen. Our boy's a secretor, AB to be precise. That represents only about five percent of the population. Highly unlikely that two guys with that blood type would commit the same kind of murder. So, we've narrowed it down to about two-hundred-and twenty-five thousand New Yorkers, give or take fifty thousand."

"Wonderful," quipped Davis. Turning to his partner, he added, "Chris, have we got blood types on the two husbands?"

Freitag pulled his notebook from his breast pocket. He flipped through the worn pages, finally finding what he was searching for.

"Here we go," he said. "Let's see – husband number one, type O; Spiros, type A."

Davis shut his eyes, and replied in deadpan, "So, let's see, we can *definitely* eliminate the two husbands. Great! Now we're really *getting* somewhere."

Ahearn grabbed Davis's arm. "You know, you just might have something there," she said, earnestly.

"Oh, really?"

"I'm serious, Matt. The fact that both women were *married*. Maybe *that* means something —"

"And maybe it doesn't," Davis quickly replied. "Maybe we'll just have to wait until we've got a dozen in the morgue before—"

"Oh, come on, Matt. I'm only trying to help."

Davis rubbed his eyes. "Sorry, Cathy," he said. "I'm just frustrated."

"Maybe both women were having an affair with the same guy?" offered the ME.

Davis seemed to brighten at the suggestion. "I guess that *is* a possibility. Yeah, what the hell. Anyway, it's something. We'll check that out. Won't we, Freitag?" His partner rolled his eyes at the ceiling and answered in a mock slave-like tone," Whatever you says – "Massuh."

CHAPTER 14

11:17 a.m., Wednesday, March 22

"Bingo!" said Freitag, as he burst into Davis's office.

Startled by the sudden intrusion, Matt nearly fell backward off his chair.

"What the—?"

"Matching prints!" said Freitag. "The same guy was at *both* scenes."

"And this means what?" said Davis, somewhat amused.

"Well," said Freitag, "after we eliminated the husbands' prints, and anybody else with an alibi, we still had prints left over. Turns out they belong to the same guy."

"And that would be?" asked Davis.

"Don't know yet. Not until we get the report."

"But, the same person was at both scenes?"

"Yep. And if he's got a record, we've got our guy."

"Big if," said Matt.

"What about the blood?" asked Chris.

"Useless," said Davis. "Blood came from the victim at both scenes, and the husbands don't match. The semen shows our guy as AB, but that won't help until we come up with—"

Freitag finished the sentence, "—a suspect, I know, I know. Sounds like a fucking nursery rhyme. How long before we get the DNA results back from the semen?"

"Probably won't matter," answered Matt, "unless..." his voice trailed off. He finished the remainder of the thought in his head: *unless we have a suspect.*

All semen samples were sent to Life Codes, a lab in the Westchester County town of Valhalla, where it usually took about two weeks for DNA identification. If a suspect was arrested, a sample of his DNA could be obtained for comparison with the evidence from the crime scene. A match nearly always resulted in a conviction.

"Okay" said Davis. "So, let's see, we *do* know that the same guy was at both apartments, because we've got his prints, right?"

"Right," replied Chris.

"And we've got *somebody's* semen at both scenes—"

"But, we don't know *whose*," said Freitag.

"Right," said Matt. "But, let's assume for a minute that it's the same guy who left the prints."

"Okay," said Freitag. "Then we got him. Assuming we can find him."

"Maybe," said Davis.

"What do you mean *maybe?*"

"Well, they thought they had O.J. nailed, too" said Matt. "And look what happened with him. He walked."

"Yeah," said Chris. "But, they didn't have any prints, remember? They only had" – he paused for effect – "the glove!"

"How can I forget," said Matt. "'If it doesn't fit, you must acquit,'" he said, mimicking Simpson's high-profile defense attorney, Johnny Cochran.

"But *we've* got prints," said Freitag, with mock enthusiasm.

"Great," replied Davis. "Now all we need is—"

"Yeah, uh huh," said Chris.

"Right," said Matt. He stood up and stretched his arms over his head. "Okay," he said. "So, what *else* do we have?"

"Well, we know both women were seeing other men besides their husbands," said Chris. "Neighbors can vouch for that."

"So?" said Matt.

"Well, actually only the first one was," said Freitag.

Davis scratched his head, and then addressed his partner with deliberate patience. "Let me get this straight. Both women were seeing other men, except that the *second* one wasn't, only the *first*. Is that right?"

"Well, sort of. The first victim, Mrs. Simpson, was seeing the same guy for about the last six months."

"And?" said Matt.

"He's a night watchman up in the garment district. You know the drill, husband works days, boyfriend works nights, that kind of thing. Anyway, we checked him out, and it turns out, the day she was killed, he's in Atlantic City."

"Did he win?" asked Davis.

"Huh?"

"Did he win or lose?"

"Oh—he lost—big time!" said Freitag. "He's got toll receipts, parking stub, the works. Apparently, he writes it off of his income taxes. A real jerk. He even declares his winnings."

"Actually, I'd say that makes him an even *bigger* winner," quipped Davis.

"What do you mean?" asked Chris.

"It gives him an airtight alibi."

"Oh," smiled Freitag.

"Anyway, forget about him. What about Mrs. Spiros?" asked Davis.

"Well, her old man's on the road a lot," said Chris. "But, we knew that already. Neighbors say she brings strange guys home. Different guy every time."

"Anybody see anything *this* time?"

"Nope," replied Freitag. "It was a shitty night, remember? Rained like hell."

"Well, check with all the cab companies," said Matt. "See if anyone remembers a fare being dropped off. It's a long shot, but you never know."

Freitag made a note on his memo pad.

"So," continued Matt. "Let's see. We've got two different women, both seeing guys other than their husbands, but no witnesses and no suspects. Right?"

"Right," said Freitag. "But, don't forget, we've got the semen and the fingerprints."

"Big fucking deal," murmured Davis.

They both stood there in silence lost in thought. Finally, Davis plopped the autopsy report down on his desk and looked up at the clock. "Let's go get some lunch at Ratner's. I think better on a full stomach."

Freitag didn't need a written invitation.

CHAPTER 15

Freitag was busy wolfing down a pastrami sandwich; his attention focused on the abundant slabs of meat pressed between thick slices of rye bread that he held between his oversized fingers. A bright yellow smear of mustard colored the corner of his mouth. Across the table, Davis fiddled idly with his corned beef counterpart and finally said what was on his mind.

"Maybe we're barking up the wrong tree," he said.

"Huh?" said Freitag, his voice muffled by a mouthful of pastrami.

"What if they're just the guy's initials? What if the J and the C are just his initials? *Then* what?"

"You mean no religious connection?" said Freitag, taking a huge swallow of cream soda, and belching loudly. He smiled proudly.

"That's exactly what I mean," said Davis, ignoring his partner's breach of etiquette. "What if we're just following the obvious and ignoring something really significant. Maybe we should be looking at every guy in the neighborhood with J.C. as his initials."

"Well, I guess we could do that," answered Freitag. "But, it ain't gonna do much for narrowing down the list of suspects."

Davis took a bite of his corned beef sandwich. He started to chew, then stopped suddenly. "Let's go," he said.

"Go where?" asked a perplexed Freitag.

"I want to talk to CSU. See if they found anything else that might be of religious significance in the Spiros's apartment."

The pert technician at CSU clicked her chewing gum when she spoke. "Well, we did find a bible—a New Testament—but that should have been on the inventory," she said.

"I don't know how I could have missed that, but I did," replied Davis. "Can I see it?"

"Sure," replied the tech, "just give me a minute, and I'll bring it out for you."

She disappeared down the hall, her ample behind swaying side to side as Freitag watched in amusement. Davis frowned.

"What?" said Chris, with a grin.

"You're an asshole," muttered Matt.

"Hey, I'm not dead *yet*."

The woman reappeared several minutes later carrying the book. Davis took the bible and began thumbing through it, looking for something of significance, anything at all. Somewhere around the middle of the book, he found it. It was a bookmark. "Here, look," said Matt. He held the book out to his partner, the pages exposed.

Freitag leaned over Davis's shoulder and peered at the pages. A vacant look spread across his face. He obviously did not see anything of significance in front of him. As if reading his partner's mind, Davis said, "Right here. This passage here – EPHESIANS, Chapter 5."

"3 But fornication, and all unclean-
ness, or covetousness, let it not be once
named among you, as becometh saints;
4 Neither filthiness, nor foolish talking,
nor jesting, which are not convenient:
but rather giving of thanks.

    5   *For this ye know, that no whore monger,*
nor unclean person, nor covetous man,
who is an Idolater, hath any inheritance
in the kingdom of Christ and of God."

"I don't get it," said Freitag. "What are you saying?"

"Well, it looks as if someone was trying to counsel Mrs. Spiros about something."

"Okay. So, you think this is the connection? I mean—with the J.C. and all? Is that what you're saying?" asked Freitag.

"What I'm saying is, I think we need to go back and check on the Simpson homicide," answered Davis. "I'll lay you odds that we'll find a bible there, too."

He was right.

The bible had been inventoried, right along with the jewelry, coffee cups, cigarette butts, and so forth. A quick examination of the book revealed a similar bookmark in the same location, with the same passage underlined.

"I guess we can say that there's a little religious significance now," remarked Davis.

"Yeah—I guess so," said Freitag.

Maybe they were finally getting somewhere.

"Why don't we go talk to Father Richter," suggested Matt. "Tell him about the bibles. See if it rings any bells."

"Can't hurt," said Chris.

Richter greeted the detectives in his study. "Is there anything wrong?" he asked.

"Not another murder, if that's what you're thinking." said Matt. "But, there is something we'd like to run by you. Get your take on it."

"Whatever I can do," replied Richter.

"We found a bible at both scenes," said Davis.

"Nothing unusual about that, is there?" asked the priest. "Most of my parishioners have a New Testament in their homes."

"I agree," said Matt. "It's what we found *inside* the bibles that got us thinking."

"And what was that?"

"Underlined passages relating to infidelity."

"EPHESIANS, Chapter Five?" asked Richter.

"Yeah," said Matt. "How'd you know?"

Richter walked over to a bookcase in the corner of his study, and retrieved a copy of the New Testament. He thumbed through it as he returned to the detectives. "Hmm," he said. "Let's see, EPHESIANS—." He flipped through the pages, stopping when he had reached a particular spot. "Here it is." He began to read: *"But fornication, and all uncleanness, or covetousness, let it be once named among you, as becometh—"*

"Yeah," said Freitag. "That sounds like it. What's it mean?"

"Well, in a nutshell," said Richter, "it relates to infidelity. It basically says that if one is unfaithful to one's spouse, that person faces the prospect of not going to Heaven."

"Well," said Matt. "That would fit – sort of. If they were running around on their husbands, but the husbands have alibis tighter than a duck's—"

"I think I get the picture," said the priest. "Look, there's something you might as well know. I apologize for not telling you sooner, but I wasn't sure how to handle it. I had counseled both women regarding some indiscretions in their lives. I'd rather not go into too much detail. I hope you understand."

Davis nodded. "Then you knew about the bibles?" he asked.

"Not exactly. I knew both women were having trouble in their marriages."

"Did you suggest that they consult their bible?"

"We refer to it as the New Testament," answered the priest. "Actually, I recommended those passages to them over the phone. My guess is they underlined them themselves. That would explain it, wouldn't it?"

"Yes it would," said Matt. He reached out and shook Richter's hand. "Thank you very much for your time, father. It certainly clears up the business about the bibles – uh – I mean New Testaments. It must be difficult dealing with these murders. I mean, both women in your own parish, women that you knew." Richter looked away. When he turned back, his eyes were moist. "It's most difficult, I assure you."

"Well, we won't take up anymore of your time," said Chris.

CHAPTER 16

Baltimore, Maryland

*B*y the time John had turned six, he had begun talking again. His speech was limited and resembled that of a mildly retarded youngster. He attended kindergarten at a nearby parochial elementary school. It was apparent that he was slow, and he was left mostly to himself. It was not surprising that he failed to respond to the average teaching methods employed at the school. John was often observed with large bruises on his arms and legs, and when inquiries were made, Marie always told the school officials that the injuries were a result of falls.

"Baby John doesn't walk that good," the young mother would say.

Each day, upon his arrival home from school, John would be greeted with a scowl, and asked the same question.

"You didn't tell 'em nothin', did ya? Did ya'?" The boy knew she was referring to the beatings, and, over time, learned to play the game. Instead of speaking, he would just shake his head no, hoping to avoid further punishment.

Right after he turned seven, John Curran was admitted to the emergency room with a fractured finger. His mother told the nurses that her son was clumsy and had fallen off his bicycle. Actually, Marie had discovered him wearing a silver ring that had been missing from her bureau. When she tried to remove the ring from his finger, she bent it backwards so hard that it had snapped.

One night when he was eight, his mother brought home an especially rough sailor, already drunk – and particularly nasty. The man was a Negro, talked with a strange accent, and kept calling Marie "Bitch," which she seemed to like.   He ordered John to stay in the living room, while he and Marie staggered into the bedroom, leaving the door ajar.   The little boy busied himself with a coloring book, trying to ignore the sexual sounds coming from the other room. In a little while, the laughter stopped and the tone of the sailor's voice grew ugly. Soon John heard the unmistakable sound of violence, including slapping and crying.   He tried not to cry, but after a few minutes, tears sprang from his eyes.

Suddenly the man emerged, naked, from the bedroom. He was swearing and holding a shiny leather belt in his huge hand. He began swinging it at the helpless child. At first, the boy was able to duck the blows successfully, but eventually the sailor connected with the buckle end of the belt and drew blood from the youngster's arm. He continued to hit the child, as Marie screamed from the bedroom for him to stop.

Mrs. Antonucci, the downstairs neighbor, tried to ignore the noise coming from Marie's apartment.   After all, it was Marie, herself, who had often told the elderly widow to mind her own business. However, this time it was different.   The shouting grew louder and louder, and the screams of the little boy became more hysterical.   At last, the old woman could stand it no longer and called police.

Five minutes later a patrol car pulled up to the apartment building and two officers rushed upstairs.   Mrs. Antonucci stood there, eyes wide, as they rushed past her into the unlocked Curran apartment. What they found made the two police officers sick.

Apparently, little John had still been sleeping in the tiny crib in Marie's bedroom, although he was already eight years old. And that was where they found him, naked, with ugly red cigarette burns on the head of his penis and on his testicles. His entire body was covered with welts from the sailor's belt, and the mattress was stained from urine and feces. He was barely conscious.

An ambulance took the now-unconscious boy to the emergency room. Marie screamed, "It was the nigger that did everything." The police dragged her out in handcuffs, along with the drunken serviceman. When they were led past Mrs. Antonucci's apartment, the woman crossed herself, then cursed at them in Italian. Marie cowered like the wild animal she had become, and avoided the woman's eyes as she passed quietly by her in the hallway.

The next day, Mrs. Antonucci received a request to testify in family court. So did the members of the parochial school staff that had witnessed the endless array of John's "injuries."

At the hearing that followed, witness after witness testified to the abuse of the eight-year old by his mother. It was no surprise when John, Jr. was removed from Marie's custody and placed in the care of the Holy Angels Foster Home, a Catholic orphanage on the West Side of Baltimore.

Marie convinced the judge that the sailor had inflicted the bulk of John's punishment. She received only a suspended sentence, and avoided jail time. But, she was unable to persuade officials to return her child to her, and soon gave up trying. She reasoned that life was a hell of a lot simpler without the child to complicate things. She had never really wanted him, and now she was free of him.

Ironically, six months later Marie Curran was struck dead by a drunk driver, and little John was finally rid of her!

Although little John lost his mother to a drunk driver, he would never truly be rid of her memory and the scars that accompanied it. During his first three years at Holy Angels, his life was a continuation of the horror that had haunted him in the past. Fellow orphans teased him unmercifully, nuns beat him whenever he misbehaved, and his bedwetting, and nightmares followed him from sleep into consciousness. He was constantly exhausted and confused. It was not until John

Curran was nearly twelve years old that love finally entered his miserable life. It arrived one snowy winter's day in the person of Sister Francis. A transfer had brought the thirty-eight-year-old nun from an order in Akron, Ohio, to the orphanage. From the beginning, she and the boy were drawn to each other as parent to child. She was like the mother he had always wanted, and he the son she could never have.

Immediately John began to blossom. Under the guidance of Sister Francis, he began to speak more clearly, study more effectively, and even blend with the other youngsters on a social level. Soon, his life had taken on a new meaning.

Indeed, it appeared, there was a God in Heaven.

Unfortunately, there was also the Devil.

CHAPTER 17

8:15 a.m., Monday, March 27

M en, I'd like to introduce the newest member of our squad, *Miss* Rita Valdez, detective third-grade." Although it was Foster who was speaking, it was the reputation of the female detective standing before them that was on the minds of most of the men gathered in the squad room. Rita Valdez was trouble – at least that's what Matt had heard. According to interdepartmental scuttlebutt, the vivacious addition to the Tenth Precinct's elite membership was a potential home wrecker, even if only *half* the rumors about her were true. Apparently, she had been involved in an affair with every one of her commanding officers along the way, and this stop at the "One-O" would be her last unless she wised up.

Matt studied the woman. She certainly was attractive. Fairly tall, dark hair, great figure – he figured her to be one side of forty or the other. Val certainly wouldn't like her. There were a few catcalls and a whistle or two before Rita spoke. "I'd just like to say that I've heard a lot of good things about you guys here in the One-O, and I'm looking forward to becoming part of the squad." There were a couple of murmured responses, like "us, too" and "any time, baby," before Foster held up his hands to restore order.

"Okay, okay," he said, "That's it. Let's all get back to work." He grabbed Rita gently by her upper arm, and looked over at Matt. "Can I see you for a minute?"

Oh boy, here it comes, thought Davis.   "Sure, Boss. What's up?"

Foster motioned to Davis and Valdez to follow him into his office. Rita led the way, and Matt brought up the rear, closing the frosted glass door behind him. The captain pulled two chairs up to the front of his desk, and beckoned the two detectives to have a seat. Leaning back in his swivel chair, Foster clasped his hands behind his head, and rocked slowly back and forth behind his massive desk. "Okay," he said, "here's how it's gonna be. Rita will be your responsibility, Matt – at least for a while. I want her to go wherever you and Freitag go – and that means *everywhere*. Show her the ropes, and don't hold anything back. She's a fast learner, so it shouldn't take long."

Matt sat quietly, while Rita looked back and forth at the two men.

"Is there a problem with that?" asked Foster.

"No, no," replied Matt. "I just thought—"

"Don't think," said Foster. "That'll only get you into trouble." He looked at Rita, whose face had turned a medium shade of red, and smiled. Rita smiled back. "Look," said Foster, "we're all adults here. Rita, I don't think it's any secret why you're here, am I right?"

Valdez sat up straight and took a deep breath. "Yeah, well, I'm little Miss Home Wrecker, and I'm on probation, right? So, what else is new?" Matt shifted nervously in his seat, pretending to study the various diplomas and framed awards on the wall behind the captain's head.

"Look," said Rita, "it takes two to tango, so let's not put all the blame on me."

"Forget all that bullshit," said Foster. "It's ancient history as far as I'm concerned. You know what's at stake, and I trust that you'll do the right thing. Now, Matt is my number one guy, and I figure if there's anyone you can be safe with, it's him. Just follow his lead, keep your nose clean and everything will work out just fine. Any questions?" Both detectives shrugged and shook their heads. "Good," said Foster. "So, get to work."

CHAPTER 18

After locking the door to his study, Father Pete set his coffee down alongside the new desktop computer, and pulled up a chair. He had only gotten the Gateway about six weeks ago, and was still getting used to his new "toy." He reached down and started the computer, took a sip of coffee, and rolled out the keyboard from within its sanctuary beneath the desktop.

He clicked the mouse on the familiar AOL icon on the screen, but nothing happened. Then he remembered that he had to double click, and immediately the screen came alive. After a few seconds, the sign-on screen appeared, and he logged on, using his main screen name, GOLFNUT1. Then he entered his password, *Confessor2*, and waited until his home page appeared. He checked the weather report, saw that the Yankees had lost the night before to Cleveland, and noted his IBM stock was off a point.

Clicking on FAVORITE PLACES, he quickly scrolled down the growing list to the one reading Yahoo, and double-clicked on the word. Soon he was into a game room, sipping coffee and quietly amusing himself with a game of Hearts. *Amazing little device.*

After winning twice and finishing second in a third game, he became bored. He closed out the Yahoo screen and returned to the familiar AOL home page. He scanned the display until his attention was drawn to a box at the top, designated *"People."* He clicked on the icon and scanned the list of options. He selected one marked *"Chat"* and opened the box.

CHAPTER 19

*T*he killer clicked the mouse on "Find Chat Now," then double-clicked on "Manhattan Singles." This was his favorite room, but before entering, he changed his screen name to the one he most preferred, and again clicked on "Who's Chatting." Ordinarily he would just jump into the room, and ask "Anybody here from Chelsea?" That way, he knew he wouldn't be wasting his time. Tonight, however, he had someone special in mind. He scrolled the list of colorful names. There were some 25 people in the "room." Some had names that were obviously related to the individual's occupation, like **StockMarketMan** or **TheMotorDoc**. Others, it seemed, were sexual in nature, like **MakeMeCum4U** or **MaidenFormDD**. At last he found the screen name he was looking for, **2Sexy4U**. He double-clicked, and a box appeared with several choices. He selected one marked "Send Instant Message" and double-clicked. In less than the blink of an eye, a box appeared and he quickly began to type:

SexualGuy1:   Hi!

For a moment, the word stood there by itself – all alone – just like he was. But soon it was accompanied by a reply.

2Sexy4U: *Hi to U!*

Before long, the message box began to explode with conversation:

SexualGuy1:   So, what's going on?

2Sexy4U: *Not much, U?*

SexualGuy1:   Same old...same old.   What are you wearing?

2Sexy4U: *Bra and panties...*
SexualGuy1: What color?
2Sexy4U: *Black*
SexualGuy1: Hmmmm...I like...
2Sexy4U: *I'm glad...*

    The killer enjoyed the exchange. It was extremely titillating to talk so intimately with someone he didn't even know. In the "real world" he wouldn't have had a chance. Women rarely spoke to him in public, and, when they did, it was strictly in a detached, business-like manner. Sexual talk was out of the question. He continued typing:

SexualGuy1:   Wanna play?
2Sexy4U: *Sure...you wanna start?*
SexualGuy1: okay...
2Sexy4U: *I'm ready...*
SexualGuy1: I'm kissing the back of your neck....
2Sexy4U: *mmmmmmmm.........*

    The chat session continued along those lines, all the while becoming increasingly sexual in nature. Soon he had removed his trousers and under pants, and was seated at the computer, naked from the waist down.

2Sexy4U: *I'm swirling my tongue beneath the head of your cock...*
SexualGuy1: Oh, yesssss.........it feels so good....
2Sexy4U: *I'm taking your cock inside my hot, wet mouth...*

    In just a few more minutes, the individual on the other end of the connection had, essentially, made "virtual" love to the killer, bringing him not only to a "virtual" climax, but to a real one, as well. He hoped he had done the same for "her." After all, who really knew anything about anyone "out there," he thought. The best part about the whole idea of cyber sex, was the fact that there were no limits whatsoever on one's imagination.

    He said his good-byes and logged off. The next time, he thought, I'll ask her to meet me. After wiping himself with a

Kleenex, he turned the computer off, got undressed, and went to bed.

CHAPTER 20

7:00 p.m., Thursday, March 30

Except for an elderly couple, praying quietly in the front row, the church was empty. Votive candles flickered irregularly, casting shimmering shadows that moved like dancers on the smooth, plaster walls behind. There was a faint smell of incense, a reminder of the church's ancient ties to the past. It was early evening. The stained glass windows admitted no light, but glowed from the reflected light within.

One of the narrow, bronze-sheathed doors at the rear of the building opened slowly. Cindy McKenzie – screen name: *2Sexy4U* – entered the vestibule, and peered through the darkness into the church beyond. Satisfied, that there was no one there who would recognize her, she paused, dipped her fingers into the font of holy water and crossed herself. She quietly seated herself in a pew located near the rear of the church.

St. Jude was one of the oldest Catholic churches in Manhattan, dating back to the late 19th Century. There were high ceilings, supported by wide marble columns, which, if located in a ballpark, would have been considered obstructions. For Cindy, who deliberately chose to sit behind them, they provided protection from prying eyes.   She was dressed modestly in a red pullover sweater, black polyester skirt, and black flats, run over at the heels. A dingy tan raincoat and a requisite kerchief, that covered her mousy brown hair, completed her outfit.

After praying silently for a few moments, she stepped out into the aisle, and moved to the confessional booth, located against the right wall of the church. She pulled aside the velvet curtain that covered the entrance to the confessional, entered, and kneeled on the padded rest. As she crossed herself, the cover of the small, woven-mesh window that separated penitent from priest slid open in response; a masculine cough indicated it was time to make her confession.

"Bless me father, for I have sinned," she began. The words seemed uncomfortable on her tongue, but she forced herself to continue. "It has been ten years since my last confession. I have been—"

"Ten *years*?" asked the priest, incredulously.

"Yes, but—"

"No, no, my dear," said the priest. "There's no need to explain. Please, continue."

"I have been unfaithful to my Lord. I have not attended mass, and I have sinned grievously in thought and in deed."

"And what is the nature of your sin?"

"Well, I love my husband, but—" she hesitated.

"What is it?" encouraged the priest.

"I don't know how—"

"Just say it, my dear."

"Well," she began again, "I've had impure thoughts about another man—"

"And?" said the priest. His curiosity had been peaked.

"—and I've been going on the Internet and—"

The priest chuckled aloud. "I don't really think that going on the Internet is a sin. Do you?"

"No, it's not just that—I—well—I've been chatting and—"

"My dear," laughed the priest. "I don't believe chatting is a sin, either. I do it myself on occasion."

There was no response.

"Are you chatting with other men? Is *that* what's bothering you?"

"Yes—and—well—there's more." The young woman was obviously embarrassed.

"If you'd rather not—" he began.

"No!" she exclaimed, much too loudly. Her voice grew more restrained. "I mean—no. But, I need to get this off my conscience. I've—well, I've been having—cyber sex." She breathed a sigh of relief, for it had taken a good deal of courage to say the words. Then, embarrassed, she added, "I mean—oh, my God—you probably don't even know what I'm—"

"What? What you're talking about?" asked the priest.

"I'm sorry," she said.

"We're not exactly in the Dark Ages here," he said. "Yes, I understand." There was a long silence. "How many times has this happened?"

"Five—maybe six—times," she whispered.

The priest waited for more details, but none were forthcoming.

"With the same man?" he asked, unsure of where to go with his questioning.

"Yes," replied Cindy.

Another awkward silence followed, and then she spoke again. This time, the words she said caught the priest by surprise. "The thing is" she said, "I want to meet him."

"Excuse me?" said the priest.

"I said I want to meet him," repeated Cindy.

The priest was quiet for a moment.

"Father?" said Cindy. "Do you—"

"That would be a mistake," he said.

"You're right, of course," she agreed, unconvincingly.

"Is there anything else?" asked the priest.

"No," came the terse reply.

"Very well. For your penance, I want you to say ten Our Fathers and twenty Hail Marys."

"Yes, Father," she answered.

"And, young lady—" started the priest.

"Yes, Father?"

"We'd like to see you at Confession more than once every *ten years*." It came out as a command, rather than a suggestion.

The words stung the young woman like a slap in the face. "Yes, Father," she answered quietly. "Is there anything else, Father?"

"Why, yes, your Act of Contrition, of course. God bless you, my child."

Cindy McKenzie struggled with the familiar words of repentance, "Oh My God, I am heartily sorry for having offended Thee and—"

When she had finished, the priest spoke briefly in Latin, and finally said, "Go in peace, my child."

The door to the window slid shut with a bang, and Cindy hastily exited the confessional, moved to a nearby pew, kneeled, and crossed herself. She began praying almost immediately, eager to be relieved of her burden.

When Confession was over, Father Pete moved silently about the church, turning off the lights one by one. Finally, he kneeled at the altar and crossed himself. He remained in that rigid posture for several minutes, then rose and left the church. His mind was filled with many confusing thoughts.

CHAPTER 21

8:28 p.m., Saturday, April 1

*I*t was getting late. If he didn't make his move soon, he'd miss his chance. He had been online with Cindy since quarter to eight. Cindy's husband was a Merchant Marine, and was often out of town for prolonged periods. Cindy, a teacher, had taken up chatting to fill the void left by his absence. It wasn't something she was proud of; in fact, she was hoping to quit – but not quite yet. She thought briefly of her recent confession, then dismissed the thought of it. She could always go again; that was what being a Catholic was all about, wasn't it?

The killer stared at the flickering image on his screen. He was getting good at this. He typed some more:

SexualGuy1: So…uh…Cindy…when are we going to get together?

2Sexy4U: *I don't know…how about tomorrow night?*

SexualGuy1: You're kidding. Really?

2Sexy4U: *Well, my husband's not due back 'til next Wednesday…*

She had already told him where she lived, so it would only be a short walk from his residence to hers. Why not? She sounded really hot. Maybe he could really turn her on. Not like that other one. What was her name? Marlene? Maureen? It was something like that. Well, it didn't matter. He'd fixed her ass. He'd fixed her good, the bitch. Hope her husband got a good surprise, he thought.

2Sexy4U: Hey!!! Are you still there?

SexualGuy1: Yeah…I'm still here…what's up?

2Sexy4U: *Well…how about it? Do you want to come over?*

> *She really wants it, he thought. Well, I'm just the one to give it to her.*

SexualGuy1: Sure, baby…what time?

2Sexy4U: *How about 9?*

SexualGuy1: Sure. What's the apartment number?

2Sexy4U: *It's 3B…just ring the bell downstairs, and I'll let you in. Try not to make*
> *2 much noise, ok?*

SexualGuy1: Sure! NP…see you at 9!!!

> *I won't make a sound, he thought. But, I'll make sure that she makes plenty of noise. It'll be a great April Fools Day.*

CHAPTER 22

5:45 a.m., Sunday, April 2

It had been several weeks since the Spiros murder, and Davis and his men had been working almost uninterrupted, around the clock. With no real leads other than the fingerprints, hearts, and bibles, and with no particular direction in which to go, Matt decided he needed a break – or, at least, Valerie did. The previous night, at her urging, they had decided to make a trip to the Catskills to do some early-season trout fishing. It would be the day after the actual Opening Day in New York state (a day he normally avoided), and he had initially resisted fishing so close to that dreaded date. But, Val had insisted that a little diversion would be good for him, and he couldn't disagree. So, it was set. He couldn't remember the last time he had ventured out on the initial day of the season. One look at his fly fishing calendar, which showed that it was time for a *Quill Gordon* Mayfly hatch, and he had known it was the right thing to do. He hadn't fished a full-blown *Quill Gordon* hatch in nearly ten years.

Now, in the early Sunday morning hours before dawn, Matt and Valerie were busily preparing for a rarity – a day off – together. Matt scrambled around the spare bedroom, gathering up rods, reels, waders, and other specialized equipment. The water in the Beaverkill River would be cold. After all, it was only the second day of the season. He'd better bring his thermal underwear and neoprene gloves, he thought, with a shiver. He located them, and packed both items into a duffel bag. Then, he found his fly boxes and checked the contents to be sure he had the right flies.

"Shit," he muttered aloud, "no *Quill Gordons*." He'd have to purchase some size 14's when they got to Roscoe. Early season fly-fishing was a crapshoot to begin with; no point in going out unarmed. Hell, the best fishing didn't start for another month. *But, at least we'll be together*, he reflected. Matt and Valerie both worked shifts: she at the hospital, he at the disposal of the NYPD. Days off together were hard to come by.

Valerie moved efficiently about the kitchen, preparing lunch. She had fried up some chicken the previous night. She carefully wrapped the crispy breasts and legs in plastic wrap, before packing them into the Styrofoam cooler. She slid a container of German-style potato salad into the far corner of the chest, and placed a bunch of red grapes on top it. She added a jar of sweet gherkin pickles (Matt's favorite), the chicken, and a flat ice pack from the freezer, and closed the lid. Then, she filled a paper bag with plastic spoons, napkins, and little disposable shakers of salt and pepper, and set them next to the cooler.

"Don't forget the thermos for your coffee," Matt reminded her, as he strolled into the kitchen.

"Thank you, *dear*," replied his wife, theatrically.

"We'll stop at the diner and get it filled when we get to Roscoe."

"Oh *really*? You mean like we *always* do?" she replied in the smart-ass tone of voice that drove Matt crazy. It was a little game they played.

"I'll go get the car," said Matt. He grabbed his gear and hurried downstairs, car keys rattling in his hand. He crossed the street and entered the parking garage that housed the Jeep. It was nearly impossible to find a parking space on the crowded streets of Manhattan, and despite the hefty monthly rent, Davis truly cherished his long-held spot within the underground parking lot. He pulled the old Jeep Wagoneer to the front of the building, and double-parked while he waited for Valerie. Five minutes later, she emerged from the lobby, carrying the cooler and a folding chair, wearing a frown.

"Shit," muttered Matt. "I should have helped her with the cooler."

"Sorry, honey," he said, as he took the chest and chair from Valerie and stowed them in the back of the vehicle.

"It's okay," she smiled. "You can't do everything."

Matt started the engine and they were on their way. The Manhattan streets were all but deserted except for those individuals who habitually occupied the shadows, regardless of the time of day. Streetlights shone ineffectively, as their emissions were neutralized by the first rays of the rising sun, the golden color reflecting off the glass fronts of the high-rise apartment buildings located across the Hudson River.

As the Jeep traversed the George Washington Bridge, large drops of condensation dripped down from the massive steel girders above. Without fanfare, the one-car caravan crossed over the swiftly flowing river separating New York from New Jersey. The two states almost touched one another, but were light years apart in character. Automatically, Valerie shoved a Willie Nelson tape in the car's ancient cassette player, and the city was officially left behind.

It was a two-hour ride to Roscoe, New York, home of the most hallowed fly-fishing stream in the Catskills. They drove quietly through northern New Jersey without talking. The only sounds came from the humming of the tires on the highway and the music of the tape player. They passed mall after empty mall, and maneuvered through deserted cloverleaf intersections. Neither Valerie nor Matt liked New Jersey, but tolerated it like a pastured horse endures its attendant flies.

They passed the former site of the old Ford factory in Mahwah – now occupied by a tall, monolithic hotel building – and moved across the state line, out of New Jersey and back into New York. They breathed a collective sigh, and looked at each other with a smile. It always went this way. It was something they shared in common. They were free.

Before long, they had traveled through the mundane suburban areas that tied the city to the countryside, and were moving into the rural portion of the Catskills. The Jeep moaned and groaned mechanically, as it made its way slowly up the long six-mile continuous grade from Ellenville to Wurtsboro. This section of road was famous not only for its considerable incline, but also for its pea soup fog that often brought early morning traffic to a standstill. Mercifully, the fog was moderate this morning, and soon they had reached the top of the slope. They began to pass familiar Catskill landmarks: White Lake, Monticello, and eventually, the town of Liberty. The sun had crept above the mountains and Matt was beginning to relax, to breath deeper and more slowly. He looked over at his wife and thought how beautiful she was.

Valerie lay with her head against the headrest of the reclined seat. Her eyes were shut and a soft smile creased her ample mouth. She was only forty-two, and had no gray yet in her chestnut brown hair. She was wearing it short these days – a concession to her occupation – and he marveled at the grace of her neck. He was struck by a sudden impulse to kiss her. As carefully as he could, he leaned over to brush her forehead with his lips. She sighed. For a second, the Jeep swerved wildly, and he laughed aloud, as he regained control.

"Matt!" cried Valerie, as she awoke with a start.

"Relax," he said. "It's okay. It was just a deer."

He inhaled deeply, caught a whiff of her perfume, and smiled contentedly. He was a lucky man. Twenty minutes later they passed the billboard advertising their upcoming destination, the sleepy little town of Roscoe. The local Chamber of Commerce had erected the garish sign that featured a gigantic trout, years ago after officially dubbing the place "Trout Town, U.S.A.," at the urging of local business owners who catered unabashedly to the seasonal fishermen. To most travelers, however, Roscoe merely represented the halfway point between Manhattan and Binghamton, as they headed west along U.S. Route 17. More importantly, perhaps, it was known as the home of the famous Roscoe Diner.

As Matt steered the Jeep around the curving exit ramp, the recently refurbished stainless steel eatery stood alone, like an old friend, waiting with open arms to greet them at the end of their journey. Matt glanced at his watch. It was exactly eight a.m. – two hours on the nose as usual.

CHAPTER 23

After filling the thermos with steaming hot coffee, Matt ordered a hot chocolate for himself. He exchanged a few words with Gus, the owner of the restaurant, and then went outside. Valerie was leaning with her back against the side of the car, face angled upward towards the sun, luxuriating in the early morning warmth of day. Her eyes were closed. Matt walked over, placed the thermos and container of hot chocolate carefully on the roof of the Jeep, and leaned down to give his wife a kiss. Sensing his presence, Valerie lifted her head up and met him halfway. The kiss was slow and lazy, just like the day promised to be. As they broke the kiss, Valerie opened her eyes, squinting against the sun, and grinned.

"Yes?" asked Matt, with a grin.

"I do, you know," said Valerie, the grin spreading into a smile.

"Do what?" he asked.

"You know," she blushed.

"Oh, that," he said. "Well, I love you too."

"And what else?"

"And I'm so glad to be here with you today."

"Good," said Valerie.

Then Matt patted her on the hip. "Let's shoot some pool, Fast Eddie."

Matt drove the Jeep slowly toward Main Street, two blocks away. He made a left at the light, and guided the car into a parking stall across from his favorite fly shop, "Catch a Rising Trout."

A group of fly fishermen were already standing outside the door studying the hatch information on the weathered slate board attached to the outside of the building. Each of them wore waders, a vest – with specialized gadgets attached to the latter – and a hat. As usual, Budge, the owner, was late, and even though it was Opening Day, since there was no particular necessity to be early on the river this time of year, no one seemed to mind.

As Matt and Valerie approached the shop, heads swiveled in their direction, all eyes drawn immediately to her shapely figure and earthy good looks. Today, she was wearing jeans and a flannel shirt. Matt thought there was something sexy about a woman who fished. By the reaction of the other fishermen, he judged he was right. He smiled smugly; proudly acknowledging the blatant stares of a few younger men who gave her the once over. Matt leaned over and whispered something in Valerie's ear and she turned towards him and smiled. He gave her a peck on the cheek, possessively patted her on the hip, and pushed her through the open doorway. Budge stood off to the side, holding the door. He bowed as the couple entered.

The fly shop was familiar territory to Matt. In the twenty-five years he had been fishing the Beaverkill, the business had endured three droughts and seen four different owners. Budge Mallon had purchased the place around the same time Matt and Valerie had married, and he and Matt had become good friends almost from the start. He was a large man, with a belly that draped over his belt, and a swath of tanned scalp dividing the white hair on his head. His blue eyes glowed with intelligence beneath thick snowy brows that threatened to overrun his forehead.

"So, what's new in the 'Big City,' Matt?" he asked.

"Same old, same old, Budge. Car bombings, murder and mayhem," he joked. It was his standard reply. Budge clapped him on the back with one of his enormous hands and guided him toward the array of fly boxes against the far wall.

"Enough of that bullshit. Let's talk fishing. We're expecting *Quill Gordons* today. You got enough?"

"Haven't got a one," replied Matt. "Why the hell else would I come into this God-forsaken place?"

Both men laughed. Matt walked around the shop with Valerie at his side, poked and picked among the numerous fly boxes and finally selected half a dozen of the small, dark flies, marked "#14, Quill Gordon Dry." He placed them into one of the little plastic cups stacked neatly alongside the boxes of flies, snapped a lid on the container, and presented it at the counter for payment. As usual, Budge refused to accept his friend's money.

"Sorry," he said. "Register's busted. I'll catch you next time."

Matt smiled, and accepted his friend's largesse as repayment for some help he had given him in apprehending a couple of shoplifters during his first visit to the shop.

A few minutes later he and Valerie said their good-byes and filed out of the front door. They drove the short distance out of town to Old Route 17, then turned left and headed to the river. The Beaverkill is a beautiful trout stream, considered by many to be the birthplace of fly-fishing in America. To fly fishermen it is sacred water. From its confluence with its tributary, the Wilowemoc, the river flows approximately ten miles west alongside the old highway until it merges with the East Branch of the Delaware River. Their first stop was Hendrickson Pool; always a good bet during a hatch *of Quill Gordons.* Matt exited the Jeep, looked carefully in both directions, then took Valerie by the arm, and guided her carefully across the road to the other side. A guardrail framed the river below, and Matt put his right foot on its metal edge, resting his elbow on the elevated knee, his chin cradled in his hand. He stared down at the sparkling water, looking for signs of fish. Valerie stood quietly alongside him, just enjoying the fresh air.

"Look," said Matt, pointing down at the water, "look there."

Valerie stared hard at the surface of the water, expecting to see trout. Instead, she saw nothing but the steady flow of the current across the rocks.

"No, not the water," said Matt, "over there, on the far bank. See it? It's a heron."

"Where? Oh, yeah! God, it's huge. Matt, you are so amazing."

Valerie watched the large slate-blue bird, perched motionless along the bank of the river. It was so still, in fact, that it could easily have mistaken for a stuffed decoy. Val turned and looked at her husband. He was staring intently at the water now, much like the bird, and she marveled at the complexity of the man. She admired everything about him. She loved him more than life.

Matt squinted in the bright, early morning sunlight, and continued studying the flowing river. He loved it here. Maybe one day they'd move up here. Buy a little cabin. Retire. Fish the rest of their lives away. Suddenly, the vision of Melina Spiros' ravished body flashed through his mind and he had to force himself to see the water again. He sighed.

"What's the matter?" asked Valerie.

"Oh, nothing. I was just thinking of that poor woman."

She gave him a hug and leaned her head against his shoulder.

"I'm sorry, Matt."

"It's okay," he sighed. "Come on. Let's go fishing."

They spent the rest of the morning enjoying the sunshine and the fresh mountain air. Matt drifted his fly through the tumbling pocket water above the pool, then carefully waded to the side of the river, and fished down through the run entering at its head. Normally, Matt would have worked his way upstream, approaching the fish from below, but in the heavy, early-spring current, it was unlikely that he would disturb any fish, and it was easier to move with the water – instead of against it. Valerie sat on the guardrail above the river and watched. She wasn't quite ready to join him in the water.

In the first hour, Matt caught three fish—all small—on dry flies, and he urged Valerie to join him. She changed into waders, donned her vest, and rigged her fly outfit. Soon she was alongside him, positioned about thirty feet downstream, flailing away as usual with no success. Catching fish was of little importance to Valerie, but being with Matt was everything. Around one o'clock, they reeled in their fly lines, and crossed the river. They climbed up the steep bank to the road, walked to the car and stowed their gear, then drove about a half mile downstream and parked on the shoulder of the road.

Matt retrieved the cooler from the backseat, and Valerie brought the Thermos. They moved to a large rock overlooking Cairn's Pool. It was Matt's favorite spot on the river, and they always had their lunch there. They watched as fishermen covered the water with their casts, the long, silky fly lines waving gracefully in the air like loose threads from a spider's web. As her husband sat eating a chicken breast, Valerie sat alongside and watched him intently. She never felt closer to him than when they took these little day trips together. She longed for things to be the same back in Manhattan. She wished they could bottle these moments and uncork them in times of need. Unfortunately, the reality was that they rarely saw each other in the day-shift night-shift atmosphere of their daily lives.

After lunch, Matt joined the line of other fishermen waiting their turn to fish the pool. As the angler at the head of the pool caught and landed a fish, he would move to the tail end. This was called "rotating the pool," and allowed for the next fisherman in line to move up and fish the prime water. Older, more experienced anglers still observed the tradition, but newer fishermen considered it more of a nuisance. Fortunately, they were still in the minority.

The afternoon passed all too quickly, and soon it was time to leave. During the ride back to the city the couple sat in silence, as if rehearsing for the inevitable return to their "real lives" back home. However, it had been a lovely day, and its memory would sustain Val until another took its place.

Tomorrow would be a different kettle of fish.

CHAPTER 24

T hat night, Matt had the same dream he always had after spending time on the river.

He was the guest of honor at his retirement dinner at the Waldorf Astoria Hotel. He and Valerie danced the night away, he in a finely tailored tuxedo, she in an exquisite gown. The chief of police got up and toasted Matt's many years on the force, and, of course, paid tribute to his solving of some particularly heinous murder.

Following the affair, they spent the night at the Plaza Hotel—courtesy of the NYPD—and the next morning boarded a jet for a flight to New Brunswick, Canada. They were met there by a fishing guide, who escorted them to a remote salmon-fishing camp on the Miramichi River. A red-jacketed butler showed them to their room, remarking off-handedly, that "the fishing has been quite good lately."

The next morning, after an elaborate breakfast of corned beef hash, eggs, potatoes O'Brien, and homemade biscuits— plus a mug of the finest hot chocolate Matt had ever experienced—it was time for fishing. All the necessary gear had been arranged on a trunk at the foot of the bed in their room, and Matt dressed carefully while Valerie leafed through rare horticultural catalogues. There was a knock on the door and their guide announced that they "better hurry," as the fish were "jumping all over the pool."

They stopped at the kitchen where the cook gave Valerie a wicker basket containing their lunch, along with a thermos of hot chocolate for Matt and another of coffee for Valerie. Then

*the threesome walked a short distance to the river where Matt
proceeded to catch fish after fish. Matt had stood knee deep in
the cool water, the passing river forming an eddy behind him.
His rod was bent with the weight of a large salmon that was
hooked securely in the corner of its mouth by one of Matt's
hand-tied flies. With an eye out for the fish, Matt glanced at
Valerie seated on a blanket on the shore. She was deeply
absorbed in a romance novel. She lifted her eyes and turned
them toward the water, smiling when she noticed Matt gazing
lovingly at her. He returned the favor.*

*"Sweetheart," she said. "Why don't you stop fishing and
come join me for lunch?" He pointed downstream at the
jumping fish, and said, "As soon as I land this salmon." The
guide removed the net from behind his vest and moved into
position just downstream from the salmon. "I'll net him for
you, sir. That way you and the Mrs. can have your lunch..."*

The sound of the water faded quickly from Matt's
memory. The dream always seemed to end there, and Matt
usually awoke ravenously hungry, almost as if the dream were
real. The following morning was no exception.

CHAPTER 25

10:05 a.m., Wednesday, April 5

T hey found Cindy McKenzie's body just like they found the others. The woman had been raped and strangled. The signature heart was carved into her left breast, two sets of initials neatly crafted within it. Now, *three* young women in the prime of their lives were dead, and for no apparent reason. But there was always *some* motive—as convoluted as it might seem—it *was* there. There had to be some common thread connecting the pitiful victims with their even more pathetic killer. It *was* there, and it was up to Davis to find it.

There hadn't been any sign of forced entry. Apparently, she either knew the killer, or at the very least was expecting him. What kind of person could smile at a woman, spend time with her, and then kill her? These were the thoughts that wandered through the heads of the detectives as they examined the gruesome murder scene.

"Check for a bible," ordered Davis. *New Testament* seemed a bit pretentious to Matt, so he had decided on *bible –* except when he was with Father Pete.

"I'm kind of hoping we don't find one," said Chris. "If we do, we're fucked."

"Tell me about it," said Matt.

They both knew that if another book showed up— especially one with underlined passages in it—there would be little doubt that they had a serial killer on their hands. Chris donned a pair of paper-thin latex gloves, and moved from room to room, breathing a sigh of relief as each compartment failed to yield a bible.   Finally, he entered the kitchen.   A yellow Formica-covered table stood in the center of the room, bracketed by two chairs covered in matching Naugahyde.   A small glass vase containing an arrangement of silk flowers sat in the center of the table, sections of newspaper strewn to one side. Chris circled the table warily, as if the objects presented a tangible threat.   Then he leaned over and gently lifted one section of newspaper, then another and another, until he found what he was looking for. *Shit! Not another one?*

"Matt," whispered Chris, a frog in his voice. There was no response. He cleared his throat and called out again, this time louder.

"What?" answered Davis.

"It's here."

 "What?"

"The book – the friggin' bible – I found it."

"Shit," sighed Matt.

"That's what I said," said Freitag.

Davis entered the kitchen, where Chris stood with the copy of the New Testament cradled delicately in his huge hand. Matt extended his own latex-covered hand toward his partner, and gently relieved him of the book. Leafing through its pages, he stopped at a section marked by a plastic bookmark. There was a passage underlined; it was from EPHESIANS, just like the others.

"Damn it," he murmured.

"Guess we better break the news to the Captain, huh?" said Chris. "You wanna tell him?"

"I'll flip you for it," said Matt. He extracted a quarter from his pocket and tossed it in the air. "Heads," he said. The coin landed in the palm of his hand, heads side up. "Sorry, pal. You lose."

Freitag leaned over and examined the coin, then frowned.

"Two out of three?" he implored.

"NFW," replied Matt.

CHAPTER 26

8:45 a.m., Thursday, April 6

The Spiros slaying had occurred about three weeks after the first killing. This one had taken place exactly sixteen days later—or a little over two weeks. Was there significance in the time differential? Probably not, thought Davis. But, one thing was certain. The murders were getting closer together. *Not a good sign*, he thought.

Matt was sitting in the sanctuary of his study. He rubbed his eyes with the back of his hands. Nine days had passed since Cindy McKenzie's body had been found. School officials were surprised when she hadn't shown up for work that Monday, since she was a reliable employee, not prone to absences. But when she failed to appear on Tuesday, they grew concerned and placed several calls to her home, without any answer. Finally, the school secretary called the police.

It took a day to contact her husband, who'd been on a freighter off the North Carolina coast at the time of the murder. By the time he showed up at the morgue to identify the body, he had already been eliminated as a suspect. Davis stared at the autopsy report of the latest homicide, which sat like a coiled snake on his desk. He decided to strike first. With more than a little anxiety, he picked up the document and began to read:

"CLOTHING
     The body is nude. Received along with the body are: a pair of blue bikini-style underpants,

torn; a matching blue brassiere, with the clip anterior, stretched and torn. Both garments bear the label "Victoria's Secret, Medium." One slip, blue nylon, bearing label "Sears;" tan corduroy skirt, label "Dress Barn, medium;" pink angora sweater, pullover type, no label (perhaps handmade); two sneakers, white leather, size 8, Nike brand. All garments found alongside victim in single pile.

EXTERNAL APPEARANCE
Body is that of a well-developed, well-nourished white female, appearing consistent with the stated age of 34. Rigidity complete in the hands and jaw. Partial rigidity in the knees and elbows. Anterior lividity is present. Head is covered by shoulder length blond hair, approximately 14" long. Eyebrows, eyelashes light brown. There is some bluish discoloration of the lateral portions of the lower lips. Some drying and bluish discoloration in the tip of the tongue. Multiple small petechial-type hemorrhages are noted in the cheeks, bilaterally. Chest and abdomen unremarkable..."

Matt laid down the report and closed his eyes. *Unremarkable indeed,* he thought. He wondered if the parents of poor Cindy McKenzie would agree with the clinical findings. He couldn't begin to imagine what it must be like for a parent or loved one to have to read such a detached description of what had once been an alive, vital human being. He picked up the report again and continued:

"...Normal breasts with extended nipples. However, there is a heart-shaped incision on the lateral surface of the right breast. Incision is approximately .3

centimeters deep and measures approximately and measures approximately 7.5 centimeters by 5.0 centimeters. Located within the heart-shaped incision are two sets of initials. They are "J.C." and "C.M." Incisions appear to have been made with a sharp knife or probably a razor blade. Dried material with the appearance consistent of semen is present around the *labium majorum* and on the interior aspect of right and left thighs.

The teeth are natural with minimal decay. Petechial hemorrhages are observed in the gingival and in the buccal surfaces of the lips. The ears are unremarkable and each is pierced once. Normal female genitalia with some evidence of trauma, consistent with rape or forced sexual activity. Light brown curly pubic hair. Back is unremarkable. Anus appears normal. Lower extremities are unremarkable.

INTERNAL EXAMINATION
CRANIAL VAULT & BRAIN
Reflection of the scalp reveals multiple petechial hemorrhages or foci of congestion on the inner surface of the scalp. In addition, there is a 5.0-centimeter by 2.5-centimeter band of diffuse hemorrhage in the soft tissues of the scalp. This band is oriented coronally and located just to the left of the vertex. Shaving of the underlying hair reveals no injury to the external surface of the scalp. No skull fractures.

No epidural, sub dural or sub arachnoid
hemorrhage. Brain weighs 1270 grams,
and is unremarkable..."

Davis sighed and reflected upon the last
statement. There was that word again, "unremarkable."
Damn it, thought the detective, they weren't
unremarkable – any of the victims. Each one had been a
living, breathing person, with ideas, hopes, dreams,
friends, and relatives. He couldn't accept that insipid
word, "unremarkable." He was determined to make
their lives count for something. He forced himself to
continue reading:

"...Incision made through a 2.5 centimeter
panniculus. No excess fluid or adhesions. A
few hemorrhages up to .3 centimeters in
diameter are noted in the diaphragm..."

Matt skimmed the remainder of the report, until he came
to the final line, entitled "CAUSE OF DEATH." The words
were the same as in the others: "Asphyxia by Strangulation,
HOMICIDE." The autopsy report was dated April 12, and was
signed: Catherine D. Ahearn, Assistant Medical Examiner.
Attached was a copy of the toxicological report that revealed
nothing abnormal other than the fact that the victim had
consumed a chicken sandwich before her death.
     It was too soon to expect the results of the DNA tests on
the semen, but Davis had no doubt that the profile belonged to
one messed up individual. This guy was a one-way trip to hell.
Matt only hoped he could stop the train before it made too many
more stops.
     He gingerly placed the four-page combined document
on the far corner of his desk. He regarded it with distaste, as if
it contained a life of its own, which of course—in a manner of
speaking—it did. The detective rubbed his eyes, and was

suddenly very weary. He reflected upon the details of the latest homicide and grew even more upset.

The circumstances surrounding Cindy McKenzie's murder had been identical to the others, except for one detail: she hadn't been bound to the bed. Perhaps she was already dead by the time her body was defiled, eliminating the need for the ligatures? Often times there were discrepancies in the details of serial killings, but these were generally outweighed by the similarities. The papers would say that she had been brutally raped and strangled like the two previous victims, but there would be no mention of the heart and the initials. Those details were being withheld at all costs to avoid inflating the killer's ego, and to discourage anyone else from becoming a "copycat killer."

But, it wasn't the newspaper stories, the autopsy report, or the toxicological report that disturbed Davis so much. These were routine occurrences, but he never got used to them. No, it was a simple bit of information that gnawed at him like acid on an empty stomach. It was the fact that, upon further investigation, it had been discovered that earlier that evening, according to a neighbor, Cindy had been to Confession at St. Jude's.

According to the autopsy report, the victim, thirty-four-year old Cindy McKenzie, had eaten a chicken sandwich – nothing abnormal about that was there? No, certainly not. But, then, as if anticipating her fate, the young woman had visited St. Jude and made what amounted to her final confession, and final Act of Contrition. Was it merely a coincidence, or did her actions provide some sort of morbid clue? What, wondered Davis, had been in that confession and perhaps more important, who had heard it?

CHAPTER 27

Baltimore, Maryland

*J*ohn Curran entered puberty when he was thirteen. At the same time he entered his own personal hell. In the beginning, all of the boy's feelings of sexual arousal were accompanied by a competing sense of apprehension and fear. His scarred penis and testicles were a fierce reminder of the various tortures administered by his mother and her partners. Every erection brought with it both excitement and revulsion.

One evening, though, while lying in bed and unable to sleep, John subconsciously allowed his mind to wander to the image of the fresh, innocent face of Sister Francis. He became ashamed. He tried desperately to turn his thoughts to a non-sexual subject. He thought of cars, sports, and even food – anything but Sister Francis. But, his attempts at misdirection only brought the image of his surrogate mother more clearly into focus. Try as he might to dismiss it, the image only became clearer, and with the image came the erection. He wasn't aware of exactly how it happened, but John soon found himself on the brink of orgasm. Before he realized what was happening, the first-time experience was over. The warm, wet fluid from his ejaculation had spread over the front of his under shorts and he was left relieved, but also confused. The exhausted boy immediately drifted into a deep, untroubled sleep. When he awoke in the morning, he felt oddly refreshed – even cleansed – but with no memory of the shame of the *previous evening. From that day forward, however, all feelings of sexual arousal were to be forever linked to the image of John Curran's one true love—Sister Francis—and were to be accompanied by a deep feeling of shame...*

CHAPTER 28

8:45 a.m., Friday, April 7

The Tenth Precinct headquarters is situated in the middle of the block on 20th Street, between Seventh and Eighth Avenues. Nobody knows for sure how old the building is, but it is generally considered a safe bet that it pre-dates the turn of the century. At first glance, it appears to be just another apartment building, sandwiched in between two others. However, upon further inspection, its large double doors and twin globe lights that illuminate its entrance give it away for what it is—a police station. Davis shuffled up the ancient metal stairs to his office on the second floor. The day was warming quickly, and he removed his heavy topcoat before signing in on the movement sheet. It was about nine when he decided to phone St. Jude.

Margaret Flynn, the seventy-eight-year old housekeeper, answered the phone on the fifth ring. Except for being a little hard of hearing, she was as spry as the day she left her native Ireland to come to America, almost sixty years ago. She had been employed by the church ever since.

"It's for you, Father Pete," she shouted from the large, white-tiled kitchen, adjacent to the head priest's study.

Richter put down the latest copy of *Golf Magazine* and picked up the extension. He waited for the click, which signaled that Margaret had hung up, then spoke clearly into the phone. "Hello, this is Father Richter."

"It's Matt Davis, Father Pete," said the detective, remembering the priest's request for informality. "I was wondering—" he hesitated briefly, carefully phrasing his request "—I was wondering if it would be possible to find out who was hearing Confession last Friday afternoon?"

The silence on the other end of the line was palpable.

"I really *need* to know," he said, quite forcefully. He immediately regretted the tone of his voice *and* his choice of words.

"Well, hello to you, *too*, Matt," said Father Richter, as if he had never heard the detective's question. "And how are you?"

Oh boy, thought Davis, *I was right. I pushed too hard.* He forced himself to respond. "I'm sorry, Father Pete. I'm fine. And you?"

"Great, Matt. So, what can I help you with?" His voice sounded more relaxed.

"Well, I guess you heard about the McKenzie woman, right?"

"Yes, I'm afraid I did," replied Father Richter, with a sigh. "In fact, her funeral is tomorrow morning. I didn't know her very well, though."

"No, no, I'm sure you didn't. I understand she hadn't been to Confession in over ten years."

"I wouldn't know about that," answered the priest. "Is that what her husband told you?"

"Yes, that's right," said Davis. "That's why it's so important that I speak with who ever it was that heard her confession. Maybe he can give us some idea of what was troubling her."

"Well, the funeral mass is at ten tomorrow morning," replied Father Richter. "And, of course, it is the weekend. Perhaps, sometime Monday afternoon? Would that be okay?"

Matt sensed some reluctance on the priest's part, and answered quickly. "Actually, I was hoping for a little sooner.

But, I guess Monday would be fine. Do you *know* who it was, that heard the confession, I mean?"

Father Richter's voice smiled as he replied. "Well, not right off the top of my head, Matt. I'd have to look at the assignment sheet, talk to the other priests. But, I'll tell you what: I'll find out who it was and make sure they're here when you come by on Monday. Is four o'clock okay?"

Matt breathed a sigh of relief. "Four o'clock will be fine, Father. I'll see you then."

"Okay, Matt. So long."

Father Richter hung up the phone and clasped his hands behind his head. He leaned back in his chair and propped his feet up on his desk. He imagined a grizzly picture of Cindy McKenzie's corpse and shuddered. Swiveling the chair around, he stopped short when his gaze fell upon the photograph of Sister Francis that hung upon the nearby wall. Without thinking, he quietly crossed himself, rose directly from the chair and left the room.

Mrs. Flynn was still in the kitchen, and she offered the priest a cup of tea, which he gratefully accepted and began sipping from almost immediately. He held the vessel reverently in his hands, allowing its warmth to spread through his fingers, as he walked toward the window that overlooked the street. To the housekeeper, it appeared that the priest seemed to be upset.

"Is there something wrong, Father?" asked the housekeeper.

"Huh?"

"I mean – the detective – is there anything wrong?"

The priest stirred his tea slowly, then looked up.

"I hope not, Margaret. I certainly hope not."

Around ten, Matt was heading for the men's room to relieve himself of the burden of his morning hot chocolate, when he passed Captain Foster's office. His superior's familiar voice rang out. "Is that you, Matt?"

"Yeah, boss. What's up?"

"*That's* what I was going to ask *you*."

Davis ducked his head inside the captain's doorway. "I'll be right back. I've gotta see a man about a horse."

"Make sure you don't piss on your shoes," shouted Foster. "And make it fast. We need to talk."

Davis returned in a moment and sat down opposite the other detective. "So?"

"Which do you want first? The good news or the bad news?" asked Foster.

Matt considered Foster's tone of voice and thought he knew what his boss was going to tell him.

"Hey, you know me. I'm a sucker for bad news, so let's have it," said Davis.

"Okay," sighed Foster. "They're asking for a task force."

Matt had been partially correct.

"So, what's the good news?" he asked.

Foster squinted his eyes, and affected a stage whisper. "What if I told you that I can keep the whole thing down here? Right here in the One-O?"

"I'd say you had rocks in your head."

"Well, I don't have rocks in my head—*and*—I already did it."

"No shit. How?"

"Well, I promised the PC that you'd have it wrapped up in three weeks☐"

"Three weeks!" shouted Davis. "What are you, nuts? Never mind. Don't answer that."

The two men sat quietly, each staring past the other. Finally, Matt broke the silence. "Okay, how many men do I get?"

Foster swiveled his chair around to face the window and looked out, his back to Davis. His silence was a wordless statement that only reinforced Matt's sense of dread.

"Well?" asked Matt.

"Well what?"

"How many men?"

"Five," said Foster, almost in a whisper.

"*How* many?"

"Five, god damn it!" shouted Foster. "Matt, it's the best I can do," he added, meekly.

Davis stood up and began pacing back and forth. "Let me get this straight. You tell the PC I'll have this thing all tied up in a neat package in three weeks, and then you only give me *five* men. Is that what you're telling me?"

"Matt, I—"

"You *are* nuts! Look, it's bad enough that—"

This time it was Foster's turn to interrupt. "It gets worse."

"What do you mean?" asked Davis.

"The five *includes* you, Freitag, and Valdez. It's the best I can do, Matt. I swear it. Otherwise they wanted to go outside the One-O. And we don't want *that* do we?" It was a rhetorical question with only one answer.

Matt answered it anyway. "No," he said, quietly.

A task force was a detective's worst nightmare. Its specter haunted every serial homicide investigation. It not only threatened confusion, but an invasion by outside agencies. It guaranteed the one thing that every homicide detective feared most of all – loss of control. Task forces invited risk taking, along with glory seeking officials, *ad nausea*. Davis knew the odds were against him.

"So?" asked Foster. "What do you say? Give it a shot, alright?"

"What *can* I say?" shrugged Davis. "It sucks, but, sure, we'll give it a shot."

"Attaboy, Matt," said Foster. "I knew you'd see it my way. Besides, if you can just get some kind of *lead* working, well – you know – then they'll *probably* let you hang onto it."

"Lucky me," mumbled Davis. He pulled out his notebook, flipped through the pages and stopped. "Okay, look, I've got to go over to St. Jude Monday afternoon and meet with that priest who took Cindy McKenzie's confession."

Foster nodded his approval.

"In the meantime, how's about getting those *other* two guys into my office? You know what they say: 'Use 'em or lose 'em,' right?"

"Right!" said Foster. He had to admit that he admired Davis. Matt was his best shot at not only keeping the investigation local, but in solving the case as well. "I'm giving you Martini and Wolinski. I hope you don't mind?" It wasn't really a question.

Davis winced at the mention of Adam Wolinski. He was the oldest detective in the Tenth Precinct. Foster couldn't help but notice Matt's discomfort.

"Hey, he's good, Matt," he said. "I know you don't like working with the old guy, but Wolinski is top drawer."

Davis shrugged his shoulders.

"Okay, okay, he's not exactly Sherlock Holmes – but, he's a warm body *and* he's got plenty of experience. And, besides," added Foster, "he'll give you an experienced perspective. Who knows, it just might be helpful on a case like this—"

"Yeah, yeah," replied Matt. "Well, we'll just see."

Davis looked uncomfortable, and Foster sensed a need for reconciliation. "Hey, Matt," he said.

"What?"

"At least you've got Rita. She ain't exactly hard on the eyes – *if* you know what I mean?"

"Fuck you, boss. Try telling that to my wife."

Davis picked up his topcoat and left the office without saying goodbye. He marched down the hall to his own cubicle, slamming the door and flopping down into the chair behind his desk. Things were really going to shit. First Valdez and her bad "rep," and now Wolinski. Retirement couldn't come soon enough.

A knock on Matt's office door was followed almost immediately by a small procession that filed into his already overstuffed cubicle. First, came Freitag, followed in turn by Detectives Third-Grade Rita Valdez, Frank Martini, and the aging Wolinski. A beaming Foster brought up the rear, closing the door behind him.

Matt had to admit that Rita Valdez was truly a knockout. The combination of her Italian and Puerto Rican heritage left her with the soft, sultry appearance of the former, and the fiery temperament of the latter. At thirty-nine years of age, she was "old enough to know better" and young enough to not care. She was wearing a low cut blouse beneath a conservative navy blue pants suit. Her dark brown hair was stacked loosely atop her head, and held in place with a thin red ribbon. She had deep blue eyes which, along with her olive complexion, combined to give her a truly unique appearance. She took Davis's breath away whenever he encountered her. Today was no exception. He wasn't tempted, but he wasn't blind either.

Frank Martini, on the other hand, was easy to overlook. He was around fifty years old, five-ten, overweight, and slovenly. He was, however, one of the finest detail men in the department. He excelled at the day in, day out, grunt work that everyone else found so boring. Davis was glad to have him on board. As for Wolinski? Well, Wolinski was Wolinski. He was a live body.

Foster stood fidgeting by the door, and finally spoke. "Okay, everybody, listen up. You know why you're here. We've got a bitch of a case here, and Matt can use all the help he can get—and you're it, for now. So, do the best you can, and let's get this damn case solved. Matt will—"

"Okay, boss, I'll take it from here," said Davis.

Foster grinned, and beat a hasty retreat through the door, scurrying back to the security of his own office. That left Davis alone with Freitag, Valdez, and the two newcomers to the case.

"Alright," he said, looking at Martini, "Frank, I want you to re-canvass the neighbors of all three victims."

Martini started to say something, but stopped.

"I know they were canvassed already," said Matt. "But, find out if anybody saw *anything*. Go through the entire neighborhood. See if there were any unusual cars in the area, strange-acting men hanging around, regular visitors, *irregular* visitors – anything at all that you can find out that might help us. Wolinski, you're with Martini."

He looked over at Rita and sighed. Valdez didn't help things any when she leaned across his desk, showing off her ample cleavage that swelled over the top of her revealing blouse. "And what about *me*?" she asked, batting her considerable eyelashes at Davis.

Matt felt a twinge of guilt as he briefly enjoyed the view, then quickly willed himself to concentrate. He had never cheated on Valerie, and he wasn't about to start now. He cleared his throat and said, "Rita, I assume Foster filled you in on most of the details?"

"Uh huh. But, what do *you* want me to do, *Detective?*" The way she put the emphasis on 'Detective' caused Davis to wince. He knew that Valdez's professional reputation was beyond reproach, and assumed she was just having a little fun. He wished he could enjoy it, but he couldn't. Instead, he pressed ahead.

"Look, Rita, if we're gonna be working together on this thing, just call me *Matt*, and let's skip the 'Detective' bullshit, okay?"

"Sure thing – *Lou*."

Davis rolled his eyes, a smile on his face. "Give me a break, will you, Rita?"

Rita removed herself from the top of his desk, taking the view of her breasts with her—much to Matt's relief—and stood up straight, pulling her suit jacket closed across her blouse. That suited him just fine. He certainly didn't need any rumors circulating around the precinct.

"Well, for starters, suppose you see if you can track down where those three bibles came from. They're all the same, so maybe there's something there. Start with Father Richter. Hell, maybe he can save us all a lot of time."

Rita headed out the door towards the evidence room to pick up one of the bibles. Freitag shut the door behind her, and turned toward Davis, an exasperated look spreading across his face. Wolinski and Martini took the cue and exited promptly.

"I know, I know," said Matt. "Don't piss her off; it'll only make it worse, right?"

"Right," smiled Freitag.

"Don't worry. I can handle Rita. I just want to make sure we're all on the same page." He turned and caught Freitag snickering.

"Isn't that right, Chris?" asked Davis.

"Oh, yeah. Whatever you say – *Lou*."

Davis couldn't resist laughing. "Okay, let's get moving," he said. "I think we've *all* got plenty to keep us busy."

The two men exited the office and hurried downstairs to the street. Martini and Wolinski climbed into the little black Dodge that had been assigned to them from the motor pool, while Freitag and Davis jumped into the Impala. Both cars sped off in opposite directions.

The funeral mass for Cindy McKenzie was uneventful. Afterwards, the killer sat unnoticed, in the rear of the church, while close friends and relatives mingled. At the conclusion of the ritual he kneeled, crossed himself, and left.

CHAPTER 29

*T*he killer was having difficulty separating the events of his daily routine with those that filled his private hours. He hadn't intended to kill any of those women. It just happened. How much, he rationalized, could a man take? They had only themselves to blame. How dare they not accept him? They were so shallow. They pretended to want his advice and his companionship, yet when he gave in to them, he always came up lacking. He knew what they really wanted. They weren't any different from the whores he saw frequenting the area around the bus station at 42nd Street. They were all whores – just like his mother.

The simple act of just getting through his daily routine was becoming increasingly more difficult. He struggled to control his desires, and fought to maintain a hold on his anger, which was considerable. It simmered just below the surface, and, on the occasions when he gave vent to it, his rage had been so terrible that he had been unable to control it at all. The result was three dead women. Well, he thought, they deserved it. Women always disappointed him – always!

And that damn computer. It sat there like some sort of demon. And, of course, he was too weak to resist. His mother always said he was weak. Lately, he found himself drawn to the chat rooms almost every night. He would sit there like a zombie, trying desperately to be whoever or whatever the naive housewives wanted him to be. Sometimes he was a stockbroker; sometimes he worked in construction. He always pretended to be anything but what he really was. He wished he could stop *chatting and just have a normal life like everyone else. But, he knew that wasn't possible. Not any more, at least.*

As time went on, the line between reality and fantasy began to blur. Sometimes he scarcely knew who he was when he awoke, covered in perspiration from some nightmare or other. Other times when he awoke, he wasn't sure whether he had been dreaming, or if he had awakened from a re-enactment of the actual nightmare he had perpetrated the night before.

Things were definitely getting out of control.

CHAPTER 30

Rita entered her Volkswagen Jetta and started the engine. She hated having to use her own car, but until one was available from the motor pool, she had no other option. Driving downtown toward St. Jude's, her mind raced with the thoughts of the previous day's farce at headquarters. She hadn't minded the formal introduction or even the catcalls, but the little scenario in Foster's office – well, that was another story altogether. She absolutely *hated* the "let's be a good little girl" lecture by the captain, and despised the fact that she would be walking on proverbial eggshells as long as *he* deemed it necessary.

As she cruised down Broadway, and threaded her way through the crowded streets of Chelsea, Rita began to reconsider her position. Maybe Foster was right. After all, she really had nobody to blame but herself. The crap she purported about needing "two to tango" was just that – crap. *She* was the one who had initiated each encounter. *They* were only doing what came naturally to *all* men – following their dicks to the source.

No one would ever know how painful her first affair had been. Everyone thought: "sex," but she knew differently. Bill Connor had been a wonderful man, and she had loved him deeply. Rumors around the precinct had indicated that his marriage was in trouble, but Rita had resisted – that is, until her boss had given her the opening, inviting her to accompany him to a PBA dinner when his wife was out of town. Still, she hadn't intended for anything to happen. It just did. And then, the floodgates had opened, and all bets were off. It lasted less than two years, but in that time, Rita had a glimpse of what a deep, meaningful relationship could be like – and she liked it, and gladly paid the price for the experience.

In the end, however, it was Connor's wife who had prevailed, and Bill being the good, decent man he really was, had broken off the relationship in spite of the love he obviously felt for Rita. After that, Valdez became reckless, going after first one, than the other, until things became a blur. But, there was always an emptiness – a feeling of futility – that had attached itself to each relationship. Now, she was paying a price that was not only very dear, but totally undeserved as well. She imagined Foster could have declined her transfer into his squad – but, he didn't. So, perhaps it showed he wasn't such a bad guy. And, maybe, just maybe, she could finally get it right. Then, she pictured Davis, and let her imagination wander a bit.

"Fuck!" she exclaimed. "There I go again. Get a grip, girlfriend." She smiled at her momentary lapse, and vowed to do better.

She maneuvered the small car through the crowded streets of Chelsea, and eventually found her way to St. Jude's, slipping the car into a tight parking spot in front of the imposing structure. She shut off the engine, tossed her identification placard on the dashboard where it could be seen through the windshield, and grabbed the copy of the New Testament she had signed out of the evidence room. Her spiked heels clicked loudly as she made her way along the concrete path, leading to the side door that she assumed was the entrance to the rectory. A slightly elevated portion of the pavement caused her to trip, and while struggling to maintain her balance, she subconsciously regretted her choice of shoes for the day's work. *No more heels.* She rang the bell and waited.

Presently, a rather plain-looking woman with white hair answered the door. "May I help you?" she asked. Valdez detected an Irish accent. She flashed her badge. "Detective

Valdez of the Tenth Precinct. I was wondering if I could speak with Father Richter for just a moment?"

"Oh, dear, is anything wrong?"

"Oh, no, I was just hoping he might save us some time with a case we're working on."

"Well," said the woman, "let me see if he's free."

Rita waited patiently until the woman returned. "Why don't you come in?" she said, and motioned Rita into the vestibule. "He should only be a minute."

Looking about the sparsely decorated anteroom, Rita reflected upon the life of religious personnel – if, indeed, that was a term that could be used in such a context. It was probably a lot like these surroundings: plain, even barren. Certainly not a life for her. A quiet cough roused her from her reverie. She turned and saw a strikingly handsome older man, standing quietly with his hands at his sides, dressed in navy slacks and a tan turtle neck sweater. *Very interesting. He couldn't be Richter, could he?*

As if on cue, the man extended his hand and answered the question for her. "Father Richter," he said. "And you are?"

"I'm sorry. I'm Detective Valdez," she replied, shaking his outstretched hand. "Lieutenant Davis asked me to stop by and ask you a question about the case we've been working on." She flashed her identification, and the priest scrutinized it briefly, before nodding his approval.

"Well, Miss Valdez, I'll be happy to help," he said. "Would you like a cup of coffee – or some tea, perhaps?"

"Oh, that's not necessary – but, thank you." She handed him the New Testament. "We found copies like this at all three crime scenes, and we were wondering if you knew where they might have come from?"

Richter studied the book, riffling the pages gently, almost lovingly, and handed it back to Valdez. "Could be any place. In fact, they could even be from here. We get them from a religious publishing house somewhere in the Midwest. All the Catholic churches use them." He turned and pointed to a collection of books stacked on a countertop in the corner of the vestibule. "You see, we have a veritable stockpile of them. I wish I could be more helpful."

Valdez reached into her purse and extracted one of her old business cards. She had crossed out the outdated information on a stack of them, and hastily replaced it with her new precinct address and phone number. She didn't like using them, but they'd just have to do until her new cards were ready. She apologized for the card's condition, and gave it to Richter, who studied it for a moment before stashing it in his pants pocket. "If you think of anything else, please don't hesitate to contact me," she said.

"It would be my pleasure," said Richter. Something about the remark made Rita smile; it was probably because she never connected pleasure with clergy. She extended her hand once more, and Richter took it graciously in his and bid her good day. She walked out the door and down the sidewalk to the Jetta. Before entering the car, she glanced back over her shoulder, she saw Richter standing in the rectory doorway. Without thinking, she waved, and the priest smiled and waved back. *Nice guy*, she thought, and drove off.

CHAPTER 31

Valerie moved efficiently about the narrow kitchen as she prepared dinner for Matt and herself. Although the cooking area was barely adequate, Valerie was proud of how she had organized it. Everything was right at her fingertips. The sun was nearly gone as she paused to look out the little window at the end of the galley. The view of the city, silhouetted by the receding sunset always brought her pleasure. Unlike a painting, this picture changed daily. Tonight, the glow behind the buildings had a reddish – nearly pink – cast to it. *What is it they say about a red sky at night? Sailor's delight – that's it!*

The meatloaf was just about done, so she called Matt to the table. It was his favorite dish, and she always served it the same way: with freshly made mashed potatoes, frozen peas (better than canned), steamed carrots, and homemade gravy. Valerie had prepared it in the hope that it might take her husband's mind off his work, if only for an hour or so. She turned from the kitchen to the table, hot platter in hand, and was surprised to find her husband missing.

"Matt!" she shouted. "Come on, honey. It's going to get cold."

"I'll be right there," he answered from the living room.

As he wandered into the dining area, he was engrossed in reading the autopsy report he carried in his hand.

Valerie frowned. "Matt, for God's sake. Can't we just eat dinner alone?"

"Huh?" he asked. His face showed not a trace of comprehension.

Valerie pointed at the report in his hand.

"Oh," he replied. "I'm sorry." He placed the papers on the floor next to his chair and sat down. They ate in relative silence, punctuated only by the sounds of knives and forks scraping the ancient dinnerware. A dinner that had been planned as special had suddenly become very ordinary – just another supper.

But, Valerie wasn't giving up without a fight. When they were done, she quickly cleared the table and placed the dishes alongside the sink. Turning to her husband, she said, "Honey? Why don't you put on a little music?" She looked at him with a little twinkle in her eye. "Maybe we could dance?"

Matt seemed lost in thought, and so Valerie, without waiting for a reply, stripped off her apron, hung it on the refrigerator handle, and walked over to the aging stereo resting on its aluminum-framed stand. She fingered a stack of Frank Sinatra albums, and eventually selected *September of My Years*, which she carefully placed on the turntable. Most of their friends had progressed from records to cassettes to CDs, but Matt insisted that the best sound still came from a turntable. She switched on the receiver, and gently placed the needle in the wide starter groove at the outer edge of the record. In a second the familiar scratchy tones of the title song filled the room. Matt wasn't *always* right, thought Valerie.

Matt was still seated at the kitchen table, again poring over the autopsy report. He turned when he heard Sinatra begin to sing. With a smile, he placed the report on the table, slowly got up, and moved to the living room to join his wife. With a little bow at the waist, he looked at Valerie and said, "May I have this dance?"

She blushed, and put her arms around his neck.

They began to move slowly to the music. Matt inhaled the fragrance of Valerie's perfume and sighed. It was *Shalimar*—his favorite. He kept her well supplied, and she never failed to wear it. Matt nuzzled Valerie's neck with his chin, causing her to shiver slightly. After several more songs, she pulled away from her husband and looked him directly in the eye. "Hey, big boy. Don't you have a bed in this place?"

Matt laughed. Valerie's question was a reference to their first date. On that occasion, he had been so shy that he had barely been able to kiss her. She had then asked the now-famous question, and the two of them had ended up making love, much to Matt's surprise—and pleasure.

Now, he accepted the question for what it appeared to be – an open invitation to lovemaking. Without a word, he took Valerie's hand and led her to the small but cozy bedroom. He turned his back to her, unbuttoned his shirt, and removed it, tossing it haphazardly into the corner. His shoes followed suit, and finally his trousers. At the same time Matt was disrobing, Valerie was removing her dress and underclothing. She slid quietly beneath the covers. Matt walked around to the other side of the bed, and slipped in beside her.

Valerie immediately turned and embraced her husband, kissing him hard on the lips. She was naked. Matt's hand reached automatically for her left breast. It was a routine perfected through the three years or so of their marriage. Valerie moaned softly and pressed herself to him. Preliminaries were neither elaborate nor very necessary, and soon they were both fully aroused.

Gently, Matt inserted himself and they began to move in unison. Caught up in the moment, Valerie whispered familiar words into her husband's ear, while Sinatra continued to croon unheard in the other room. Soon, she felt the familiar warmth and tingling that signaled she was nearing orgasm. She gripped her husband tightly, and ground herself hard against him, moving faster and with more urgency. Together, they moved as one, in the timeless rhythm of love, until they both had attained the release they so desperately sought. Afterwards, they lay quietly in one another's arms, their breathing shallow and quick, as they regained their strength. Presently, Valerie sensed a

change in the rhythm of her husband's breathing; it was slower
– more deliberate. Val opened her eyes and looked at Matt's
face. He was fast asleep. She smiled. *Sweet dreams my love.*
Had she know the nature of his fantasies she might not have
been quite as pleased.

*...Matt had been summoned to the scene of a murder.
When he arrived, he found himself in his own apartment, only
the walls were painted a violet color and the ceilings were
remarkably high. As he moved down the hallway toward the
bedroom, the corridor narrowed progressively, until by the time
he reached the end its walls were touching his shoulders. His
entire being was filled with an inexplicable sense of dread.
Archbishop Romero stood at the end of the passageway,
wearing a long black gown. His face was shrunken and evil
looking. He extended a bony hand, and beckoned Matt to
follow him into the bedroom.*

*The interior was bathed in a soft, golden light. There
was a small bed, like in a dollhouse, positioned in the center of
the room – and nothing else. Suddenly, Matt felt himself
growing taller and taller. He and the archbishop stood side by
side, looking down at the postage-stamp sized bed. His
confusion grew and he turned to the cleric for enlightenment.
The archbishop raised his hand and pointed a finger at the bed.
Matt felt his body growing feathery light, and he began to fly
over the bed, circling it like a hawk covering its prey.*

*He swooped down, and was startled to discover Valerie,
lying nude on its surface. She was dead. In silent agony, he
turned back toward the archbishop, who stood alongside the
bed, pointing an accusing finger in his direction. Romero
began to laugh, louder and louder, until the sound was like
cannon fire hitting Davis's ears. It was deafening...*

Matt awoke with a start. His upper body was drenched with perspiration and his hands trembled violently. It was well past midnight. Faint traces of the nightmare still clung like cobwebs to his subconscious. The sky flashed with lightning, and a clap of thunder shook the apartment. Matt sat on the edge of the bed, his heart beating furiously, his breathing ragged. He listened to the sounds of the rain and occasional thunder outside the apartment. Valerie lay sleeping peacefully next to him, her slow, even breathing in marked contrast to his own syncopated efforts. *Thank God, she's safe*, he thought. With a smile he placed a hand on her rounded buttocks, and gently massaged the curve of her hip. Then he patted her behind softly and stood up. He dressed quietly, mindful not to wake her, and slipped out of the bedroom and into the kitchen.

Soon, the kettle was steaming aggressively on the stove, a thin trail of steam disappearing into the air. Matt dumped some cocoa into a cup, filled it with boiling water and stirred it carefully, then topped the whole thing off with a squirt of whipped cream from a can. He rummaged through the cupboard and found a half-empty bag of Hershey-ets candy and poured the contents into a small bowl. He looked at the kitchen clock. It was one-fifteen a.m. With the cup of hot chocolate in one hand and the bowl of candy in the other, he moved down the hallway to his study.

Davis sat down at his fly tying bench. In front of him were the tools, hooks, and delicate materials germane to his hobby. He selected a tiny hook and clamped it into jaws of the Regal rotary vice that Valerie had bought him on their first wedding anniversary. It was the finest tool of its kind and he took great pride in using it.

He decided to tie a gold-ribbed hare's ear nymph. There were literally thousands of fly patterns to choose from, but this particular one was an old standard. A stack of instructional manuals lay undisturbed at the far corner of the worktable. He hardly needed them anymore. In the beginning, when he was first learning to tie, Matt had been forced to rely upon books to help him through the process. Now, he prided himself in his knowledge of the construction of the various patterns, and could make most of them without consultation.

Working effortlessly, he had soon tied half a dozen of the tiny insect imitations, each an exact duplicate of the others. Consistency was what it was all about, he thought. As he finished each one, he used a small needle dipped in vinyl cement to carefully coat the wrappings of thread that made up the head of the fly. Then, he placed each one neatly in a row on a magnetic strip that he had affixed to his tying bench to let them dry.

The apprehension that Matt felt upon waking from the nightmare had begun to dissipate. As the tension faded, so, too, did the memory of the details. He got up and moved to the hall closet, retrieving his notebook from his jacket pocket. He returned to the study, sat down at his desk, and removed a piece of paper from the drawer. He took a pen and wrote down the names of the three victims: Ida Simpson, Melina Spiros, and Cindy McKenzie. Next, he printed alongside each victim's name her age, marital status, and race.

Each was white, each was married, and each was about the same age – in her thirties. Then, he added the word "cheating" next to the first two names. Davis knew that that information was probably important, but exactly *why* was still a mystery. Simpson's lover had been in Atlantic City at the time of her murder, so, of course, that information had eliminated him. And Spiros' killer could have been any one of perhaps a dozen casual pick-ups described by "helpful" neighbors. Only God Himself knew how many men she had been with. Naturally, the detectives were trying to track down anyone matching the various descriptions they had been given. Nevertheless, it was like looking for a needle in the proverbial haystack.

All three husbands had been cleared initially by airtight alibis, and then through blood typing. Bob McKenzie, the most recent widower, decried any knowledge of infidelity by his wife. It was further proof that "husbands were always last to know." Maybe she *had* been cheating? Perhaps that's why she had gone to Confession for the first time in ten years? None of the husbands had had any reason to doubt the faithfulness of their spouses, and yet each of their wives was dead. Matt hoped he would learn something tomorrow when he met with Father Pete.

He reached into the bowl of Hershey-ets and extracted a handful, popping just one into his mouth. Following his usual ritual, he allowed the warmth of his mouth to soften the chocolate within the hard candy shell. Then, he cracked the casing, and separated the morsel into two halves. Finally, using his tongue, he sucked out the chocolate from one half, then the other. He repeated the process until the bowl of candy was gone.

With his candy "Jones" sated, Matt turned his attention once more to the piece of paper in front of him. He drew pictures of three hearts with the initials "J.C." inside each of them. Then he added an additional set of initials – the victim's own – to each drawing. He studied the sketch, trying to make sense of what he saw. It seemed too simple. Too *damned* simple, he thought. But, it *couldn't* be that simple, could it? There had to be something he was missing – some connection. But what the hell was it?

There was one other thing. All three women had belonged to the same church. Not much to go on, but maybe *something*. It reminded Davis of the famous "Rosary Murders" back in 1955. Seven nuns had been brutally raped and stabbed in Chicago. Each had had a set of rosary beads forced into her vagina. It turned out that the murderer had been a caretaker in a convent, rejected by a nun. Once he started killing, he couldn't stop. The police had finally caught him by using a decoy. Davis guessed that that technique might prove useful at some point, but not until he had more to go on. Right now, he had nothing.

He rubbed his eyes, yawned, and stretched his arms in the air. He was bone weary, tired of murders, and tired of the nightmares. He laid his head down on his desk, and closed his eyes. Soon, he was asleep, with images of fly-fishing for salmon filling he head. He was still dreaming when Valerie gently nudged him awake in the morning.

CHAPTER 32

Baltimore, Maryland

B   *y the age of fourteen, "little" John Curran had matured into a physically striking young man. His shoulders were wide, his hips narrow, his blue eyes alive with a kind of electricity that conveyed intelligence and wit. He was six feet, three-inches tall, and was the dominant figure in any room full of his peers. It was during this time that he became possessed by an uncontrollable temper. Perhaps it was the pubescent surge of Testosterone coursing through his system, or perhaps something entirely different. For no apparent reason, he would often pound other boys into submission in violent fits of rage. On several occasions, the police had to be called to the orphanage. Each time, Sister Francis was able to convince the officers not to arrest the teenager, but his reputation as a troublemaker was growing.*

Finally, one night, driven by a wild desire to experience every possible thrill that life had to offer, young John went too far. He convinced two other boys to sneak out of the orphanage. They "borrowed" a car and went for a high-speed joy ride, side swiping several vehicles in the process. The police apprehended the trio, but only after John had unsuccessfully tried to negotiate a corner at high speed and crashed into a parked car. After being treated for minor injuries, the two other boys were released to the care of the orphanage and returned to the home with Sister Francis. However, John – because of his previous scrapes with the law – was arrested and charged with grand larceny, albeit as a minor. After a hearing before a no-nonsense magistrate, he was sent to a state work farm for minors. He would remain there until he was sixteen.

The day he left for the penal institution, Sister Francis paid him a farewell visit, and gave him a picture of her to remind him of the one that loved him. John Curran was to keep that photograph with him for the remainder of his life...

CHAPTER 33

7:56 p.m., Friday, April 7

Rita Valdez was tired of being single. The affairs had been exciting, but ultimately not very fulfilling. She enjoyed the constant activity and diversity of her professional life, but abhorred her private one. In fact, she didn't have one. She had an existence. She lived in a second-story apartment in an ancient tenement building on East 23rd Street. Not far from her residence sat the School of Visual Arts. During the day, longhaired students of each sex flooded the streets on their way to and from the avant-garde institution. After dark, a different class of pedestrians moved silently in the shadows, pursuing less altruistic forms of gratification. They had one thing in common: they were all young. Rita envied them their youth. Time was running out for her. If she didn't marry soon, she'd end up an old maid.

As she stood naked in front of the full-length mirror mounted on the back of her bedroom door and examined her figure. She ran her hands through her dark hair, then over her breasts, admiring their firmness. *Pretty good.* Not much sag – yet. Her hands roamed over her stomach, which was still fairly flat, then lightly touched the thick carpet of hair above her *pubis.* She licked her full lips and blew a kiss at her reflection. Then, she turned her back to the mirror and, looking over her shoulder, admired her buttocks. She smacked the firm skin with the palm of her hand. Thwack! Still tight, she thought. Her waist was getting a little thick, but she could disguise that deficiency with the right clothes. In all, it was a pretty sexy package.

At her age, being good looking was a double-edged sword; sure, she could attract almost any man she wanted, but more often than not her steamy Latin looks scared away the ones she really wanted—the marrying ones.

Recently, a friend of hers in Florida had married a man whom she had never seen in person, up until their wedding day. The two of them met in a Yahoo Internet chat room. They spoke to each other frequently on screen, graduated to phone conversations, eventually marrying after a six-month Internet romance. Not too traditional, she thought, but practical. Maybe she should try it herself. Hell, who did she think she was she kidding? She wasn't even on the Internet yet. *First chance I get – I'm getting connected.*

Rita entered the glass enclosure of her stall shower and turned the control knob towards hot. *The hotter the better.* When steam began to fill the limited space around her, she stepped under the hard-flowing water. Taking a disposable razor from the little suction cup holder, she quickly shaved first one leg, then the other. Satisfied with the results, she grabbed one of the many bottles of shampoo that she kept on the shelf opposite the glass door, and massaged a dollop of the thick liquid into her hair.

She worked up a thick, full lather and then rinsed, allowing the soapy remains to run down her body. She picked up a bar of perfumed soap and began rubbing it slowly over every inch of her skin. She paid special attention to her private parts, letting her fingers penetrate the outer lips of her vagina, the middle finger of her right hand pressing against her clitoris. She loved to play with herself in the shower. No guilt, only pleasure. As her finger lingered on the engorged organ, she rubbed it in a circular motion, and felt it grow harder. She enjoyed the warm tingling sensation that spread throughout her loins.

She closed her eyes and pictured an imaginary lover running his hands sensually over her body. For a moment, she envisioned Freitag – all six feet, four inches of him – standing close to her, pressing himself against her. Sometimes she found Chris extremely attractive, his raw physical power a real turn on. Yet, at other times, his boorish manners and ignorant speech were outright repugnant. She smiled and thought of Davis. Oh, to be sure, he wasn't much to look at. But he had a certain kind of gentleness, and a mind like a steel trap. If only she could find someone who possessed the characteristics of both: Freitag's raw sexuality and Davis's warmth and intelligence.

Her reverie was interrupted by the persistent ringing of her cell phone, lying on the vanity, beside the sink. She opened the shower door a crack and reached her hand out, groping along the Formica surface of the countertop until her fingers closed around the ringing object. She pressed the "speak" button and placed the instrument to her ear.

"Hello?" she said.

"Hey!" It was Jan, her best friend and bowling partner. "Are you almost ready?"

"What time is it?" asked Rita.

"Almost eight," said Jan.

"Shit!" said Rita. "I didn't realize it was so late."

"Are you still in the shower?" asked Jan.

Embarrassed at being found out, Rita lied, "Of course not. I'll be ready in twenty minutes, okay?"

"Sure," replied Jan, "Just don't be any later than that."

"Yeah, yeah, I know," said Rita. "Otherwise all the good ones will be gone."

"You got it!" laughed Jan.

"I'll meet you downstairs."

"Just hurry up!" said Jan.

The two women hung up simultaneously. Rita finished rinsing and stepped onto the bathmat to dry her body. They had planned to "bar hop" along the Upper East Side. Rita was so worn out by the ongoing investigation that the evening's plans had completely slipped her mind. She had been looking forward to lounging around the apartment and maybe just watching a little TV.

She began using the blow dryer on her hair. Taking a pick, she ran it through her still-damp locks to loosen up the curls, then sprayed the results. A little lipstick and eye shadow finished her from the neck up. She removed the cap from the bottle of *Tresor* perfume, and ran it to along the sides of her neck, then the insides of her wrists. Next, she brushed it against her breasts, along her belly, and the insides of her thighs. Finally, she lowered it to gently caress the lips of her vagina, sending a shower of sparks through her body.

No bra tonight, she thought, as she slipped a light pink, cotton sweater over head. The fabric felt rough against her skin, and caused her nipples to become erect. *Hope you like 'em, boys.* In a way, she felt a little guilty dressing this way. After all, it wasn't really sex she was after, but marriage and a family. But she couldn't very well wear a sign, advertising: "No sex! Long-term relationship wanted," could she? She grabbed a pair of black thong panties from her overstuffed underwear drawer and stepped into them. Then came a pair of skintight jeans, black leather pumps, and a matching belt with a large gold buckle. She was ready to roll.

She pulled a long, black leather coat from the hall closet, grabbed her shoulder bag from the top of the kitchen counter, flipped a few light switches, and exited the apartment. She stopped outside the door, turned around, and checked her purse for her keys. She carefully secured the door handle lock, then the heavier deadbolt above. Returning the keys to her handbag, she was startled by a noise at the bottom of the stairs. She turned and stared down at the dimly lit landing.

The entryway was rather dimly lit, and Rita could just make out the outline of someone standing in the shadows.

"Hello," she said, almost in a whisper.

There was no answer – nothing.

"Who's there?" she added, a bit louder, but still sounding meek.

Silence.

Shit, she thought, *I hate this damned city.* She reached in her purse and extracted the .38 snub-nosed Smith and Wesson service revolver she was required to carry. She undid the safety. *Okay, wise ass; see how you like this.*

Feeling more secure with the loaded firearm in her hand, she shouted down the stairs, "Hey, asshole! I've got a gun. Now move into the light, where I can see you."

Slowly, the figure stepped out of the shadows and into the dim light cast by the overhead fixture at the foot of the stairs. It was Jan. She looked up at Rita, smiling sheepishly. "Hey! Take it easy," she said. "I was only fooling."

"Not funny, Jan," said Rita, engaging the safety, and lowering the gun to her side. "You could have gotten your ass shot off."

Realizing she had acted foolishly, Jan fumbled an apology. "Sorry, Rita," she said. "I guess that wasn't too smart, was it?"

"No, it wasn't." Rita placed the pistol back in her bag.

"I'm really sorry," said Jan. She slowly climbed the stairway, stopping several stairs short of where Rita stood on the landing, reluctant to come any closer. "Forgive me?" she asked.

"Yeah, yeah, sure," sighed Rita, "It's okay. Honest." She reached out and patted Jan lightly on her shoulder. The girl smiled, feeling the tension leave her body.

"What do you say we take a cab?" said Rita.

"Sounds like a good idea to me," answered Jan. "What the hell, I'll buy."

"And I'll let you," laughed Rita.

The two women walked slowly down the stairs, exited the apartment building, and hailed a passing taxi.

Friday nights on the Upper East Side of Manhattan have a Mardi gras air about them, with crowds of young people everywhere, all seeking partners. Nearly every building houses either a bar or a restaurant, each sporting bright lights and plenty of patrons. The gaudy establishments literally overflow with singles hoping to meet that "special someone." Mixed among the many bachelors and unmarried women are individual spouses wishing that they, too, were unattached – each of them having decided that their "special someone" wasn't so special anymore.

Joe Carey was a one of those "single wanna be's." Like Rita, he was also thirty-nine. He was a transplanted Texan, who was doing his best to ward off the inevitable "Big Four Oh." His marriage of fourteen years had grown stale, and he regularly prowled the singles scene seeking to rekindle the fire missing in his ample belly. He had posted himself strategically by the front door of the bar, waiting in ambush for a suitable candidate to help him through the night.

Around eight-thirty, the taxi bearing Rita and Jan pulled to the curb in front of O'Hearly's Irish Pub, located on Third Avenue, between 82nd and 83d Streets. True to her word, Jan paid the fare, even tipping the Indian driver seventy-five cents (a generous amount for her). The two women giggled loudly as they made their way toward the bar. Jan's long blond hair and skin-tight leather pants attracted most of the stares, and that suited Rita just fine. The two women couldn't have had more different taste in men.

Their laughter caught the attention of the lanky, longhaired stranger who stood by the open door. He watched closely as the pair exited the taxi, smiling to himself as they passed him on their way inside. He paid particular attention to Rita, and decided she was perfect. He liked her dark hair and complexion. Besides, his wife was a blond, like the other one, and he'd had enough of her type to last a lifetime. He waited until they had seated themselves at the bar and ordered their drinks, before approaching them. Casually, he walked over and pressed himself against the ancient mahogany structure, standing immediately to the left of Jan. Ignoring the women, he hailed the passing bartender, and ordered a gin and tonic. When he had his drink, he faced the two women, and raised his glass in a mock toast. Concentrating on Rita, he drawled, "Here's to y'all."

Jan assessed the man's rugged good looks, decided she liked them and his accent, and raised her glass of white wine in response. Already bored, Rita blew a sigh, and turned her attention to the TV that was located in the upper corner of the bar. The Mets were playing the Yankees in an inter-league game, and trailing badly after only two innings, 7-1. If the present score was any indication, it might be a long night for the boys from Flushing.

"Come on, you bums," said Rita, rooting on the home team. "Let's score some runs." She hated the Yankees. The only team she hated more was the Atlanta Braves.

"Mets fan?" asked Joe. He was looking past Jan, his question obviously directed at Rita, who stood with her back to him, facing the TV. When she didn't respond, he tapped her lightly on the shoulder, and repeated the question. "I *said*, are y'all a Mets fan?"

Rita turned around, looked down at his hand, which was resting on her shoulder, and grimaced. "Nope. Just can't stand the Yankees."

"Me neither," answered Joe. He had made no effort to remove his hand, and in fact was giving her an uninvited massage. Rita decided that he was trying a bit too hard to suit her tastes.

"Oh, really?" she said, removing the offending hand from her shoulder. "And what team do *you* root for?"

"Texas Rangers," he drawled. His accent made the word sound more like "Range-uhs."

"Cute," said Rita. "And what are you, a cowboy?" She deliberately looked past him and laughed out loud towards Jan, who reflected her amusement.

"Well, not exactly," replied the stranger. "But, I am from Texas."

"That's nice," she replied. "And what brings you to New York?" She exaggerated her own accent, pronouncing the last word "Yawk."

"The usual," he replied, with a laugh. "Work. I'm an engineer with Con Edison."

"Ah ha," said Rita. "'Dig we must', huh?"

"Well, you could say that, except that I mostly spend my time in an office."

"You mean when you're not bothering strange women in bars?" Rita had already decided she wasn't interested in this one, and wanted to send a message.

"Look, maybe we got off on the wrong foot. My name is Joe Carey," he said. "Can I buy you ladies a drink?"

"I'm fine," said Rita. She glanced back at Jan, hoping for support, but received an icy stare instead. Reacting quickly, Rita added, "But, maybe my friend would like one. How about it, Jan?"

Jan smiled her appreciation. "Sure," she said. "I'll have a white wine and seltzer on the rocks…and thanks. By the way, I'm Jan."

Realizing that pursuing Rita was a losing cause, Joe turned his attention away from her and concentrated instead on her enthusiastic companion. He extended his hand, and Jan eagerly accepted it.

"Pleased to meet you, Jan," he said.

Rita finished her drink, stood up and said, "I'm gonna hit the ladies' room." She winked at Jan behind the man's back and waved good-bye, making the traditional good luck sign before leaving Jan on her own. Weaving through the crowd, she made her way toward the back of the bar. After using the ladies' room, Rita returned to the crowded floor of the bar. As she looked towards the front of the bar, Rita saw Jan and "the Con Edison man" leaving through the front door.

Con Edison, my ass. More like Con Man!

Two hours and three drinks later, the Yankees had beaten the Mets, 13-3, and Rita had rebuffed a half dozen potential "leading men." She decided she'd had enough action for one night, and took a taxi home to her Chelsea apartment on 17th Street. She checked her handbag as she entered the building, reassured by the weight of her Smith and Wesson nestled inside. As she entered the hallway, she glanced back over her shoulder and was surprised to see a man standing across the street smoking a cigarette. She glanced at her watch. It was only ten-forty five. Not really that late, she thought, but still...what was he doing there?

For a second, she was afraid. Then, looking again, she recognized the man as Ken Callahan, the delivery clerk from the neighborhood market. She breathed a sigh of relief. *What's the matter with me? I'm starting to imagine things.* It was the damn case. It was getting to her.

Ken was a Vietnam vet on a disability pension, who supplemented his meager Army income by delivering groceries on a three-wheeled bicycle that was fitted with a basket. He was polite but a bit shy, probably because of the burn scars that covered most of one side of his face. If anyone was harmless, she thought, it was certainly him. In spite of the scars, he really wasn't that bad looking.

Relieved, Rita waved at the man. "Hi Ken," she said, feeling a little guilty.

"Hi, Miss Valdez," he replied. He flipped his cigarette into the gutter, and started to cross the street.

Rita smiled. "What's up?" she asked.

"Ah, not much. Just enjoying the nice weather."

The two exchanged small talk for several minutes, and finally Rita said goodnight and went inside. *Poor man. He probably got nailed with Napalm or something in 'Nam. What a shame.* No wonder people hated the Vietnam War, she thought.

Rita let herself into her apartment, and made sure to double lock the door. *Can't be too careful.* She hung her coat in the closet, and as she did, noticed the lingering aroma of cigarette smoke that clung to the garment. It obscured the natural scent of the leather, and she shook her head in disgust, thinking just how much she hated the bar scene.

"Today, the bar scene, tomorrow the Internet!" she announced to the walls.

She passed her answering machine and noticed the light flashing on and off, indicating a new message. She pressed the button marked "play," and heard the sound of a woman's voice. The sound was barely audible, and she had to turn the volume all the way up before she recognized the voice as belonging to Jan.

"Hey, it's me," Jan whispered. "I've got 'Tex' at my apartment. He's in the john. God, Rita, he's fantastic. You really blew it, but thanks. Anyway, I'll talk to you tomorrow."

Rita erased the message and frowned. One of these days her friend was going to pick up the wrong guy. She didn't want to think about it. She undressed, took a quick shower to remove the smoke from her body, brushed her teeth, and slipped into bed. She quickly drifted off into a dreamless sleep.

CHAPTER 34

Monday, April 10

I
t was precisely four o'clock in the afternoon. Father
Pete greeted Davis, Freitag, and Valdez at the door to
the rectory and led them into his office. He was
accompanied by a young, boyish-looking priest, whom he
introduced to the two detectives as Father Anthony.

"Father Anthony," began Davis. "Did you hear a
confession by Mrs. McKenzie on March 30th—a few weeks
ago—on a Thursday evening?" His question apparently caught
the young priest slightly off guard.

"Well, I...I..." he stammered. His face flushed and he
looked at Father Pete for assistance. Matt watched as the two
clergymen exchanged knowing looks.

"Uh, Matt," said Father Pete, "Father Anthony couldn't
tell you even if he wanted to. In fact, there's not even any way
he can be sure it was *her* confession he may have heard."

"Well," said Davis. "Perhaps I should rephrase the
question." He began again, "Father Anthony, did you hear a
young woman's confession on that particular Thursday night?"

"I heard the confessions of a number of people. But—"

"Yes, but how many of them were young women?"
asked Matt. He was growing mildly impatient.

"Well—I was going to say—only *two* of them were
young women." He coughed nervously, then continued.
"Anyway, I—"

"—Do you suppose one of them was Mrs. McKenzie?"

"I imagine so. But, Detective—"

"—and what did she say?" asked Davis, impatiently.

Father Pete stepped between the two men, shaking his head. "Matt, please. Let's be fair. You know we can't divulge a person's confession—not *even* to solve a murder."

"Sorry, Father Pete. I had to try."

Freitag spoke up. "Father Anthony, was the young woman a 'regular customer' so to speak?"

Davis gave his partner a dirty look. "I apologize for my partner's insensitivity, Father. Let me rephrase his question. Did the woman's voice sound familiar?"

"No. In fact, she said she hadn't made a confession in over ten years. I remember specifically, because it was very unusual."

The two detectives looked at each other, then back at the young priest.

"I thought you couldn't reveal somebody's confession?" asked Davis.

Father Pete smiled and said, "Yes, Matt. That's true. But, technically, what Father Anthony just told you was not part of the young woman's confession. Besides, we *are* trying to help you. If you know what I mean." The older priest winked demurely.

"Well, we certainly appreciate it," replied Matt.

He addressed the young priest again. "You see, Father Anthony, it appears that the first two victims were both cheating on their husbands—"

"I see," said the priest.

"One was having an ongoing affair," said Matt. "And the other appears to have been quite promiscuous. We don't necessarily think that there's a definite connection there, but if all *three* were cheating, well, you see, then maybe we might be on to something."

Father Anthony shifted from one foot to the other. He looked extremely uncomfortable. Davis looked at Father Pete. The priest rubbed his cheek slowly with the palm of his hand, then whispered into his young colleague's ear. Father

Anthony's face tightened at first, then relaxed. He nodded, as if in some kind of agreement with his mentor.

Father Pete spoke. "Perhaps, Matt, I might offer a suggestion."

"Fire away, Father Pete," he said.

The elder priest moved closer to Davis and whispered into his ear, just as he had done with Father Anthony. Then he moved back and said aloud, "Would that be alright, Matt?"

"Yes," said Davis. "I think that would work okay. Let's try it."

Freitag stood quietly watching the charade, wondering just what in the hell was going on. He didn't have long to wait.

"Father Anthony, are you happy here at St. Jude's?" The priest nodded in the affirmative, a quizzical look spreading across his face.

"Good," said Davis. "Do you root for the Mets?"

This time the priest shook his side to side in denial.

Davis frowned, in mock disapproval. Then he continued. "Father Anthony, did you hear any confessions last Saturday evening?"

Again the priest shook his head, only up and down, in a positive response.

Freitag smiled. He was catching on to the game. If the priest didn't *say* anything, he wouldn't be guilty of violating his vow of confidence. Of course, at this rate, he thought, it might take a week to get anything meaningful out of the young priest.

"Now, Father Anthony, did this young woman confess to adultery?"

Father Anthony hesitated, looked at Father Pete, then turned back to Davis. "You know, detective, it's gets very confusing in the confessional sometimes. I *do* recall one woman confessing to adultery—"

"Yes?"

"—and another woman confessing to having violated her Lenten vows. But, I honestly can't remember which was which. I'm sorry I can't be of more help."

"That's alright, Father. My mistake for asking." Davis glanced at his watch, noted the time, and extended his hand toward Father Anthony. The young priest smiled and accepted the detective's hand, and shook it vigorously.

"You've been most helpful, Father Anthony. Thank you."

Father Anthony then quickly left the room. Father Richter turned to the two detectives and said, "Perhaps the three of you will join me for some tea *or* a cup of hot chocolate?"

Davis whispered something in Freitag's ear, then turned back to the priest.

"Detective Freitag and Miss Valdez have got a little errand they have to run, but I'll be glad to join you for a couple of minutes." Chris, Rita, I'll need you back here in about a half hour, okay?"

"You got it, boss," replied Freitag. Rita nodded her assent. They each shook Father Pete's hand and Rita said, "Thanks for the offer, Father. Maybe some other time."

Davis waited until the two detectives had left the room before turning to the priest, who sat quietly, seemingly lost in thought. The next words Matt spoke came as a surprise, both to the priest and to himself.

"Father Pete, you're the expert on religion. What do *you* think? Do we have a religious fanatic running around killing these women, or what?"

Father Richter's face blanched. The detective's frankness had caught him off guard, and it took a moment for him to compose himself.

Davis realized he might have gone too far. "I'm sorry, Father Pete. That was really out of line."

"Yes, well, perhaps[]"

"I guess I'm kinda desperate, Father. I think I just said the first thing that popped into my head. I'm really sorry."

Richter smiled a forgiving smile. "I guess I can understand that, Matt. After all, three women, all having affairs or cheating. All members of the same church. To use your expression, there *must* be some kind of 'religious fanatic' running around. I would tend to agree with you."

"Well, I guess I could have phrased it a little better."

"No problem, Matt. Hey, how about some of that hot cocoa? Maybe clear the old mind a bit, huh? What do you say?"

Davis grinned sheepishly. "I think that would be fine."

When Father Richter had disappeared into the kitchen, Davis stood up and began absentmindedly roaming around the priest's office. The bookshelves were full of standard Catholic publications, including books, magazines, and a dozen copies of *The Baltimore Catechism.* There were also a number of different versions of the Bible, and even a Torah. Several titles caught the detective's attention; most especially one entitled *Children with Aids and the Celebration of Life,* by Tolbert McCarroll. *Things sure have changed,* thought Matt. Scanning the lower shelves, Davis was surprised to find books of another kind. These were books on golf. The titles greeted him like old friends. There was even a copy *of Golf Shot Making With Billy Casper,* an old paperback that Davis, himself, had purchased a copy of back in the late sixties. He opened it and was shocked to see the price of only "one dollar" printed inside the front cover. Things definitely *had* changed, he thought.

"That one was given to me by Mrs. Flynn," said Father Richter. He had returned with a wooden tray bearing a silver teapot, two bone China cups, two silver spoons, and a large Danish pastry. One of the cups held a heaping pile of instant cocoa, obviously intended for the detective. The other cup contained a tea bag.

Startled, Davis turned around in embarrassment, his face flushed, caught, red-handed, rifling the priest's personal library. "Sorry, Father. I just couldn't resist," he said. "It's an occupational habit, I guess."

"I understand completely," said the priest. "Do you play?"

Davis smiled. "I try," he said. "*Some* people actually *play* golf. Me, I play *at* it."

"As long as you enjoy the game. That's the important thing."

Judging from Richter's athletic build, Davis thought he was probably a pretty good player. "I'll bet you hit a pretty mean ball, huh, Father?"

Father Pete raised his eyebrows, and looked at the ceiling in a display of false modesty. "Let's just say...that I ...do okay."

"Oh, come on," said Matt. "Don't be so modest. What's your handicap?"

"Well, since you asked, it's a four," said the priest. "But," he quickly added, "I also get to play rain or shine—uh—*religiously*—twice a week—no pun intended."

Again, Matt was struck by the gregarious nature of the man.

As if sensing Matt's envy, Father Richter said, "Perhaps we could get out together some time?"

"I'd like that a lot, Father," replied Davis. "That is if you wouldn't mind putting up with a five hour round and maybe a little cursing."

The priest chuckled.

"Where do you usually play?" asked Matt.

"Van Cortland Park," answered the priest. "It's the only place I can still afford." He was referring to the city park in the Bronx, which only charged a nominal fee to residents.

"That's one of the reasons I don't get out more often, myself," said Matt. "That, and my job, of course. Never enough time."

"I used to play out at Beth Page," added Father Richter, "but, now that they've played the Open there, everybody and his uncle wants to play it, and it's impossible to get a tee time."

"Van Cortland is just fine with me," said Matt, with a laugh.

"Well, I think maybe we ought to set a date right now," challenged Father Richter. "Before you have a chance to back out."

"Well...I don't know," said Davis, a note of hesitation in his voice. "With the investigation going on and all...." His resolve weakened. "I guess I might be able to squeeze in nine, but that's probably it. Maybe on a Wednesday afternoon sometime, but—"

"Good. Then it's a date. Check your schedule and let me know which Wednesday is good," said Father Richter.

"Well—"

"I usually try to play on Mondays *and* Wednesdays," added Father Pete. "So, that shouldn't be a problem, but if you need to—"

"No, no," insisted Davis. "I'm sure I can get a couple of hours on a Wednesday. I just have to check my calendar, that's all."

"Good. Maybe even *next* Wednesday," said Richter. "Just let me know as soon as you can, okay?"

"I promise," said Matt. He was already looking forward to playing.

"Now, how about some hot cocoa?" said the priest.

"Probably more like *warm* cocoa, by now," quipped Davis. "You know, I always have difficulty with my chipping. Maybe you could help me with a problem I..."

For the next fifteen minutes the two men chatted away, each surprised at having struck up such an unexpected friendship. Finally, Matt jotted his home number on the back of one of his cards and handed it to Richter. They promised to get together soon.

Exactly thirty-one minutes had elapsed when Freitag knocked sharply on the rectory door, signaling to Davis that his little break was over. Although it had not been an uninteresting half-hour, he realized he had failed to glean any truly earth-shattering news. He *had* learned, however, that most probably Cindy McKenzie was having some sort of an affair. That much had been made quite clear from his little interview with Father Anthony. *And*, that made it three for three. He felt certain that their luck was beginning to turn.

CHAPTER 35

Baltimore, Maryland

*I*n *August of 1960, John Curran, Jr. was nearly nineteen-years of age. He had been living with a foster family ever since his release from reform school nearly two years earlier. His foster parents had been left childless after their own son had been struck down by polio in 1952. The couple was pleased to have John join their family. They felt the boy possessed an innate intelligence that would eventually blossom as he matured. The fact that he resembled their own son, physically, made him that much easier for them to love him.*

During his incarceration John had continued his high school studies and now, after receiving his diploma, it was time to think about college. His foster parents were upper-middle class residents of New Castle, a suburb of Baltimore, and had already decided that young John should attend Benjamin Franklin University in Lewisburg, Pennsylvania. Since John's foster father was an alumnus of BFU (and a generous contributor to his alma mater) it was quietly arranged for the boy to be admitted without the usual red tape.

Things went well at college until midway into John's sophomore year. One evening, while he and several other students were drinking beer and playing darts in a local pub, he noticed a young girl alone at the bar. He offered to buy her a drink, and the two sat down together at a table to become better acquainted. As the evening progressed, John became increasingly intoxicated. His attitude toward the girl, initially playful and amorous, grew belligerent, sexual, and confrontational. Finally, when he had made one offensive remark too many, the girl got up to leave. In a rage, John grabbed her wrist and began shouting obscenities. The young woman matched him, curse for curse. Suddenly, without warning, John slapped her hard across the face.

The girl panicked. She flung her beer into his face and screamed. John continued slapping the girl viciously until, at last, the bartender charged over to the table to stop him. A nasty fight ensued, and John was arrested for assault and battery. Again he was fingerprinted and forced to spend a night in jail before being released the following day on bail.

A week later, John's foster father drove up to the college and hired a lawyer. Before the case ever came to trial, he, John, and the attorney met with the local judge. They arranged for John to be moved through the judicial system by way of a pre-trial intervention. Under this agreement, the court would postpone the trial for six months, during which period John would do community service, and be on a kind of probation. If, at the end of the half-year period, he had remained out of trouble, the case would never come to trial, and the record of the arrest, along with John's fingerprints, would be expunged. It would be as if the offense had never occurred.

John did his community service at a local juvenile home, and more than lived up to the expectations of the court and his foster parents. Now, it was six months later, and the record of his crime was to be officially deleted, and his fingerprints removed from the police files. He would be free to move on with his life.

But, fate was to attach a very long string to John Curran, one that would forever connect his past to his future. It came in the form of a politically-appointed seventy-four year old court clerk named Agnes Short. Agnes was a lovely woman, a lifelong Democrat, and a grandmother of five. Unfortunately, she was also suffering from undiagnosed Alzheimer's disease. The day John's records (including his fingerprints) were to be removed from the files, Agnes was stumbling through a particularly bad day. She not only locked her keys in her car and forgot to feed her cat, but, more importantly, she neglected to expunge John Curran's records. Now, thanks to a well-meaning, but forgetful public servant, John's arrest record and his fingerprints would remain on file in the Lewisburg police records forever, and, once again, the rage that he carried against women would cost him dearly.

CHAPTER 36

Father Anthony was thirty-one-years old. He didn't want to do *anything* that might place his job in jeopardy. He had only been at St. Jude's for about two years, and relished his position at one of the more active parishes in Manhattan. Its location in the Chelsea district of the city, with its proximity to museums, theaters, and art galleries, made it an ideal post for a man like him, one who was consumed by the arts.

Now, however, he was consumed by something entirely different—guilt! He paced nervously back and forth in the small room he shared with Father James. He hadn't really done anything wrong, he thought. After all, he rationalized; he had answered all the detective's questions as openly and honestly as the conditions would permit.

Three women were dead, he thought – three innocent women. *In the eyes of God, we are all innocent – assuming we are contrite.* Certainly, the McKenzie woman was contrite, wasn't she? And yet, she was dead. Raped and strangled by a madman. A madman that *he*, Father Anthony, could probably help the police to find. After all, he thought, didn't she say that she had been chatting with him on the computer? Didn't she confess that she wanted to meet him; the man she had been talking to on the Internet? Perhaps if the police had this information it would help them track her killer.

The young priest knelt in the corner of the room, and bowed his head in whispered prayer: "Dear God," he prayed. "Tell me what to do. Show me the direction to take. Guide me in this time of indecision. Lord Jesus, I know I am sworn to secrecy, but can it be a sin when the woman is already dead? I want to do the right thing Lord. Help me. Tell me what to do."

Tears appeared at the corner of Father Anthony's tightly closed blue eyes, and his body heaved with emotion. He continued praying, "Father, let me do the right thing. I'm sure *you* can understand that I *must* tell someone. I can't let this man go free. What should I do? Who can I tell? Help me Father." He waited several minutes for an answer.

In the end, however, the young priest decided that he would maintain his silence as he had vowed he would. He would leave it all in God's hands. That was what his religion taught him, and that is what he must do. He hurried through an *Our Father* and several *Hail Mary's*, crossed himself and rose to a standing position. As he looked out the small, plain window, he thought, *if it happens again, I must tell them. Please, Lord; don't let there be another one— please!*

CHAPTER 37

6:55 p.m., Saturday, April 22

*T**he killer pushed the last scraps of his dinner into the sink and ran the water, while at the same time flipping on the garbage disposal unit, which burst into operation with a loud grinding sound. He hadn't planned on going out tonight, but when he had checked his email and found the invitation from Linda, a.k.a. Hot2Trot, he couldn't resist. She had been on his Buddy List for about two weeks now. He found her brand of hard, raunchy sex to be just the thing to turn him on lately. He wasn't due at her place until nine, so he decided to go online and see if any of his other "friends" were chatting. Nearly all of the women with whom he chatted lived in Chelsea, as he did, but occasionally he enjoyed chatting with someone totally out of the area. Variety, after all, was the spice of life, wasn't it?*

*The screen slowly became illuminated, and he clicked and scrolled a number of times until at last his "Buddy List" was showing on the screen. None of the little smiley faces alongside the names was illuminated, meaning that none of his buddies were on line. A few clicks of the mouse and he was in one of his favorite rooms – "Forty Plus and Still Flirting." He always lied about his age, anyway, so it really didn't matter which room he went into. He scrolled through the "Who's Chatting" box and saw **MyPussy4U** on the list of occupants. Never heard of her, he thought. He clicked on "Get Profile" and waited while the computer loaded the individual's home page. In a few moments, the box began to fill with information:*

Age: 41

Real Name: Wouldn't you like to know…
Measurements: 38C-28-36
Location: NYC
Marital Status: Divorced and <u>loving</u> it!!
Hobbies: Sex, sex, and <u>more</u> sex!!

His eyes focused on **"Location."** *Hmm, he thought.* I wonder where in the city? *He closed down the "My Profile" box and double clicked on the words "Send PM Now," and waited until the box appeared which would allow him to send a Personal Message. He started writing:*

SexualGuy1: Dear "Wouldn't You Like To Know", I like your screen name. Are you really into lots of sex?

(He thought that was really clever. Show them he had a sense of humor; nothing like a little humor to break the ice). He waited a few moments, and then came the answer:

MyPussy4U: *Uh huh…Are you really a sexual guy?*

Oh boy, he thought. He had a live one.

SexualGuy1: What do <u>you</u> think?

MyPussy4U: *I don't know…tell me what you like…*

SexualGuy1: Well, first I wanna know if your pussy is nice and wet?

MyPussy4U: *Oh, baby…I'm dripping already …I'm so wet…why don't you eat me?*

SexualGuy1: Would you like that?

MyPussy4U: *Oh, baby…you know I would…*

SexualGuy1:   Good…first let me start by running my tongue along the outside of your cunt lips. Can you feel that?

MyPussy4U: *Oh yes, baby…my clit is so hard…I want your hot tongue…let me feel it now….now, baby!!*

SexualGuy1: I'm licking along the outside of your pussy lips…now I'm forcing my tongue between your lips and inside your hot, moist cunt…

MyPussy4U: *mmmmmmmmmmm…*

SexualGuy1: Oh yes, baby….yes…you're so hot…

Before long he had brought his new "friend" to climax, and was working on his own fulfillment. He began stroking himself while she urged him on.

MyPussy4U: *Are you good and hard, baby?*

SexualGuy1: Oh, yes......so hard........yessss!!!

MyPussy4U: *My tongue is running up and down your shaft...feeling your balls tighten...Oh, baby, you're so hard...I want you to fill my mouth with cum...stroke it for me, baby...make it squirt....I want to swallow it all...*

SexualGuy1: Oh God...I can't stand it any longer...I'm stroking it hard...gonna cum....soon.....oh, yes.......here it cums......Ohhhhhhhhhhhhhh..............

In a matter of seconds, it was all over. He had achieved an orgasm. He cleaned himself, and quickly typed out some more words, telling her how great she was and how they had to get back together soon. She agreed, and they added each other to their individual "Buddy Lists." He glanced at his watch and noticed it was getting late, and told her he had to go. He promised to chat with her again soon. Then he closed down his computer, went into the bathroom and brushed his teeth, combed his hair, and splashed on some cologne

It was only a short walk over to "Hot2Trot's" apartment on 21st Street, just off Eighth Avenue, but he didn't want to be late. Maybe this time it would work out – not like those others, he thought. He turned off the light and strolled out into the early spring evening. He was whistling as he walked.

CHAPTER 38

Linda heard a soft knock at the door and took a deep breath before answering. Her full name was Linda Jean Vogel, and she was thirty-eight, divorced, and very lonely. She had been chatting with *SexualGuy1* for a while now, and looked forward to meeting the man with the great sense of humor and overactive sex drive. If he was half as much fun in person as he was online, they should have a great evening together. She doubted that they would really have sex, but she didn't really care. All that stuff on the Internet was just an act anyway. She was sure he would be a regular guy who liked to listen to music and loved to go bowling. Who knows, she thought, maybe we…

Why doesn't she answer? thought the killer. He knocked softly again. This time the door opened, and there she was. Wow, he thought. She looks even better than I remembered.

"Surprised?" he asked.

"Wha—"

"So, you are surprised? Bet you never expected me, did you?"

"No, not exactly," replied Linda. "I didn't think you—"

"What? Fooled around? Sure, why wouldn't I? I'm no different than any other guy. I thought you might enjoy the surprise."

She didn't look surprised as much as she looked horrified. He felt himself getting angry. Why did they always react this way?

"Aren't you going to invite me in?" he asked.

"Well, I…I mean, I didn't expect—"

"You're not interested, are you?" he said.

It was happening again, he thought. Once they knew who he "really" was, they didn't want to have anything to do with him. Well, he would just have to show her just like he had shown the others. But, first he had to get inside.

"How about I just come in for a drink, and we can 'chat' in person for a few minutes. If you want me to leave, then I'll just leave, okay?"

"Well, I guess—"

"Oh, come on. I only want to talk, anyway." He pushed the door open and walked inside. "You really do have a nice place, Linda." He walked into the shabby living room, thinking, what a dump.

She looked around, as if seeing her own apartment for the very first time. The walls were cracked and needed painting, the drapes were faded, and the carpets were stained from her cat.

"I didn't really get a chance to straighten up like I should have. I hope you don't mind." She appeared very nervous. "I guess I didn't really expect somebody to take me up on my invitation. And you know *I didn't expect it to be you."*

He waited until she had closed the door before moving closer to her. He could smell her perfume, and could feel himself growing hard already. He could hardly control himself.

"Would you like a beer?" she asked. "I mean, I don't even know if you drink—"

"Sure," he said.

"Look," she said. "I'm sorry if I looked a little shocked, but, to be honest, you're the last person in the world I expected to show up tonight."

"Hey, no problem. It's my own fault, anyway," he said.

Certainly not a problem for me, he thought. But, it could be one for you.

She moved into the kitchen, and he followed her into its narrow confines. She turned toward the refrigerator, her back to him, and he made his move.   He put an arm around her waist, and leaned over and kissed her on the neck.

"What the—"   She turned around quickly, the fear showing in her eyes.

"It's okay—really," he said, quietly.

"But—"   She was beginning to panic.

"Shhhhh..."

He pressed his mouth to hers and simultaneously brought his hands to her throat.   Soon, she had lost consciousness, and he carried her limp form into the bedroom. The bed was small, with no posts or headboard, so he would have to tie her hands behind her, and bind her feet to the legs beneath the frame of the bed.   He tore off her blouse and removed her brassiere.   He turned her onto her stomach, and tied her hands with the bra.   Then, using his penknife, he cut off her panties.   He rolled her over onto her back again, and stuffed the wadded up undergarment into her mouth.   It was easy, he thought, so easy...

Of course, when she had regained consciousness, she had resisted, struggling furiously.   He'd had to beat her, and the sound of her nose breaking beneath his fist still reverberated inside his head. He never intended to hit them, but what else could he do? Later, he crouched over the body, and carefully used the little pearl-handled knife to precisely carve his trademark on her left breast.   He whistled as he worked, being careful to blot any blood that ran outside the finely cut lines.   Mustn't make a mess, he thought, chuckling to himself. When he was finished, he stepped back to admire his handiwork.   The heart was perfectly symmetrical, and the initials, "J.C." and "L.V." were perfectly centered within it.

Again, his attempt at a normal relationship had failed. Maybe next time, he thought, as he carefully closed the door behind him, and walked down the three flights to the street below. Perhaps he would stop for a nightcap before he went to bed. He smiled to himself, and began to whistle "Hey Jude."

Then, he changed from whistling to singing, substituting the name, Jack, for the name Jude. Much better, he though, much better.

CHAPTER 39

8:24 p.m., Tuesday, May 2

T he call to 911 came in around seven-fifteen in the evening; it was placed by a seventy-one-year old widow named Marilyn Kaufman. She complained that there was an awful smell coming out of Ms. Vogel's apartment, and went on to say that she didn't like to be nosey, but thought maybe somebody was sick or something. Anyway, she thought somebody ought to check on her, especially since she hadn't answered the door in three days.

Davis, Freitag, and Valdez pulled up to the five-story walk-up within an hour after the body was discovered. The building superintendent had let the responding officers in, and they had found the corpse on the bed, bound and gagged. The body was bloated with gases, the skin stretched taut and almost black. The putrid smell had caused the super to vomit, and the young uniformed cop had all he could do to not follow suit.

They guessed the woman had been dead about a week (ultimately, the autopsy would show that she had been murdered between noon and midnight on the 28th). As usual, there was the neatly carved heart on the left breast, with the initials "L.V." beneath the now familiar other set, which read "J.C."

The three detectives sat outside the building, in the front seat of the Impala. The engine was running, and periodically the squawk of the police radio pierced the stillness of the spring night. They were bone weary.

"So far, no bible," said Davis.

"Nope," answered Freitag, automatically. He appeared to be lost in thought.

"Do you think we're wrong? About the religion thing, I mean?" asked Valdez.

"I don't know," answered Freitag. "Maybe."

"Or maybe he's deliberately trying to throw us off," said Davis.

"Either way, we're still nowhere with this thing," said Rita.

Matt didn't say a word. He didn't have to.

"Hey, anything come back on those prints yet?" asked Chris.

"Nope. Nothing yet," answered Davis. "I hope we get *something* soon."

The fingerprints gathered at the various scenes were sent to One Police Plaza, or, as it was referred to by the men in the department, "The Puzzle Palace."   There they would be classified, and run through the massive computer to see if they matched those of any local criminals. Then they were sent to the FBI for possible identification and comparison with those of any known felons who might be wanted by the federal agency.

Of course, all the technical information in the world wouldn't help if they couldn't come up with a suspect.

Driving up Broadway, on their way back to the precinct, the three detectives observed one of the many storefront mosques that were springing up an alarming rate in the city. Even at this late hour, bearded men in turbans moved quietly within the dimly-lit confines of the makeshift house of worship. Ever since the events of 9/11, Matt had struggled with an undeniable tendency to want to mistrust middle-Easterners at first sight. The only way he was able to suppress his negative feelings was by constantly reminding himself of how blind prejudice had negatively affected his ancestors when they emigrated from Ireland to America. Conversely, Freitag made no pretext of hiding his all out distaste for "those fucking camel jockeys," as he angrily referred to anyone with skin darker than his own.   Whenever Matt would berate him for his biased opinions, Chris would jokingly refer to his partner as a sappy liberal, and urge him to get in touch with his "true feelings." Ironically, at the present time, the reality of the recent murders made the imagined transgressions of unwanted immigrants seem relativity insignificant, and the detectives rode past the mosque in silence.

It was nearly midnight by the time they arrived back at headquarters. The usual gaggle of reporters was waiting for the detectives when they burst through the battered front doors of the precinct lobby.

"Alright guys," said Matt. "Take it easy.   One at a time."

"Is it the strangler?" asked Donnelly from *the Daily News*.

"We can't be sure, Dave, but it certainly looks like a possibility." Davis wished they would all just go away.

"Do you have any suspects?" asked Tim Ryan from *Newsday*.

"Presently, no," answered Matt. "But, we have a couple of leads that we're running down which *might* provide us with a possible direction."

It was all "double speak," of course, but he had to say *something*. What he'd really like to say is that he didn't have a fucking clue, but he sure wished he could come up with one.

Harry Cohen, of *the Post*, stood off to the side, waiting for an opportunity to get Davis alone. Gradually, the various reporters filtered out the front door until at last, the wily scribe got his wish. Rita had headed for the ladies room, leaving Matt and Chris to deal with Cohen. The seasoned scribe walked up to Davis and Freitag, and spoke directly to Matt.

"So—uh—Matt," he began. "I've really been patient…"

Here it comes, thought Davis.

"You promised me if I laid off, you'd let me know when you had something. So, how 'bout it?"

"Harry," said Matt. "We don't have a *damn* thing, honest."

"Oh, for the love of God," said Harry. "You've got four murders now—all done by the same guy—and you're telling me you don't have a *thing* to go on?"

"That's the truth," said Freitag.

"Oh, great," said Cohen. "You've even got *him* believing it." He jerked his thumb in Freitag's direction.

"Look, Harry," said Matt. "I'd love to help you out, but it's after midnight, and I'm tired as shit. You have my word. Anything happens you'll be the first to know about it. Now, if you'll excuse me, I'm gonna go home and get some shuteye."

Cohen shrugged his shoulders, stuffed his reporter's note pad inside his jacket pocket, and started walking down the hall. He made a quick left and entered the men's room.

Freitag looked at Davis and whispered, "Let's get the fuck out of here while the old bastard's takin' a leak."

"Good idea," said Matt. "Rita can show him the door."

Both detectives laughed and headed out the door, and were soon on their way home. Tomorrow would be a new day, and, hopefully a better one.

Five minutes later, the *Post* reporter quietly opened the door to the men's room and sneaked a look back down the hall. Being familiar with the layout of the old building, Cohen used the back stairway to get upstairs to Davis's office. He prayed that the door wouldn't be locked. He wasn't disappointed.

Keeping his back to the door, he looked around the darkened hallway, and then slowly opened the door. Cohen had never done anything like this before, but he was getting a bit long in the tooth, and this story had the potential to boost his career big time. He needed the edge that this information could provide. He shrugged his shoulders, and tiptoed over to the detective's desk. Reaching inside his pocket, he extracted a small flashlight, and carefully adjusted the beam until it was as small as possible. He moved the light quickly back and forth over the top of Davis's desk. Several manila folders caught his attention. One was marked *Spiros*. Two others bore the names *McKenzie* and *Simpson*. He quickly flipped through the paperwork contained in the *Spiros* file, until he came to several photos, located in the back.

"Hmm?" he asked, rhetorically. "What've we got here?"

His eyes focused on the image of the heart on Melina Spiros' nude body. He stared hard and brought the two sets of initials into focus. "Well, I'll be damned."

He grabbed up the other two folders and began rifling through their contents. In each one he found a photograph similar to the one in the Spiros file. The only difference was that, in each of the others, there was a different set of initials accompanying the ones reading "J.C."

"Holy shit," whispered Harry to himself. "That son of a bitch. He's known about this all along." He thought of what Davis had told him: "As soon as I know anything, Harry, you'll be the first to know."

Oh, yeah? Bullshit! Well now I know, so kiss my ass, Davis!

The reporter continued to study the three folders, until, at last he was satisfied that he had gleaned all he could from them. He turned off the flashlight, exited the office, and slipped quietly down the back stairway, leaving through the rear door of the building.

I'll fix that prick. He fired up the engine to the battered '91 Nova. *Not only am I the first to know, but we'll see how he likes it when twelve million New Yorkers know, too.*

CHAPTER 40

Upstate New York, 1964

*E*arly in his probation, John Curran came to realize that his sexual attitudes toward women had become a real problem. The scars he carried from childhood virtually guaranteed he would never marry. He decided his life needed a new direction. By the time John was graduated in June of 1964, his compass had been set. He had chosen to give his life to God.

That fall, with his foster parents' blessings, he entered a Catholic seminary in Elmira, New York. For four years, he studied hard, kept to himself, and reinforced his relationship with Jesus Christ. Finally, it was time for him to take his vows of celibacy and enter the priesthood. As the final act in his transformation from abused child to man of God, John Curran asked his foster parents for permission to legally change his last name to theirs. Without hesitation, they agreed. Then he selected the first name he would use forever in the service of the Lord. He chose the name given the only son of his foster parents.

CHAPTER 41

9:05 a.m., Wednesday, May 3

STRANGLER HAS A CHEATING HEART!

By Harry Cohen

NEW YORK CITY – Undisclosed sources revealed that NYC detectives are searching for a religious zealot as the chief suspect in the four unsolved strangling murders recently committed here in Manhattan. Despite being told by the man in charge of the investigation, Detective First Grade, Matt Davis, that the department had no real leads, this reporter has learned that each of the victims has been found raped and strangled. And, in each instance, a small heart has been carved on the victim's left breast.

Sources reveal that within each of the hearts has been found two sets of initials – one set matching those of the victim, the other reading "J.C." Each of the victims, it has been noted, has been involved in some kind of affair...

The headline on the front page of *The Post* screamed a warning at Davis as loud as any police siren. Matt studied the article, and wondered how in the hell the veteran reporter had found out what he, himself, had tried so hard to contain. Had it been the ME's office that had leaked the information? He doubted it. He couldn't believe that Ahearn would let him down. So, how did Cohen find out?

Matt knew it was a waste of time to confront the *Post* reporter. He would merely claim First Amendment privileges, and then threaten to sue if Davis persisted. *No*, he thought, *that wouldn't do any good at all.* Well, Cohen could just wait in line at the next DCPI press conference. Let him *try* to get anything meaningful out of Deputy Commissioner for Public Information, Gil Clancy. It would be like trying to get a straight answer from Professor Irwin Corey, the double talk specialist.

"Chris, Martini, Valdez. In my office, right now!" commanded Davis. Almost as an afterthought, he added, "You, too, Wolinski."

"What's up Matt?" asked Freitag, as he filed past his boss and into the detective's office.

"Good morning, *Matt*," said Valdez. She smiled warmly as she passed by him.

"Mornin'," muttered Martini. His white shirt bore a large grease stain that threatened to overshadow the garish purple flowers on his tie. Wolinski shambled past without a salutation.

Matt had scribbled several bits of information on the large blackboard, which hung on the north wall of his office. "Everybody take a seat," he said. He crossed the room and closed and locked the door to his office.

"I feel like I'm back in high school," whispered Martini to Valdez, who just ignored him. Wolinski appeared to fall asleep almost as soon as his ass hit the chair, prompting Matt to frown in mild disapproval. He thought of waking him, and then decided against it. *Let the poor bastard sleep. If I were his age and still on the job, I'd probably want to sleep, too.*

Matt walked to the blackboard, turned his back to it, and propped one foot behind him against the already-filthy wall. He looked at his three colleagues and took a deep breath. He hadn't slept well last night, and the events of the previous evening were still fresh in his mind; especially disturbing, however, was this morning's headline. He held up a copy of *the Post* for everyone to see, like a social studies teacher holding up current events' article for his class. He pointed to the headline, which was spelled out in 60-point bold face type.

"Everybody get a look at this, this morning?"

Three of the seated detectives nodded their heads;
Wolinski just snored.

"Well, what are we going to do about it?" he asked
rhetorically.

Silence.

"Anybody have *any* idea how that bastard Cohen got
this story? Anybody?"

Davis stared at Martini. "Don't look at me," answered
the disheveled detective. "I didn't tell that bum anything." It
was obvious he was sincere.

"Valdez?" he asked.

"Sorry, boss. I don't even *know* the guy," she said.

"Chris, I'm sure it wasn't you, right?"

"Right," answered his partner.

"Alright," said Davis. "I guess it doesn't matter how he
got it. But, he got it *somehow,* and there's not a damn thing we
can do about it. Just make sure he doesn't get anything else.
For God's sake, be careful. We can't afford anymore leaks."

"Now we'll have to watch out for copycats," said
Martini.

"God forbid," muttered Freitag. "That's all we need."

"Anyway, let's concentrate on what we have so far,"
said Matt. "And, let's see if we can't get something going on
this case."

He turned towards the blackboard, on which he had
written the names of the first three victims: Simpson, Spiros,
and McKenzie. Next to the names, he had drawn several
vertical columns. At the top of the columns were the words:
LOCATION, PHYSICAL EVIDENCE, TIME OF DAY, and
SUSPECTS.

He now added to the list of victims, the name Linda
Vogel, then turned back to the others.

"Okay, so let's see what we've got." said Matt.
"Location? All four victims lived within the One-O," he said.

"Time? All four appear to have been murdered in the
evening,"

"So, that leaves physical evidence and suspects. Well, we don't have any suspects so far, but we've got plenty of evidence." Matt pointed to the column in question.

"Each victim was found with a heart carved on her breast. Each heart had two sets of initials in it. So, what does that tell us?"

Martini raised his hand.

"Yes, Martini?"

"Well, I guess it tells us that the same guy did each one," he said.

"But, do we really know for sure it *was* the same guy?" asked Davis. "I mean, we *assume* it was the same guy. For that matter, we assume it was a *guy*. But, do we really know if *either* assumption is correct?"

"Well, there *was* semen present on the first three," offered Valdez. "So we know *they* were done by a guy."

"How about this one?" asked Martini. "Any semen?"

"We think so," answered Matt. "We'll know for sure, later today."

"What about a bible?" inquired Valdez. "We had bibles at the first three scenes. Anybody turn up a bible here?"

"Nope," said Matt. "No bible."

"That reminds me," said Valdez. "I forgot to tell you. I checked out those other bibles with Father Richter. They're generic New Testaments, published by a religious outfit in the Midwest. They sell to everybody and anybody, including St. Jude. In fact, they had a stack of them in the rectory."

Davis filed that little bit of information in the back of his mind.

"What else have we got?" he asked.

The room grew quiet and remained that way for several minutes.

Freitag broke the silence. "Maybe we've got a copy cat?"

"But how *could* we?" asked Davis. "Up until now, nobody even knew about the hearts, much less the bibles. No, I don't buy it. Maybe the guy just ran out of bibles."

Again, nobody said a word.

"Okay, let's see," said Davis. "What do we know about opportunity?"

He answered his own question. "Nothin—"

"But," said Freitag, "we do know for sure that they either *know* this guy—"

"Or they don't *know* him—" said Davis. He was extremely animated. "But, they're *expecting* him—*and*—he knows *them!*"

"You mean like maybe he calls them first?" asked Martini. "Like he's selling something or—"

"Exactly!" answered Davis. "Maybe he's some kind of salesman."

"That *would* explain how he gets in so easy," offered Valdez. "Probably got a real good line of bullshit."

"Okay, I want everybody on this," shouted Davis. "Martini, I want you and Sleeping Beauty to re-canvas Simpson's neighborhood. Find out if anybody there remembers any salesman around the time of the murder."

"Right," answered Frank. He jabbed his elbow into Wolinski's ribcage, rousing the elder detective from his sleep.

"Valdez. Check out the area around the Spiros' apartment."

"Will do," said Valdez.

"Chris, you and I will go back to the McKenzie block. Then we'll nose around Vogel's place."

Freitag smiled, and began gathering up his things.

"Okay, everybody, that's it! Let's get moving," said Matt.

In less than thirty seconds the office was empty.

The next morning forensics called and told Matt that, indeed, a bible *had* been found. It was wedged between two of the cushions on the couch, and had apparently been overlooked during the original search. Davis thanked the technician and hung up the phone.

"Thank God," he muttered to no one in particular. "I don't think I could take a copycat."

CHAPTER 42

F ather Pete made sure the door to his study was locked, then crossed the room and sat down at the computer. He had never done a search before, but thought he might try to locate the web site for Van Cortland Park's golf course. He turned on the machine, waited for the screen to brighten, and then logged on to AOL. He moved the mouse's pointer tentatively around the screen until he found the area he wanted, and typed in *www.google.com*, and double-clicked the mouse. Immediately the computer transformed the abbreviated URL address into the correct form, and within seconds, Father Richter found himself face to face with the search engine he had heard so much about.

It took a few minutes, but finally the priest managed to obtain the web site for Van Cortland Park, and soon made a reservation for a tee time for a twosome at two p.m. on Wednesday, May 10. He figured that if he called the detective with a tee time already reserved, there would be no way Davis could turn him down.

Father Pete took out his little address book from the desk drawer, and scanned its contents until he found the detective's business card, wedged between the pages. After struggling with the handwriting on the back of the card, he deciphered the home phone number Davis had written down, and picked up the telephone receiver. Holding it to his ear, he dialed.

After the fourth ring, an answering machine picked up. The pleasant voice of a woman— obviously the detective was married—read a prepared announcement. He waited for the beep, and left his name and number, along with a brief message about their reserved tee time at Van Cortland, before finally hanging up.

He turned back to the computer and clicked on the task bar's "back" icon several times until, at last, he arrived at the AOL home page. He moved the pointer to *"People,"* and clicked once. Then, he scrolled down the list of options and double clicked on *"Chat."* In a few seconds he was confronted by the usual assortment of chat rooms, from which he selected *"Married But Flirting."*

I won't chat this time, he promised himself. *I'll just look.*

He clicked on the icon for *"JOIN CHAT,"* and watched in fascination as the smaller chatroom screen materialized on the main screen. He was always amazed at the variety of individuals who frequented the Internet, and the chat rooms in particular. The contents of the room's screen were like those of a movie script, with each person identified like a character, their dialogue spelled out—or misspelled, as was more often the case—next to the screen name of each participant. The most amazing thing of all, he thought, was the complete anonymity afforded by this unique medium.

Father Pete leaned back in his chair, his arms behind his head, and just watched the screen:

ImASlut32571: *He told me he lived in Australia…*

Stud4U69: *Any hot women out there? PM me now…*

2KidsNoMan*: They always give you a phony name. Do you really believe him?*

KissMeNow36DD: **What makes you think I'm a virgin?**

The priest was amazed by how many different conversations could take place at one time in a chat room. The screen scrolled as each new entry appeared, and if there were 15 individuals chatting in the room, there could be almost as many conversations going on as that. In fact, some individuals carried on chats with more than one other person at a time. He noticed that some people appeared to have no interest at all in being heard, but just wanted to make a statement about some topic or the other:

IlikeCunt69Me: *SUCK MY COCK!   SUCK MY COCK! SUCK MY COCK!*

KissMeNow36DD: Fuck You! Asshole!!!

IlikeCunt69Me: *FUCK YOU 2 ASSHOLE!*

The vulgarity was incredible.   The priest was mesmerized and just sat there as the dialogue continued unabated. Several times he thought about joining in. But he had promised himself he wouldn't chat this time, and resisted the temptation. Suddenly, a box appeared in the center of his screen, partially obscuring the ongoing dialogue of the chat room.   The   words   **"INSTANT MESSAGE FROM LindaLuvsIt2 "** appeared at the top of the box, and within the box was:

LindaLuvsIt2: *What are you? A watcher?*

Father Pete felt his face flush, and his mouth went dry. For an instant he was paralyzed. He didn't know how to react. This was the first time anyone had *ever* contacted *him*. Did he know her? More importantly, did she know *him*? He searched the frame of the small box on the screen, and found the familiar smaller box labeled *"REPLY,"* located near the bottom. He hesitated, then moved the mouse until the pointer's arrow rested on the box.   Still unsure of his actions, he double clicked. Instantly, his screen name appeared within the box, below that of the other chatter. Without thinking, he typed in the word *"What?"* next to it, and clicked on *"SEND."* Now, the solo word he had typed joined the other words within the box, just like those on the chat room screen:

LindaLuvsIt2: *What are you? A watcher?*

GolfNut1: What?

In a moment, another message appeared:

LindaLuvsIt2: *Do you come here often?*

The priest drew a shallow breath. Without thinking, he answered back:

GolfNut1: Not really. Do you?

My God, he thought. *I'm chatting again. I shouldn't be doing this.* His mind was racing. He felt every kind of emotion flooding through him: guilt, embarrassment, anxiety, curiosity, and arousal. The screen jumped again:

LindaLuvsIt2: *a/s/l?*

Instinctively, Father Pete answered:

GolfNut1: What does a/s/l mean?

He waited. In a few seconds he read the answer.

LindaLuvsIt2: *age/sex/location…how old are u? your sex?/ where do u live?*

He read the words out loud. It made sense of course, he thought. *Am I a jerk, or what?*

Should I answer? Oh God, I can't do this. He felt himself becoming more aroused. At the same time, blood was rushing to his cheeks. His hands trembled. He lifted them from the keyboard and wrung them out, his eyes closed tightly. He opened his eyes and looked. It wasn't his imagination. The question was still there. He answered.

GolfNut1: 58/male/USA

He clicked send.

LindaLuvsIt2: *37/f/NYC*

Then, before he could respond, another message appeared in the box:

LindaLuvsIt2: *I like older men. Where in the USA?*

Immediately, the priest directed the pointer to the upper right hand corner of the ***INSTANT MESSAGE*** box, and clicked on the *X* to close it. The box went away. He breathed a sigh of relief.

In a moment, the box re-appeared. *Oh my God,* he thought. Without reading its message, he again clicked on the *X*, closing the box. Then, he quickly closed down the chat room screen, and exited AOL™. He clicked *"Start"* at the bottom left corner on his desktop screen, scrolled up to *"Shut Down,"* and double clicked on the words. In a moment the screen went black, and then lit up again, with instructions for the user to "Please Wait While Your Computer Shuts Down." Then, he heard the familiar click, and the monitor went blank.

He was sweating.

"Oh my God, I am heartily sorry for having offended Thee…" came the words. They were the familiar lines of the Act of Contrition. Father Richter bowed his head, clasped his hands together, and recited the familiar words in a feverish whisper.

He had much for which to ask forgiveness.

CHAPTER 43

11:45 a.m., Saturday, May 6

Atchison's Quality Market was located downtown in the Chelsea District. Other than for the upscale grocery store's location, it was typical of its counterparts that dotted the Upper East Side of Manhattan. They all served as culinary oases in the streets of the city's concrete desert. Each overcharged its customers unmercifully, citing high rents and even higher taxes as excuses for their inflated prices. But, in defense of Atchison's, it did carry every possible luxury food item that money could buy. From snails and oysters, to bird's nest soup and smoked salmon, the Chelsea store had it all, including ethnic specialties. In addition, the Lower Manhattan specialty store offered one more accommodation that endeared it to its loyal customers – free delivery.

Jeanine Kelly loved Irish soda bread, and Atchison's carried the genuine article. Of course, they charged more than five dollars for a tiny loaf, but it *was* fresh, and Lord knew it was authentic. The eighty-one-year old widow also knew that there was a twenty-dollar minimum order required for the "free" delivery, so, limping around her kitchen on arthritic feet, the white-haired grandmother added some basic items to fill out her order, and phoned it in.

Twenty minutes later, Ken Callahan loaded her order into the huge basket which hung from the handlebars of his three-wheel delivery bicycle and began pedaling up the sidewalk toward her West 23rd Street apartment.   He rode slowly, keeping an eye out for pedestrians while enjoying the warmth of the early May sun.   He was glad he worked in Chelsea, he thought, instead of uptown where the taller buildings all but obliterated the sunlight, and, even in spring, funneled the winds mercilessly through the narrow streets.

He thought, too, about Mrs. Kelly's attractive neighbor, Rita Valdez, and how hot she had looked the other night in her long leather coat, tight jeans, and high heels.   He'd love to throw a hump into her, he thought.   *She treats me like a nice little boy – like a ten-year old – all because of my face. I'm sick of their pity. I'll bet I could make her treat me different if she'd just get to know me.*   He recalled their recent late-night conversation.   Imagine the nerve, he had thought, telling me, "How hard it is to meet somebody." *Just try walking around with* this *face. You think you've got problems—try mine.*   And, to make matters worse, the blame – he had decided – belonged to women.

If it hadn't been for the unfaithfulness of his college girlfriend, he would *never* have dropped out of Columbia in his sophomore year; never mind that his two-point-one grade point average had him on the verge of flunking out.   It was easier to blame his dilemma on a girl, rather than on his own shortcomings.   "The bitch fucked me," he would say, whenever the subject came up. *If it wasn't for that cunt, I would've never got drafted.*   And, of course, if he had never been drafted, he would never have been sent to that hellhole of Vietnam.   And, he would never have suffered the incident that had shaped the remainder of his miserable life.   It was all so logical; it all made perfect sense—at least it did to Kenneth John Callahan.

The day it all happened, Ken was stoned.   He and one of his platoon buddies had scored some excellent Tai Stick off a fourteen-year old Vietnamese whore they both frequented.   His squad was sent out on a reconnaissance patrol, and had engaged the enemy in a firefight just outside their perimeter.   A cluster grenade had exploded just in front of him, and the white-hot magnesium fragments that struck his face had adhered like sticky glue, burning through three layers of delicate facial skin. His hands had been burned even worse when he attempted to remove the magnesium fragments from his face. His tour of duty was over, but his nightmare was just beginning.

When he returned to the States, he spent nearly four months in the Veterans Administration hospital in Fort Hamilton in Brooklyn. During that period, he contacted his old college girlfriend, who visited him once—probably out of curiosity. The visit was disastrous. The young girl was repulsed by his appearance and left the hospital in tears, leaving the wounded GI in a state of shock. Later that evening, Ken attempted suicide by cutting his wrists, and only the quick actions of a neighboring roommate saved his life.

In reality, Ken's physical disfigurement was really quite minimal. Dozens of sessions with a team of VA plastic surgeons had all but restored his face to limits of acceptability. His hands were another story, and the scar tissue that all but obliterated his fingerprints, ensured that he would never wield a hammer, or dig ditches for a living. However, while his reflection in a mirror gave little clue to his suffering, the images he saw in his mind bore the scars just as visibly as if they were real. The fact was that the unpopular war in Southeast Asia had left the veteran with emotional wounds far more severe than the physical ones he displayed on his face and hands.

In the ensuing years, Callahan underwent years of psychiatric treatment at the veterans' hospital. The clinical term for his condition was *paranoia schizophrenia*. In the beginning, he had shown promise of recovery, but, in the end, the effects of his war experiences were too much for him to overcome. Put simply, Ken Callahan felt that everyone was plotting against him, especially women.

After chaining his bicycle to a street sign, Callahan rang the bell to Mrs. Kelly's apartment. A moment later there was a loud buzz and the lock to the entrance of the apartment building released its hold on the metal-sheathed door. He trudged up the narrow flight of stairs to the second-floor landing, and was greeted warmly by the elderly woman who welcomed him into her dingy apartment. As he was about to leave, the door to Rita Valdez's apartment opened narrowly, restricted by a security chain that permitted it to open only a few inches.

"Is that you, Ken?" asked Rita.

"Yes, Miss Valdez," he answered, "it's me." *But, you can call me Jack.*

Rita unhooked the chain and opened the door wide.

God, she's hot.

"I was wondering," said Rita, "Do you think you could you give me a hand with my new computer?"

"Oh, I dunno, Miss Valdez," he said, "I'm not really that great with those things. I just use mine for sending Emails—" Then, he added, "—and chatting. You know, stuff like that. Believe me, I'm no expert. I'm surprised, with you bein' a secretary and all that you can't do it yourself."

"Oh, I know how to *run* it okay," answered Rita. "I'm just not too sure how to hook it up." Although she didn't make it a habit to lie, Rita had created a bit of a false identity in her neighborhood, preferring to be known as a secretary, effectively hiding her police connection.

"Well, I guess I could—"

"I'll pay you," said Rita.

"Oh, you don't have to do that," he answered, quietly. "I'd be happy to take a look at it for you."

Mrs. Kelly waved good bye to Rita and retreated to her apartment, locking her door behind her.

"Can you do it now?" asked Rita.

Ken looked at his watch, then back at Rita. She was wearing a navy pants suit, and he wondered what she was wearing underneath.

"Sure," he said, "I guess I could give it a look. Long as it doesn't take too long."

"Oh, great," she replied. She stepped aside, and allowed the deliveryman into her apartment. He was careful not to brush against her. Rita mistook his deliberate manner for shyness.

She had already removed the components from their cow-covered boxes, and the empty cardboard containers were stacked against the wall. Ken studied the directions for a moment, and before long had connected the monitor to the tower. He then ran the proper wires to the printer, speakers, and microphone and plugged the power cord into the nearby outlet.

"Let's give it a try," he said.

Rita pressed the buttons on the tower and monitor, and waited. In a couple of seconds the screen flickered and lit up. Soon, the familiar Microsoft waving-flag logo appeared, together with the manufacturer's trademarked black and white image. "Great," said Rita, with a broad smile.

"Believe it or not, I just want to get on the Internet so I can start chatting."

She related the story of her Florida girlfriend, and again expressed her own frustration with the dating scene. Again, Ken was struck by her naïveté.

"Have you picked out a screen name yet?" he asked.

"Nah, I haven't really thought about it," she replied. "I still have to get online."

"Well, when you do, let me know and I'll send you your first email," laughed Ken.

Rita laughed too, and showed the middle-aged man to the door. "I can't thank you enough," she said. "Are you sure I can't pay you something?"

"Nope," said Ken. "It's on the house."

"Well, thanks again. And I'll let you know when I get online."

Yeah, I'll bet.

After leaving Rita Valdez's apartment, Ken had all he could do to get through the rest of his workday. He couldn't get her off his mind. Would she really give him her screen name? He doubted it. But, what if—no, she would never give it to him. He decided that she was just like all the rest.

CHAPTER 44

Rita Valdez was quite pleased. Not only was her computer up and running – thanks in no small part to Ken—but, she had gotten a disk at a computer store that advertised "1,000 Hours Free!" The next day, she corralled Ken in the hallway, and enlisted his help in actually getting online. He walked her through the installation procedure, helped select her dial-up numbers, and moved her to the page where she was supposed to enter her personal information for her "profile." She made him turn his back while she typed in various tidbits about herself – some true, some not – including hobbies, dating preferences, astrological sign, etc. Finally, it was time to choose her screen name.

"You know," she said, "I don't have a clue what to call myself."

"Does this mean you're really going to tell me your screen name?" asked Ken, a hopeful tone in his voice.

"That's the *least* I can do," said Rita. "Especially after all you've done for *me*. Besides, didn't I promise you I would?"

"Yeah," said Ken, "but I didn't really think you would. Most girls never keep their promises."

"Well, I'm not exactly a girl," said Rita with a laugh.

"Yeah, but I'm just the grocery guy," said Ken. "You've probably got lots of guys just dying to talk to you."

Rita hesitated for a second.

"See," said Ken. "What did I tell you. You're just bein' nice to me."

"No, no," said Rita, "not at all. Honest. I'd love to chat on line with you."

"Well, okay," said Ken, apparently greatly relieved. "But, first we gotta pick you out a screen name."

"I just don't want anything too obvious," said Rita. "You know – no 'Lady Dick,' or 'Girl's Gotta Have it,' or anything like that. Just something simple. Maybe like – 'Need A Friend.' What do you think?"

Ken stared at her with a sly looking smile on his face.

"What?" said Rita.

"Well..." Ken blushed.

"Well, *what*?"

"Well, it's just that most of the girls I see on line use *sexy* names – at least, the ones *I* talk to."

"Okay, so what's a sexy name?"

"You mean it?"

"Sure," replied Rita. "What the hell? We might as well go with the flow. Give me a name."

"How old are you?" blurted out Ken.

Rita frowned.

"No, no," said Ken. "I mean, what's your age? I don't care how old you are."

"Does it matter?" asked Rita.

"No, no – that's not what I mean. I mean, you could use that as part of your name, that's all."

Rita shook her head. "I don't think so. Besides, I don't want anyone on line to know my name. There're too many creeps out there."

"No, not your *real* name," replied Ken. "I was thinking more like – 'Sexy21' or something like that."

"Well, we both know I'm not twenty one," said Rita," so that won't work."

"That's why I asked you how old you are," replied Ken.

"Okay, okay. Now I get it. Oh, what the hell. How about 'Sexy39?'"

"*You're* thirty nine?" said Ken, incredulously. "No way!"

Rita sucked in her stomach. "Why? You think I look younger?"

"Of course," answered Ken. "You don't look a day over – thirty."

Rita could remember a time when that would have been an insult. She laughed out loud. "Okay," she said, "'Sexy39' it is." *No big deal if they know my age*, she thought. *Hell, it might help weed out the kiddies.*

To test out her new moniker, Rita agreed to have Ken send her a personal message (PM) using the AOL Instant Messenger program. His screen name was "QuesanKen," which was an obvious reference to his time spent in Vietnam. On her first night on the Internet, Rita logged on and waited for Ken's message. At exactly eight o'clock, as he had promised, Ken sent Rita the PM. They chatted for a few minutes, and then he said he had to go. All of a sudden, she was alone, just she and the computer.

Rita viewed the screen for the next couple of hours, getting the hang of the lingo, and observing how others operated within the cyber world. It was fascinating. Mostly, she noted that everyone seemed to be interested in one thing—sex! Oh sure, there were rooms for those interested in hobbies, such as boating or skiing, but sex was the common thread.

After a couple of evenings of just watching, Rita entered a room designated as "Single and Looking." In it she met Carl, whose screen name was "CallMeCarl." Not too imaginative, but certainly not threatening, either. He was from Connecticut, and was divorced. He had married way too early, he explained—he was nineteen, his bride a year younger—and now, at forty one, he was ready to find his soul mate. His job as an insurance adjuster provided him with a good income, and his flexible schedule allowed him freedom to travel. His major encumbrance was his two sons, with whom he observed diligent visitation.

Rita told Carl about her friend in Florida, who had struck up a "cyber" romance with someone she met in a chat room. Naturally, she left out the part about the actual marriage that had resulted from the Internet affair. Leave that for later, she thought.

She and Carl hit it off right away. He didn't want to rush her into a face to face meeting, and that suited Rita just fine. She said she *was* interested in a long-term relationship, but wasn't really in a great hurry. However, she had joked if she didn't find someone within a year, she'd "just commit suicide; that's all." They both laughed, and agreed that that wouldn't be necessary.

So, each night they would meet in "Single and Looking," and then move into a "private room," to continue their cyber conversation. For the first time in years, Rita felt optimistic about the future.

CHAPTER 45

"**D**o you know what today is?" asked Valdez. She was standing in Matt's office, her finger tracing a trail across the face of his wall calendar.

Matt looked up and absentmindedly answered, "Yeah, it's Monday."

"Well, I *know* it's Monday," said Rita with a laugh. "But, do you know what today *is*? As in 'what occasion?'"

"Haven't a clue," quipped Matt. "But, guessing by the question, it must be *something* special. I give up. What is it?"

"It's May 7th!" said Rita. "It's been six weeks since I transferred in. I think that calls for a celebration. Don't you?"

Matt looked at Valdez over the top of his reading glasses and smiled. "Since when is six weeks a special time for a celebration?"

"It isn't," said Rita. "We *should* have celebrated after a month. But, nobody offered. And I'm *s-o-o-o-o* disappointed," she said, with an exaggerated pout.

"So solly, Missy," said Matt, in a mock Chinese accent. "Better ruck next time."

"Very funny," said Rita. "Come on, Matt. Seriously. How about you, me and Freitag tip a couple of beers tonight? No big deal. Just a tiny little celebration."

Matt frowned.

"A little bonding?" teased Rita. "Just between friends, of course," she added. "Come on. What's the matter – afraid the little woman won't approve?" Matt narrowed his eyes; Rita figured she'd hit a nerve.

"Okay, okay," said Matt. "I know I'm going to regret this – okay, but just one. Check with Freitag, and see if he can make it."

"You got it, Lou – I mean, Matt." She leaned over and gave Davis a peck on the cheek. As she floated out the door, Matt watched her ass wave goodbye and thought, watch it, Buddy, watch it!

Freitag and Valdez waltzed into Matt's office at exactly midnight. Matt sighed resolutely, put down his pen, and removed his reading glasses. He knew when he was licked. He pushed back his chair, and stood up. "All ready, are we?" he said, addressing Rita, who was fidgeting like an anxious schoolgirl.

"Yep. I'm even buying the first round." She handed Matt his jacket. "Come on, let's go," she said, "no more stalling. You promised."

"Okay, okay," sighed Matt. He looked at the other two and smiled. "What are we, like the three musketeers?"

"Egg-zactly!" replied Rita. "All for one and one for all!"

"Oh, Christ," muttered Freitag, raising his head and rolling his eyes skyward. "Here we go again."

"By the way," said Matt, "where're we going, anyway?"

Rita hesitated before answering. "How about Malone's, over on First Avenue?"

"Killian's Red on tap?" asked Matt, referring to his favorite Irish beer.

Rita nodded in the affirmative. "*And* great soda bread," she added, looking over at Freitag, who grinned in apparent approval.

"Works for me," he said, validating Rita's supposition. "Let's get the hell out of here."

It was nearly two in the morning, and Matt was feeling no pain. He sat quietly on his stool opposite the polished mahogany bar in Malone's, and watched Freitag and Valdez as they slow-danced to the strains of a baleful Irish love song that poured from the ancient jukebox in the corner. The lyrics were actually quite dreadful, and told of a sheepherder who had leaped to his death from a cliff after losing his true love to – of all things – another sheepherder.

Rita and Freitag were an odd twosome, but it seemed to work, thought Matt. As he watched the couple move awkwardly around the dance floor, he was struck by how peaceful they appeared in one another's arms. He reflected upon all the salacious rumors that had preceded the female addition to his squad, and wondered if maybe they were merely founded in jealousy. The last two hours had been filled not with ribald jokes or innuendo, but rather with poignant remembrances of Rita's love affair with her first commanding officer. As Rita understood them now, the subsequent flings with the others had probably just been her blind attempt to eradicate the memories. Instead, all she had accomplished was to tattoo her reputation with the indelible ink of rumor and hearsay. Now, as Matt watched her dancing with his best friend, it occurred to him that she had probably orchestrated this get together for the sole purpose of explaining her side of the story – and it had worked, at least as far as he was concerned. Val had nothing to fear from Rita Valdez. *Who knows, maybe the two of them could even become friends? Lord knows Val could use one.* He pictured his wife, probably asleep, and smiled. Then, he stood up, stretched his arms high, and yawned.

"Oh, shit!" he exclaimed, suddenly fully awake.

Freitag and Valdez stopped dancing, and looked over at their boss. "What's wrong?" asked Rita.

"I didn't call Val," said Matt. "I forgot. I totally fucking forgot."

Rita broke free of Freitag and walked over to Matt, who was struggling mightily to put on his jacket – inside out. She grabbed hold of the garment, quickly re-arranged it, and helped Matt to put it on correctly. "It's all my fault," she said. "I should never have dragged you out here tonight. I'm *so* sorry. I really am."

"There's *nothing* to be sorry about," said Matt. "I'm the one who fucked up."

Rita frowned.

"And, besides," said Matt, "it was actually a good idea. If anything, *I'm* the one who should be sorry – for not doing this sooner."

Rita threw her arms around Matt, and gave him a big hug. "Okay, okay," he said, "let's not get carried away." He glanced at his wristwatch. "Besides, I've gotta get the hell out of here." He looked at Freitag. "Take me home first, okay Chris?"

"No problem," replied Freitag. He looked over at Rita. "Okay with you?" he asked. Rita grabbed his arm and sighed, "Uh huh." She looked exhausted. They all were.

It was nearly three in the morning when Matt climbed wearily out from the backseat of the Chevrolet, closing the heavy door as quietly as he could. Freitag waited until his partner was on the sidewalk, and then pressed down gently on the accelerator, steering the big car away from the curb. Rita snuggled close to Chris, and looked back apprehensively over her shoulder at the receding image of Matt, who stood waving slowly at the automobile. He made his way wearily up the front steps and into his apartment, silently praying that Val was indeed asleep. No such luck.

Chris inserted a Sinatra CD into the little player located beneath the dashboard. He had had to get special permission to have the unit installed in the unmarked patrol car, but it had been worth the trouble. Now, it infused a quiet mix of the Italian crooner's eloquently sung lyrics and Nelson Riddle's accompaniment into the cozy interior of the Chevy. Rita snuggled close to Chris, and began busily searching through her purse for something with which to write. Freitag drove slowly, humming along with the melody. "What're ya doin'?" he asked.

"Oh, just looking for a pen," replied Rita. "I want to write down my new email address for you – if you don't mind?"

"No, I don't mind at all," replied Chris softly. "In fact, I kinda like it – that you want to give it to me, I mean."

Rita asked Chris for one of his business cards, turned it over to the backside, and carefully printed *rvaldez@aol.com* on it. Then, smiling smugly to herself, she added in parenthesis *Sexy39*. "I put my screen name on there, too," she said, as she carefully slipped the card into Chris's right front pocket. "But, keep *that* information to yourself, okay? I just thought that if you ever get lonely some night, you might want to chat."

"Actually, I thought I'd post it on the bulletin board, down at headquarters," quipped Chris. He reached over and gave Rita a little pinch on the arm. "What do you take me for, some kind of asshole?" he said. "Besides, why would I want to share *that* with anybody, anyway?"

"Okay, fine, don't be such a crab," said Rita. "I just wanted make sure, that's all. I don't need twenty-five horny guys emailing me with dirty jokes, that's all."

"Maybe just one," shot back Chris.

"Yeah," smiled Rita, "just one."

When Matt walked into the apartment, he could hear the TV playing softly in the living room. The lights were on, and Val was fast asleep in the corner of the sofa. He picked up the remote, turned off the set, and reached down and gently shook her shoulder. She murmured softly in response, but remained asleep. Matt sat down next to her, and whispered in her ear,

"Val, honey, I'm home." She shifted her weight, and leaned against his shoulder, sighing softly. "Sweetheart," Matt said, "it's time for bed."

Suddenly, Valerie sat upright with a start, and pulled her robe close around her shoulders. She opened her eyes wide, and looked at her husband as if he were a stranger. Apparently, she had been dreaming.

"Honey, it's me," said Matt.

"Wha—oh, Matt, it's you. I must have been dreaming." Slowly, she gained awareness, and with it came the realization of how late it must have been. "Where have you been?" she said. "What time is it?" There was a tone of annoyance in her voice.

"It's a little after three," replied Matt. "I meant to call you. I'm so sorry."

By now, Val was fully awake. "You should be," she said. "I was worried sick."

"I know, I know," said Matt. "I just forgot."

"So, where were you?" asked Val.

"I was at Malone's – I mean, we were at Malone's, and—"

"Who's *we*?" asked Val, angrily. "And is that perfume I smell?" Matt could tell that she was really pissed.

"Me and Chris" replied Matt. "And Valdez," he added. "I guess that's where the perfume came from." Then, realizing the implication of his answer, he added, "I mean *she* was the one wearing the perfume."

"Oh, great," shouted Val. "I'm here worrying my ass off about you, and you're out playing footsie with 'Little Miss Home Wrecker.' And, I suppose Chris just stood by and played lookout?"

"It wasn't like that at all," said Matt. "We were celebrating Rita's six-week anniversary, and—"

"And what, drinking and dancing?"

"Not exactly," answered Matt.

"Then what?"

"Well – mostly talking, actually. Chris and Rita danced a little, but more than anything, the three of us just talked."

"Oh, real cozy like, huh? You and the home wrecker. What did you talk about? Me?"

"*No*," said Matt, firmly, "we did not talk about you."

"Well, what then?"

"Mostly about her affairs," said Matt. He immediately regretted his choice of words. "That's not what I meant. You know, she came with a lot of baggage, and she just wanted to explain herself."

"And just how did she explain her *affairs*?"

Matt was growing weary of the subject. "Look, it's not what you think, okay? She – we – needed to clear the air, that's all. I think it worked out pretty well, actually."

"Well, I'm not so sure I agree," said Valerie. She pulled her robe tight around her and stood up. "I think you should sleep on the couch," she said softly. With that, Val turned and walked off silently to the bedroom, leaving Matt wondering why he had even bothered coming home.

The next morning, he arose at sunrise, quickly showered and dressed, and put a pot of coffee on, all before waking Val. Reluctantly, she sat and listened as Matt filled in the details of the previous night's events. He explained how desperately Rita had wanted to be accepted by the squad, and how her whole history had been distorted and exaggerated. He also described how her perfume had gotten on his clothing when she had unexpectedly hugged him in appreciation for his agreeing to go to Malone's. More than once, Matt apologized for not calling home, and promised to never again leave Val guessing. Val tried staying angry, but the more she listened to Matt, the more apparent it became that he couldn't possibly be fabricating such a story. Eventually Matt persuaded her to accept his apology, but not before Val managed to get in one last good-natured jab.

"You better be telling the truth, Buster. If I find out otherwise, you'll be sleeping in the hallway, never mind the couch."

"Yes, dear," replied Matt, in his best Dagwood Bumstead imitation.

"Oh, and Dagwood," said Val, picking up on the routine, "Don't forget to pick up a roast at the butcher's."

Things were going to be alright after all, thought Matt as he slipped out the door to greet the day.

The first thing Davis noticed upon his arrival at the precinct was that Freitag and Valdez were acting like divorced spouses at a birthday party for their mutual offspring; they appeared to be avoiding one another at all cost. Things remained like that until three o'clock, when Matt finally decided that enough was enough, and called the other two into his office.

"Okay, if anyone wants to say anything, say it now and let's get it out of the way." Freitag and Valdez shot nervous glances at one another, but remained silent.

"Look, it's no big deal," said Matt. "Nobody *did* anything, and nothing happened, *right?*" More silence. Rita started to speak at the same time as Chris, and both ended up laughing. Matt looked back and forth at the two of them. "Oh, so you're telling me something *did* happen. Is that what it is?"

"Well," said Chris, "not exactly—"

"But, it's not what you think," said Rita. Immediately, she regretted her choice of words. "I mean, you're right. Nothing happened – at least, not like you that."

"Oh, shit," said Chris. "It's no big deal. I drove Rita home – and – well, we just – uh, you know how it is. Well, shit, it's none of your business, and let's just leave it at that. Okay?"

"That's fine," said Matt, with an air of finality in his voice. "Really. Now, can we all get back to work, and stop acting like a bunch of teenagers?"

Chris and Rita looked at each other, and replied in unison, "Sure, no problem."

"Good," said Matt. "Oh, and you'll both be pleased to know that, unlike you too, *I* spent the night on the old Thomasville convertible – but, everything's cool, so not to worry."

"Oh, Matt," said Rita, "I'm so sorry. If there's anything I can do—"

"Actually, I think you've done enough already," laughed Matt. "But, seriously, Val and I had a long talk, and everything is really okay."

Rita breathed a sigh of relief. "I'm really glad, because I wouldn't want anything to happen that would screw things up for *any* of us, if you know what I mean."

"Everything's just fine," said Matt. "Now, if you don't mind, I think we should all get back to work solving crime. In case you've forgotten, we've still got a killer to catch."

CHAPTER 46

9:15 p.m., Friday, May 12

S ince spending the evening with Freitag at Malone's, and in light of their budding relationship, Rita had been slowly disengaging herself from her other "relationship," (if one could call it that) the one with her online friend, Carl.   She had pretty much told him that she wasn't interested in pursuing things, and he had actually seemed relieved. Everything appeared to be falling place – she hoped.

She was reading a news article posted on her AOL home page, when an "Instant Message" box opened on her screen.

Hunkalovin': Hi! What's shakin'?

At first, Rita was startled by the intrusion. She knew it wasn't Carl, but didn't recognize the screen name. Then, she relaxed. It must have been someone who had been in a chat room with her. *That's it*, she reasoned, *he must have written down my screen name.*

Sexy39: *Do I know you?*

Hunkalovin': Not really. Do you want to?

Do I want to? Yeah, why not?

Sexy39: *Okay, I'll bite. Who are you?*

Hunkalovin': You'll bite? Really?

Oh boy, another sex pervert. She decided to end this conversation now.

Sexy39: *Sorry, buddy. I think you've got the wrong girl...*

Hunkalovin': Do I really? Aren't you sexy Rita?

A cold chill ran up Rita's spine. How could he know her name? She never used her name on screen—just "Sexy39."

Sexy39: *Is that you, Carl?*

Hunkalovin': Who's Carl? Is that your boyfriend?

Rita was totally perplexed. Carl was the only one who knew her real name. Yet, it wasn't like him to play games like this. True, she reasoned, she didn't really know him *that* well. But, would he really try a stunt like this?

Sexy39: *Okay, Carl. If that's you, please tell me. I'm not enjoying this...*

Hunkalovin': What? You mean you don't like games? Ha! Ha!

Sexy39: *You know what I mean. This isn't like you...*

Hunkalovin': And what am I like? I mean, what's Carl like?

Sexy39: *Okay – that's it! I'm out of here*

Hunkalovin': WAIT!!!

Rita hesitated. What if it was Carl? What if he was just kidding? She didn't want him to think her immature.

Hunkalovin': HEY! I'M SORRY!! ARE YOU STILL THERE?

Sexy39: *Carl?*

Hunkalovin': No, I'm not Carl. But, I <u>am</u> sorry!

Sexy39: *Well, I think I'm still out of here*

Hunkalovin': Please! Don't Go! I really am sorry...

Sexy39: *How did you know my name?*

Hunkalovin': I got it from your profile

My profile? Profile—Oh, shit! She remembered that she had had to fill out an information questionnaire in order to obtain an AOL screen name. *So that's where he got it. Damn it!*

Sexy39: *Well, look Hunk, or whatever your name is – I'm not interested, okay?*

Hunkalovin': I'm Jack! Don't be mad, please?

Sexy39: *Look, Jack, I'm not mad. But, you really scared me...*

Hunkalovin': I didn't mean to. I was just fooling around. I'm really sorry

Rita thought about it for a minute, and then decided that maybe it wasn't such a big deal after all. She'd have to remember to take her real name off her profile, or block it – or something. Anyway, there wasn't any real harm in talking to the guy. What else did she have to do on a Friday night? Besides, wasn't that the whole idea of this chatting crap, anyway?

Sexy39: *Okay, you win. I accept your apology...*

Hunkalovin': **Thank you, Rita**

Sexy39: *Do me a favor, okay?*

Hunkalovin': **What?**

Sexy39: *Just don't call me Rita...It makes me nervous...*

Hunkalovin': **So what should I call you?**

Rita thought about it for a minute. She really wasn't comfortable with him calling her by her name, but what else could he call her? What the hell, she thought, she might as well enjoy this. Her fingers flashed over the keyboard:

Sexy39: *How about just Sexy?*

Hunkalovin': **Cool! Hey Sexy! Do me a favor?**

Hunkalovin': **Call me Jack?**

Sexy39: *Why not Hunk? That's sexier...*

Hunkalovin': **Yeah but Jack is, like, my nickname...**

Hunkalovin': **...and it gets me hot!**

Sexy39: *Maybe I shouldn't use it then...ha! ha! We don't want to get you too hot...*

Although the conversation was a bit immature, Rita enjoyed chatting with Jack. The time seemed to fly by, and before she knew it, it was almost eleven o'clock. She had learned a couple of things about him. He was single, drove a Honda, and lived in New Jersey. He had also been married once, but for only two years. He didn't think he ever wanted to marry again, but might consider it "if the right girl came along." He claimed to be a construction worker, but Rita knew that was probably crap. She told him she was a secretary, figuring he didn't need to know any more about her than was necessary. What difference did it make, anyway? They'd never meet, so let him think what he wanted. And, if they ever did? Well, she'd worry about setting the record then. No point in putting the proverbial horse before the cart. They signed off, but not before Jack got her to agree to let him "PM" her some other time.

Before she even got into bed, Rita had long since forgotten about Jack, and fell asleep with images of Carl filling her dreams.

Jack's dreams were of another variety all together.

CHAPTER 47

9:25 a.m., Sunday, May 14

Joan Swanson was really annoyed. She and Maria Caruso had a date for doubles tennis at ten o'clock, and she was anxious to get the scoop on her friend's date last night. It was already nine twenty-five, and if they didn't get moving soon they would probably miss their game. The two of them usually walked the three-and-a-half blocks to the West Side club, but now they would probably have to take a cab. She dropped her Adidas tennis bag on the floor outside Maria's apartment, and rang the buzzer.

"Come on, Maria," she shouted at the metal apartment door, "it's getting late."

After knocking loudly for almost five minutes without a response, she was no longer annoyed, but instead was becoming increasingly concerned. It wasn't like Maria to be late. Just then, the door to the adjacent apartment opened, and an elderly woman poked her head through the narrow opening allowed by the limit of the security chain.

"Are you looking for Maria?" asked the woman.

"Yes I am," replied Joan. "Have you seen her this morning?"

"No," said the neighbor, "but I think she had company last night." Then, realizing her last statement might make her appear to be a busybody, she quickly added, "We watch out for each other, you know. When I heard a man's voice, I opened my door."

"Did you see him?" asked Joan.

"Yes and no," she replied.

"Well," said Joan, "I've been knocking for quite a while, but she's not answering."

"So I noticed," said the woman. "Maybe we should call the super?"

Joan glanced at the designer watch on her wrist and considered going on alone, but a nagging sense that something was wrong made her inclined to agree with the woman. "I think you're right. Maybe we should call somebody," she said.

Moments later, the neighbor returned with the janitor, an elderly gentleman smoking an oversized, blackened pipe that spewed a steady stream of noxious, blue smoke. His head was encircled by a cloud that moved along with him much like a personal weather system. Reluctantly, he selected a key from a large metal ring attached to his trousers. "Ya know, I don't really like to get involved in other people's business," he said.

"Please," said Joan, "could you just open the door."

"Okay, okay," he said. He inserted the key in the cylinder of the deadbolt, and gave a twist. "That's strange," he said, "the deadbolt's not locked." He slipped a different key into the worn lock opening of the doorknob below and gave a twist. The door opened easily.

The first thing they noticed was how quiet the apartment was. "Maybe she's not even here," said Joan. "If she went without me I'm really going to be pissed."

The superintendent started down the narrow hall toward the bedroom, followed in turn by Joan and the neighbor. "Miss Caruso?" he called softly. "Are you there?" There was no answer.

"Maria," said Joan, "It's me. We're late."

The door to the bedroom was ajar, and Joan gently pushed it open. Then, she looked inside. "Oh, my God!" she cried.

The superintendent barely had time to react, as Joan fainted, and then collapsed silently into his arms. While struggling to hold her limp form upright, the man peered past her into the dimly lit room. He wanted to get a better look at what had caused such a reaction. Before him was a scene not unlike one of many he had witnessed countless times before in a movie – a horror movie – and he gasped for breath in order to scream. Almost immediately, as if in a bizarre show of support, came the shrill cry of the elderly neighbor, whose voice joined his in a morbid duet.

        Davis, Freitag, and Valdez got there at 9:57. By the time the detectives arrived, several uniformed patrolmen had already secured the scene; yellow crime tape crisscrossed the opening to the weathered apartment building. They flashed their badges, and hurried upstairs. The door to the apartment was open, and inside, men from the forensics lab were busy collecting evidence. Davis and Freitag donned latex gloves, and stepped inside. Rita did likewise. They moved through the hallway and entered the bedroom.
        "Just like the others, huh?" said Davis, addressing one of the uniformed patrolmen. His practiced eyes scanned the room.
        "Certainly looks like it," said the patrolman, who couldn't have been more than twenty-years of age. Matt could sense his discomfort. *He'll get used to it. Shit! Who am I kidding? You* never *get used to it.*
        "We've got three witnesses," said the officer, pulling a small pad from his pocket. "Let's see, there's a friend, a Joan Swanson; she's in the other room. And the super. The two of them discovered the body. Then there's the neighbor, Mrs. Milam. She's the one who called the super."
        Freitag left the one bedroom, and entered what appeared to be a second bedroom, which had been converted into a makeshift exercise room. The Swanson woman, who by now had regained consciousness, was sitting on a folding chair, sipping a Coke that one of the officers had brought to her. "Ma'am," he said. "Do you think you could answer a few questions?"

"Well," she sighed. "I guess so. But I don't think I can help you much."

The two of them went into the dining area of the living room and sat down at the small, Formica table. Freitag pulled out his notebook and a pen.

"Had you known the deceased long?" he asked.

The woman sitting across from him sagged in her chair, her upper body limp, nearly assuming the contours of its back. Her blue eyes were moist from crying, and her dyed blond hair was matted against her damp forehead. It was obvious that she was devastated. The use of the word "deceased" cemented the fact that, indeed, her friend was actually dead. It pushed her over the edge. Softly, she began to cry, tears cascading down her cheeks. Freitag offered her his handkerchief, which she accepted with a sigh. He waited until she had regained her composure, and began again.

"Had long had you known Miss Caruso?" he inquired.

"Almost two years," she replied.

"Can you think of anyone who might have wanted to do this to her?"

"No," she said. "Maria was a wonderful person. Everybody liked her."

"Do you know if she was seeing anyone?" asked Chris.

"You mean, like a boyfriend?"

"Exactly," said Freitag. "Usually, when something like this happens, it's somebody the victim knew."

"Well, she wasn't dating anybody," said Joan. "But, she was getting pretty friendly with some guy she had met online."

"Did she mention a name?" asked the detective.

"No, but I know she was supposed to have a date with him last night."

"Did she say where they were going?" asked Chris.

"No, just out for dinner," she said. "I don't think she wanted to say too much, in case it didn't work out."

Freitag reflected on the irony of her statement. "Well, thank you, ma'am," he said. "If you think of anything else, here's my card. Just give us a call."

She nodded, and Matt offered to have one of the patrolmen drive her home, but she declined, saying the walk would do her good.

"Oh, detective?" she said. "There's *is* one thing."

"What's that?" asked Chris.

"She met him in a chat room. You know, on the Internet. The guy she was supposed to go out with, I mean."

Freitag jotted the information down in his notebook. He'd have to impound the computer, have forensics run a search of the hard drive, and see what they could come up with.

"Thank you, Miss Swanson. We really appreciate your cooperation."

"I just hope you get the son of a bitch," she cried. "Maria didn't deserve what happened to her." Tears had begun streaming down the young woman's face again, and Chris moved closer and gently cupped her shoulder with his hand.

"I'm very sorry for your loss," he said quietly, before stepping away.

Outside the apartment, in the dimly lit hallway, a small cluster of tenants stood at a comfortable distance, their heads close together in muted conversation.

"Excuse me, is one of you Mrs. Milam?" asked Rita.

"Yes," replied a voice. "That's me."

The elderly neighbor, who had been leaning against the wall, stepped forward, her hands clasped tightly at her sides. Her face was ashen, and perspiration dotted her forehead. Rita smiled at her, trying to put her at ease. It was always hardest on these people, the ones left behind, he thought. "Do you mind if we ask you a few questions, Mrs.—" She hesitated, not remembering the woman's name.

"It's Milam," said the woman. "Margaret Milam. No, I don't mind."

"Did you hear her come home?" asked Rita.

The woman shifted nervously, not offering an answer.

"I'm sorry, ma'am," said Valdez, "I asked whether you heard her when she came in?'

"Well," She hesitated. "I don't want you to get the wrong idea," she continued. "I mean, I'm not a busybody or anything—"

"But, you *did* hear her come in," said Rita.

"Yes," she replied.

"Was she alone?"

"No," responded the neighbor.

"Did you see who she was with?" asked Davis, who had joined Rita in the hallway.

"Yes and no," she replied.

"Well, did you see the man or didn't you?" asked Rita. Matt gave her a look as if to say: *ease up.* Rita backed away.

"Sort of," said the woman. "The lighting's not so good in the hall."

"Would you recognize him if you saw him again?"

"Maybe, but I'm not sure. I'm sorry."

"It's okay," said Matt. "You've been a big help. Thank you."

"I could try," said the woman. "I mean, I liked her. I just want to help."

Davis pulled a card from his wallet and held it out to her. "If you think of anything else, anything at all. Just call me."

The old woman nodded in the affirmative, then added, "I'm old, you know," almost as if her apology weren't enough and she needed to explain. Then she silently accepted the card, turned away, and shuffled into the sanctuary of her apartment.

Several hours later, after searching the Caruso apartment thoroughly, the three detectives were convinced they would find nothing more to help them. Everything was there, of course: the body bound to the bed, the heart with the two sets of initials –

everything. Everything the same – except for one thing. There
was no *New Testament*!

"Are you sure there's no bible?" asked Matt.

"Absolutely," said one of the forensic detectives.

"That's really strange," said Chris.

"What?" said Matt. A funny look crossed his face.
"You're not thinking about that copycat shit again, are you?"
asked Matt.

"I don't know," said Chris. "I sure as hell hope not."

"Well, she's the first one that's not married," added
Rita. "That's certainly different. I just hope it's not a copycat.
I don't think I could take it."

"I know, I know," said Matt, rolling his eyes toward the ceiling.
The threesome stood quietly, not looking at one another, until at
last Matt broke the silence. "Fuck it!" he shouted. "I just can't
buy it. It's too easy! I want that fucking computer dissected
like a goddamn fetal pig. Find out who she'd been talking to,
who she knew, who her fucking pharmacist was – everything! I
want to know all there is to know about this woman!"

CHAPTER 48

9:05 p.m., Tuesday, May 16

R ita's relationship with Carl, her Internet friend, had cooled considerably; in fact, it appeared to be all but over. He meant well, she thought, but it seemed as if all his time was either occupied with work or his kids. Somehow, he could never fit Rita into his schedule, *and they still hadn't met each other face-to-face. Maybe his ex-wife knew what she was doing, after all.* Rita decided she didn't need the hassle of a man with kids, not to mention one with no time for *her.* There was every possibility that something might develop between Freitag and her, but for now she was technically a woman without a man.

Tonight, as she sat at her computer, she thought of the fellow who had surprised her recently. *What the hell was his name? Jim? John? It was something with a J.* "Jack!" she exclaimed. "That's it! Jack!"

Now, if she could only remember his screen name. *The Hulk? Hulk something? No, that's not it. Wait a minute. I think I wrote it down – somewhere. Where did I put that piece of paper?* Rita rummaged through a mess of paper scraps until she found the one she wanted. There it was, scribbled hurriedly, but legible nevertheless. It was Jack (Hunkalovin').

She quickly brought up the AOL *Instant Messenger*, and there was *Hunkalovin'* on her *Friends* list. A little "smiley" icon next to the name indicated that, indeed, he was online. *Hmm, I wonder what I should say. I don't want to—Oh, the hell with it. I'm desperate!*

She hit *"Send Personal Message."*   When the box appeared, her fingers flew over the keyboard, as she typed:

Sexy39: *Hi Jack. Are you there?*

For a second, nothing happened. *Shit, I'll bet he just signed off.* Then, like magic, a reply appeared beneath her question.

Hunkalovin': Hey Sexy. What's shakin'?

Sexy39: *Not much, I'm afraid...*

Hunkalovin': Aw that's too bad...

Hunkalovin': A sexy girl like you all alone

Hunkalovin': Want me to come over?

Sexy39: *Not tonight...*

Hunkalovin': When then?

Sexy39: *Oh...maybe some other time. I don't even know you yet*

Hunkalovin': Sure you do

Hunkalovin': OK OK I know what you mean but

Sexy39: *This is only our second "date"...remember?*

Rita regretted her choice of words almost immediately. But, it was too late.

Hunkalovin': Hey! third times a charm right?

Sexy39: *I just <u>knew</u> you'd say that...*

There was a long pause, and for a minute Rita thought she had lost Jack. She waited a bit more, before typing.

Sexy39: *Are you still there Jack?*

Hunkalovin': Yeah...I'm still here

Hunkalovin': Rita, do you like sex?

Rita's breath caught in her throat. She felt her heart beat faster, and her palms grew clammy. *What am I doing? I don't even know who this guy is. He's probably some pervert...*

Hunkalovin': Do you? Do you like it?

Rita's mind was racing. *Does he really know me?*

Sexy39: *Who is this, really?*

Hunkalovin': Do you? I'll bet your tits are hard...Are they hard...Rita?

This had gone far enough, Rita thought.

Sexy39: *Okay. That's enough! Whoever you are, I'm out of here.*

Hunkalovin': **I know where you live ya know...**

Rita gasped. She quickly typed a response.

Sexy39: *What do you mean, you know where I live?*

Hunkalovin': **I see you all the time...**

Rita's mind automatically ticked off all the recent encounters she had had. There wasn't anyone that came to mind that could behave like this. She was frantic.

Sexy39: *How do you know where I live? It's not in my profile...*

Hunkalovin': **You live on the east side...**

Rita was stunned. How did he know where she lived? How could he possibly know that? Who was this guy? Rita's fingers virtually flew over the keyboard as she typed the next question.

Sexy39: *Who are you?*

Hunkalovin': **Why?**

Sexy39: *If you don't tell me right now, I'll contact AOL immediately and find out who you are. Who are you?*

Hunkalovin': **Why do you want to know?**

Sexy39: *Because I don't like you knowing where I live. For the last time, who are you?*

Hunkalovin': **I'm Ken**

Sexy39: *But, you said your name was Jack?*

Hunkalovin': **It is....thats my middle name...Jack....my friends call me Jack.......remember?**

Rita stared at the screen in disbelief. Could it really be? She typed furiously.

Sexy39: *Are you Ken Callahan? The delivery guy?*

Hunkalovin': **Yeah.....it's me. Are you disappointed?**

Sexy39: *No, I'm not disappointed. I'm mad! Who the fuck do you think you are?*

Hunkalovin': **But you said you wanted to meet a man....I was just havin a little fun....thats all...**

Sexy39: *What's wrong with you, anyway? I trusted you.*

Hunkalovin': **I'm sorry Rita**

Sexy39: *Sorry doesn't cut it, buddy, you fucked up big time. I don't want you to ever contact me again. Is that clear?*

Hunkalovin': **But Rita....I thought we could get together...**

Sexy39: *Look, Ken, or Jack, or whatever your name really is. I'm not really a secretary. I'm a cop.*

Hunkalovin': **You're a cop?**

Sexy39: *That's right...and a damn good one. And if you tell anyone, or if you pull this kind of crap again...*

Hunkalovin': **I'm really sorry Rita...I was just foolin around...I swear**

Sexy39: *People get arrested for fooling around like that. You're lucky I know you, Ken.*

Hunkalovin': **I'm sorry Rita**

Sexy39: *Too late. You just lose this email address. Do you understand? Otherwise I'll turn you in. Do you understand me?*

Hunkalovin': **Yeah......I promise.......you won't tell anybody will you?**

Sexy39: *No. But, if I even see your name in another chat room I'll arrest you myself. Now get offline! Now!*

Rita felt strange, writing these types of things on the screen. It was all so – artificial. That was the only word that adequately described the whole process. She should have known better. After tonight, she would confine her relationships to the one-on-one, in-person kind. No more Internet chat rooms for her. She studied the screen for any signs of Ken's presence, but apparently he had taken her seriously and had signed off. She closed down the computer, and went to bed.

CHAPTER 49

9:00 a.m., Wednesday, May 17

Matt moved about the kitchen with uncertainty. Valerie was working an eight-to-four shift at the hospital, and he wasn't expected at headquarters until three-forty five. It was rare that he had the kitchen to himself, so he had decided to make the most of the opportunity.

This was Valerie's domain, he thought. His efforts at cooking were normally restricted to microwaving a cup of water for his hot chocolate, or defrosting a frozen bagel. In reality, however, he had actually become an acceptable cook while married to his first wife, Jean, whose abilities in the kitchen had been limited to unwrapping frozen entrees. He had acquired what culinary skills he possessed out of sheer necessity.

Matt rummaged through the contents of the refrigerator and came up with a hunk of Muenster cheese. A Tupperware container on the bottom shelf held some leftover broccoli, and he decided to incorporate the cheese and vegetables into an omelet. He quickly diced the cheese into small chunks, and scrambled three eggs in a bowl. He placed a blackened cast-iron frying pan on the front burner, and waited until it was good and hot. Then, he coated the pan with butter, poured the eggs into a large circle, and expertly shook the pan counter clockwise to spread the mixture evenly. When the eggs were cooked, he carefully removed them to a stainless steel baking dish. He spread the chunks of cheese and broccoli on half the circle, folded the other side over, and placed the pan inside the oven.

A few moments later, the omelet was done. He seated himself at the table, and enjoyed the fruits of his culinary labor, along with some rye toast, orange juice, and hot chocolate. It didn't get any better than this, he thought. Afterwards, he placed the dishes in the dishwasher and moved to his study.

Matt had decided to accept Father Pete's invitation to play golf on Wednesday afternoon, and wanted to firm up the arrangements. He picked up the portable telephone on his desk and dialed the number for St. Jude's. The housekeeper answered the call on the second ring.

"St. Jude's Rectory. Mrs. Flynn speaking," she said, in her thick Irish accent.

"Hello, Mrs. Flynn. This is Matt Davis, may I speak to Father Pete?"

"Why of course, Detective Davis," she replied. "I'll get him for you right away."

In a moment Matt heard the familiar voice of Father Pete. "Good morning, Matt. How are you?"

"Well, all things considered, I guess I'm doing okay. How 'bout you?"

"Just great, Matt," replied the Monsignor, "So, what can I do for you?"

"Well, actually, I got your message, and I've decided to take you up on your golf offer."

"Hey, that's great," said Father Pete. "So, next Wednesday afternoon's okay?"

"Yeah," replied Matt. "Wednesday's fine. But, I can only play nine. Actually, I shouldn't be playing at all, but—"

"Nonsense," interrupted the priest. "Besides, I'm sure you can use the break."

"Well, you're probably right about that," said Matt. "But, I'm serious about the nine holes. I hope you don't mind."

"Not at all," replied Father Pete, "Besides, I can always finish the back nine by myself."

"Well, okay," said Matt. "So, I'll meet you on the practice green around what – one-thirty?"

"Sounds good, Matt. I'll see you then."

Matt hung up the telephone, closed his eyes, and leaned back in his chair, drawing a deep breath. He sat quietly like that, for several minutes, luxuriating in the peace and quiet of the morning. His thoughts drifted back to memories of him and his late father, fishing for flounder in Sheep's Head Bay. Suddenly, the silence was shattered by the harsh ringing of the phone.

"Davis here," he said, instantly alert.

"Matt," said the voice. "This is Ron Hogarth over at forensics. I'm sorry to bother you at home, but I've got some information here that I thought you might want to know about."

Matt sat upright in the chair, rubbed his eyes, and took a deep breath. "Yeah, Ron. What's up?"

"Well, we did some analysis on those carvings on your victims. We took some pictures and made some measurements, and, as near as we can figure it—well—it looks like the 'doer' is left-handed."

"No shit," said Matt. "You could tell that from the *cuts*?"

"Well, like I said, it's not a hundred percent, but we're pretty sure. The angles on the cuts on all the victims are pretty close to identical in their pattern. Anyway, based on those angles and where the cuts begin and end, that's what we think."

"So the guy's a lefty," said Matt. "Hmm, okay. Well, thanks a lot, Ron. I really appreciate it." He hung up the phone. Wonders never ceased, he thought.

When Davis arrived at headquarters, it was around three-fifty. He hung his windbreaker on a hook behind the door, and settled into the battered swivel chair at his desk. He no sooner had sat down than Freitag burst through his office door. He was wearing a New York Mets baseball cap, sweatshirt, jeans, and running shoes, and could have passed for a college student. He was muttering to himself; carrying a batch of papers in one hand and a container of coffee in the other. He set the coffee down on Davis's desk, grabbed a folding plastic chair from the closet, and sat down next to his partner.

"What's up, Chris?" asked Matt, peering at Freitag over the top of his reading glasses.

"I thought you might want to take a look at these." Freitag handed the papers to Davis.

"What have you got?" asked Matt.

"Oh, just some information to go with our fingerprints," answered Chris.

Matt glanced at the papers casually, somewhat disinterested at first, than raised his eyebrows as he studied them more intently. He was looking at the results of the National Crime Information Center's computer search that they had run on the unidentified fingerprints found at the four murder scenes. Initially, the prints had been run through the systems computer at One Police Plaza, but had come back without a match. Now, the federal results showed a positive identification.

According to the NCIC report, the prints belonged to a John Curran. The only problem was that they dated back to an arrest that had taken place nearly *forty-five years* ago, in March of 1962, in Lewisburg, Pennsylvania. John Curran had been a student at Benjamin Franklin University, and had been arrested for assault and battery – on his *girlfriend! Nice guy.* Unfortunately, there was no current address. Still, it did fit— the type of violation and all.

Matt handed the papers back to his partner. "Very interesting. Obviously our boy's kept his nose clean for quite a while—at least up until now."

"Yeah," said Freitag. "Too bad he picked *now* to fuck up."

Oh, by the way, "Said Matt, "We've got something else."

"What's that?" asked Chris.

"Forensics called me this morning. Seems like our boy's a lefty."

"How'd they know that?"

"Well, first of all, they took a bunch of pictures of all the cuts – the hearts and the initials. Then they measured the angles, where he started, where he finished, stuff like that; anyway, according to Hogarth, it's about ninety per cent that he's a lefty."

"So," said Chris, "Looks like things are starting to fit."

"Yeah, some fit," said Matt. "This guy hasn't been seen since 1962. Now he's here – somewhere. But, the question is, *where?*"

"I don't know, but I guess we'll just have to find out, won't we?" said Freitag.

"I guess so," said Davis.

"We'll find him," said Chris.

"Yeah, well, even a blind squirrel finds an acorn." Davis's voice trailed off.

Freitag looked puzzled. "What?"

"Never mind," muttered Davis. This was going to be like trying to solve a jigsaw puzzle wearing a blindfold, he thought.

CHAPTER 50

S everal days after the incident with Ken, Rita was enjoying a rare day off, puttering around her apartment, and generally relaxing – doing nothing – when she heard a knock on her neighbor's door. Without hesitating, she opened her own door and peeked out. She was just in time to see a new grocery deliveryman entering Mrs. Kelly's apartment. She waited a while until the man left, and then walked the short distance to her neighbor's door and knocked softly. Mrs. Kelly opened the door almost immediately.

"Oh, hi Rita," she said. "Have you heard the news?"

"What news?" asked Rita. "I was just going to ask what happened to Ken?"

"That's what the news is all about," replied the old woman. "He's been arrested."

"What?!"

"Who would have ever thought that nice man was a rapist," sighed Mrs. Kelly. "I always thought he was so nice," she said. "He was a Vietnam veteran, you know."

"When did all this happen?" asked Rita.

"Yesterday afternoon, around two – at least that's the way I heard it from the new man; I think he said his name is Roy. I would have thought you would've heard about it."

"Yeah, well it's a small world, Mrs. Kelly, but not *that* small. Did they say where it happened? The rape, I mean."

"Well, I don't think he actually got to that part. Thank god. They say he was trying to tie her up when she got loose and ran out into the street and flagged down a police car. It was up in the Bronx somewhere. But, I think he lives down in Chelsea. At least, that's what I heard."

Rita turned and rushed out of the apartment. "Thanks, Mrs. Kelly," she called over her shoulder. She hurried back to her apartment to call Freitag.

"Apparently he met this woman on the Internet – in one of those chat rooms," said Matt. "I can't believe these women take chances like that. Imagine meeting a total stranger – just because he wrote nice things on a computer screen? That's just nuts."

Freitag, who knew a little about Rita's Internet adventures, tried not to smile as he said, "Well, it's not *that* crazy." Rita blushed openly, and Matt couldn't help noticing.

"What's with you, Rita?"

"You mean Chris didn't tell you?"

"Tell me what?"

"I know the guy," said Rita. "He's my grocery deliveryman."

"Tell him the rest," prodded Freitag.

"Oh, Matt, I feel like such a fool."

"Rita, what the hell are you talking about?"

"Well, remember I told you I had finally gotten online?"

"Yeah, so what?"

"Well, he was the one who helped me – this Ken. He showed me how to get online, and how to get into those chatrooms. He even helped me pick out a screen name.

"And that would be what?"

"For me to know and you to find out," teased Rita. "Anyway, the creep used it to locate me in a chatroom, and then kind of made a pass at me; got pretty gross actually, and I told him not to contact me anymore."

"So, why didn't you tell someone?" asked Matt.

"I was too embarrassed," replied Rita. "Besides, I didn't think any harm had been done, and I figured I had put the fear of god into him. Obviously, he didn't take me seriously enough."

"Well, maybe *he's* our guy," said Matt. "Did you ever think of that?"

"Not really," replied Rita. "But, now that you mention it, it could make sense."

"Yeah, well we need to interview him," said Matt. "Check out his fingerprints, get a sample of his DNA. Christ, wouldn't it be something if he's the one we've been looking for all this time."

Rita felt a chill go down her spine.

CHAPTER 51

"Chris, why don't you take a ride over to Chelsea," said Matt. "Ask around the neighborhood about this Callahan character. See what you can find out. Maybe talk to Father Pete over at St. Jude. See if he belonged to the church. If he did, maybe he knew the other women."

"You really think this might be the guy?" asked Chris.

"Hey, stranger things have happened," said Matt. "Remember that one guy who worked at the day care center? Actually *volunteered* to take those little boys home to – quote, unquote – save the mothers the bother. He molested five of them before anyone caught wise. What was he, sixty five? Who would have ever suspected? To answer your question: yeah, maybe."

"Yeah, I remember that creep like it was yesterday. Well, anyway, I'd better get moving. Talk to you later."

"Okay," said Matt. "Valdez and I will take a little ride up to the Bronx, talk to this Callahan creep. Who knows, maybe we'll get lucky?"

Freitag knocked on a few doors in the apartment building Callahan called home. No one seemed to have a bad word to say about the Vietnam vet turned attempted rapist. All agreed that "*he* would never do anything like that. They must have the wrong man."

Eventually, Chris found his way over to St. Jude. He rang the bell at the side door to the rectory and waited. Mrs. Flynn opened the door and invited him inside. Apparently, the good father was off playing golf.

"Would you mind if I just left my card?" asked Freitag. "Maybe he could give me a call when he returns?"

"No, no, that would be fine," said Mrs. Flynn. "Why don't you just leave it on the desk in his study?" She pointed down a carpeted hallway. "It's at the end of the hall."

Chris walked quietly down the dimly lit corridor, and entered the richly-appointed office of the monsignor. He made a mental note that the church must be doing quite well, if the quality of the furnishings that filled the cleric's private retreat were any indication.

Being naturally curious, Freitag couldn't help but notice the fairly expensive computer and accompanying flat screen monitor that occupied a prominent place on the priest's enormous desk. *Sure beats the hell out of the one I have at home.* He also noted that a phone line was connected to the PC, indicating that Father Pete was probably an Internet user himself. *Guess everybody's online these days – even the local padre.* He reached into his pocket and extracted one of his business cards from a rubber-banded stack he carried. He placed it carefully next to the phone at the far right side of the desk where Richter would be sure to find it. What he didn't realize was that the card he had selected was the one Rita had written her email address and screen name upon, the night they had celebrated at Malone's.

Then, feeling somewhat uncomfortable at being in someone else's personal space, Freitag tiptoed out the way he had come in, closing the heavy oak door behind him. "Thank you, Mrs. Flynn," shouted Chris, to the housekeeper, who was busy in the far recesses of the kitchen.

"You're welcome, Detective," she said. "I'll tell Father Pete you were here."

CHAPTER 52

Father Pete arrived back at St. Jude around four-thirty in the afternoon. He had barely edged out his regular playing partner in a game of five-dollar Nassau, and the effort had left him drained.

"Mrs. Flynn," he called from his study. "Would you bring me a cup of tea, please?"

"Certainly, Father, I'll be just a minute. Oh, Father Pete, one of those detectives was here to see you. He left his card on your desk."

"What did he want? Did he say?" asked Richter.

"Nope. Just said he had a couple of questions for you," replied Mrs. Flynn. "Here's your tea – one teaspoon sugar, one squeeze of lemon – just the way you like it. Did you find the card?"

Richter scanned the top of his desk until his eyes spotted the plain, white paper rectangle. "Yes, it's right here," he said, picking it up. He saw that it was Freitag's card and not Matt's, and then turned it over. *Hmm, what have we here?* He read the writing on the backside of the card: "RValdez@aol.com" and "Sexy39" in parenthesis. *Hmm, guess Detective Freitag must be getting a little on the side.* He clucked his tongue in the hollow of his cheek. *Shame on you, Chris*, he chided the absent detective.

Then, Richter took another look at the card, and something registered in his memory. Valdez, he thought, wasn't that the name of the female detective that had accompanied the other two when they all first met? *What was her first name? Rena? No, Rita. That's it!* Immediately, a mental picture of Valdez formed in the priest's mind. *Hmm, she certainly was a sexy one.* The thought made him smile. *Bet the brass wouldn't think too highly of that kind of hanky panky.*

Father Pete picked up the phone and dialed Freitag's direct line.

"Detective Freitag," said Chris, answering the phone on the second ring. "How may I help you?" He hated saying the "canned" line, but that was how Captain Foster insisted that all his detectives answer the phone – strictly by the book.

"Yes, Detective Freitag, it's Father Richter – Father Pete – over at St. Jude. I understand you dropped by this afternoon."

"Oh, yes, Father, thanks for getting back to me. I just had a few questions about someone who was arrested yesterday from your neighborhood. I know it's a long shot, but I was hoping you might know him. His name's Ken Callahan. Ring a bell?"

Richter was silent for a moment before replying, "Callahan, you say? *Ken* Callahan?"

"Yeah, he was arrested up in the Bronx. Do you know him?"

"Yes, Chris, I believe so. In fact, I'm sure I do. Not too bright a fellow, I'm afraid. Got pretty messed up in Vietnam. I think he delivers groceries or something. What's he supposed to have done?"

"Attempted rape. Seems he meets women online in chatrooms, then pays them a visit in person, hoping to get lucky."

"Lucky?" asked Richter.

"Yeah, you know. He figures if they hit it off online, they'll be willing to have sex with him in person. Apparently, this one didn't fall for his line, so he tried to rape her."

"Good God!" said Richter. "What did he do, tie her up or something?"

"Funny you should ask," replied Chris. "That's *exactly* what he did."

Richter paused, then continued. "So, what did you want to ask me?" he said.

"Well, I was wondering what you might know about him. We're thinking he might be connected with those murders we've been investigating."

"I see."

"Is he a member of your church?"

"Yes, he is," answered Father Pete. "In fact, he has been quite active in our veterans group – until recently, that is – haven't seen too much of him lately. You say he meets women online – in chatrooms?"

"Yep, that seems to have been his MO. He even hit on one of the girls in our precinct," said Chris.

"Oh, really?" said Richter, thinking immediately of Valdez. "Which one?" asked Richter, a touch of humor in his voice. "Never mind," he added, "I'm joking, of course."

"Of course," replied Freitag, not at all happy with the priest's attempt at humor.

Richter sensed Freitag's displeasure, and quickly continued. "But, seriously, Chris, what else would you like to know about our friend, Mr. Callahan?"

"Well, do you know whether or not he knew any of the victims?"

Richter hesitated, and Chris took this as a sign that, indeed, Callahan had known the murdered women. "He did, didn't he?" he asked.

"Well, I can't say for sure," answered Father Pete. "But, I would imagine he did. We are a fairly sociable church, after all. My guess is that he probably did. Anything else, Chris?"

"No, but if you wouldn't mind asking around a little. Maybe some other women in your church were approached by this guy. Maybe they could tell us something we need to know."

"Well," said the priest. "I'll certainly keep my ears open. Thank goodness he's off the streets. Hopefully there won't be any more of those horrible murders now. But, I guess that might be too much to ask."

"Let's hope not," said Chris. "Well, anyway, thanks Father Pete. We'll be in touch."

"Yes, we will," said Richter. "Have a good evening." He hung up the phone, and sat quietly at his desk, studying the card Freitag had left him, turning it over and over. *Hmmm – Sexy39 – very interesting, Miss Valdez – very interesting.*

CHAPTER 53

1:05 p.m., Wednesday, May 17

"Shit," cursed Matt, under his breath. *I'm never gonna get there on time.*

"Shit! Fuck!" he shouted again, this time out loud, and hoped no one could hear him. He rarely cursed, and *never* in public, but the present situation virtually demanded it. He couldn't find his golf shoes, and he was due to meet Father Richter in less than an hour. Finding his cracked, vinyl golf bag, filled with mismatched clubs, had been relatively easy. However, locating his ancient pair of spikes was proving to be a much more daunting task.

The humidity of the apartment house basement clung to his skin like a damp towel in a steam bath. He was wearing a pair of outdated plaid golf slacks that he had bought for an outing back in the seventies. The faded, short-sleeved Banlon golf shirt wasn't much newer, and, like the pants was a bit too tight for comfort. As he continued to probe the contents of the chicken-wire storage cubicle, he was struck by how much useless crap he retained in his possession. Where would one possibly use a croquet set? Didn't lava lamps go out of style in the late sixties?

Finally, after more searching and cursing, Davis located the shoes, stuffed inside an old athletic bag. The canvas *and* the footwear smelled the same—musty! Probably just like his golf game, he thought. He grabbed the bag of clubs, and the shoes, turned out the light, locked the cage, and left the basement. Minutes later he was headed up the Harlem River Drive on his way to meet Father Pete.

As he drove the ten-or-so miles to Van Cortland Park, he debated the wisdom of playing golf while a serial killer still roamed the streets. *Screw it*, he thought. He had so many days owed to him that he'd never use them all. Besides, maybe taking a break would clear his head; help him think better. *I just hope I don't embarrass myself.*

Van Cortland Park Golf Course is the oldest public golf course in the United States, having been founded in 1895. It's located in the Bronx, and doubles as a venue for cross-country skiing in the winter season. Most residents of this northernmost borough of New York City have never seen a ski slope, let alone tried their hands at the overland version of the sport. They glide along its gentle slopes, and for the most part, feel safe in the park as long as they have a means of escape strapped to their feet. Those who frequent the links during the golf season feel equally secure, armed with steel golf clubs that can double as weapons if needed.

Matt brought the Chevrolet to a halt on a spot in the gravel parking lot, and slammed the transmission into park. Sitting on the edge of the generous trunk, he removed his black work shoes and stepped into his golf shoes, making a mental note to put them where he could find them next time. He grabbed the golf bag and slid its tattered shoulder strap over his head. When he looked up, he was surprised to see Father Pete standing beside him. At first, Matt didn't recognize him. The priest was dressed in an elegant pair of pleated beige slacks, a brown alligator-skin belt, and a navy short-sleeved shirt. He wore brown and white saddle-style golf shoes, with tassels decorating the uppers. The outfit looked as if it had cost a small fortune. In contrast, Matt's apparel appeared amateurish and cheap. He reached out his hand and smiled. "Where'd you come from?" he asked, jokingly.

Father Pete pointed to the electric cart he had driven into the lot. He was strictly business. "All set?" he asked

"Ready as I'll ever be," replied Matt.

"Good. Put your bag on the cart, and let's get going."

The huge old clubhouse loomed majestically in front of them. It was over a hundred years old, and its colorful men's dressing room had served as the set for the famous locker room scene in the movie *Wall Street*. It had character. So, too, it turned out, did the golf course. Playing to 6,100 yards, from the tips, the municipal layout boasted a par-five hole that measured over six hundred yards, and a par-three that spanned more than two hundred in length.

Davis tossed a wooden tee into the air at the first hole and was relieved when it pointed to the priest, indicating it was his turn to tee off first. Matt stood off to one side and watched as Father Pete went through a series of stretching exercises. He was surprised by the priest's agility, and marveled at the obvious athleticism of the man.

Father Pete used the ball to press the tee into the teeing ground, precisely measuring its height against the face of his driver. Then, he stepped away and took several graceful practice swings. Immediately, Davis was struck by something odd about the priest's form. What was it that looked so different? He couldn't quite figure it out. Then, he smiled and realized the obvious. Richter was left-handed.

Davis watched as his playing partner stepped behind the ball and sighted over it to an imaginary target down the first fairway. Then, Richter moved to the right side of the ball and took his stance. Without hesitation, he made a slight press forward with his left knee, and initiated a graceful back swing. Then, easily transferring his weight forward, again, he made a smooth, but powerful forward swing that sent the ball flying on a high trajectory down the middle of the fairway. His follow through was high and professional looking. The ball landed softly around two hundred and forty five yards away. It was no wonder Richter's handicap was a four, thought Matt.

Now, it was the detective's turn. Father Pete stood quietly to the side, waiting for Davis to hit. Like most "hackers," Matt had no defined warm-up routine, nor did he have a plan of attack. He stuck the wooden tee into the ground, placed a faded ball atop it, and took his stance. He wiggled the club head back and forth (as he had seen the professionals do many times). Then, he took a short, choppy back swing, and followed with a lunging forward swing that sent the ball bouncing weakly about a hundred yards down the fairway.

"Mulligan?" offered Father Pete.

"Nah, I'll just play that one," answered Matt.

Three more shots by the detective brought the two players to where Richter's ball lay waiting in the short grass in the center of the fairway. With only 115 yards to the center of the green, he chose a pitching wedge, and sent the ball expertly toward the waving flagstick. It landed softly beyond the hole, and spun backward, narrowly missing the cup.

"Great shot!" exclaimed Matt. Father Pete nodded in agreement, and stood by as Matt attempted his approach.

Davis selected an eight iron, and quickly sculled it off line into the sand trap guarding the front right side of the green. Three hacking swings later he had managed to free the ball from the hazard, landing it within ten feet of the hole. He squatted behind the ball and lined it up with the cup. His first putt was short by half the distance to the hole, and his second effort ran by the target by almost as much. He made one more stroke to within two feet, and was able to sink the remaining putt, giving him a twelve for the hole. Father Pete then stepped up to his ball and tapped it in for a birdie.

"I guess I'm a little rusty," apologized Matt.

"Really?" said Father Richter, his face totally serious. "What makes you say that?"

"Well, I—"

"Just because you made a twelve?"

Davis was starting to sweat. Maybe this hadn't been such a good idea after all, he thought.

Suddenly, Richter lost it. He exploded in a fit of laughter. Matt looked at him in amazement. Father Pete was laughing so hard he had tears running down his cheeks, his face growing bright red.

Davis didn't know what to say. "But, I thought—"

"Thought what?" roared Richter, between fits of laughing.

"I wasn't sure," said Matt. "I thought maybe you were mad at me. I mean, you were so serious."

Richter put his arm around Davis. "I couldn't resist. *You're* the one who's too serious."

"Well, I—"

"Relax, Matt. I was only kidding. It's just a game."

"Then you're not mad?" asked Matt.

"Of course not," replied Richter. "Come on, I'll show you how to handle the next one." Richter steered the detective to the golf cart, and together they drove to the next tee.

The second hole at Van Cortland is a monstrous par-five that measures 605 yards in length. Bunkers located around 250 yards from the tee guard the fairway on both the left and the right sides. Father Pete drove his tee shot into the left-hand trap, while Matt managed to loft his drive about 180 yards down the right side, leaving him with a second shot that would have to carry over the fairway bunker. He stood by the ball, uncertain of how to proceed.

"Now what do I do?" asked Matt.

"Well, the smart play for you would be to use an eight iron and just make sure you get over the trap."

Matt had never before played with anyone who had such a command of the game. He followed Richter's advice and was pleased when his ball landed safely in the fairway, some 30 yards beyond the bunker.

"Good shot, Matt," said Father Pete.

"Thanks," said a relieved Davis.

"Now you can't get into any trouble – well, at least not for a while." He smiled at Matt.

"So how are you gonna get out of that trap?" he asked the priest.

"Come on," said Richter. "I'll show you."

They ran the cart up next to the trap, where Davis watched in amazement as Father Pete sent a three wood whistling up the fairway, picking it cleanly from the firm sand of the bunker.

"Wow!" he exclaimed. "That's incredible!"

"Not really. Not if you know what you're doing."

"Yeah," replied Matt. "Well, that leaves me out," he laughed.

Richter looked around to make sure they weren't being pressed from behind, and dropped a ball into the trap. "Go ahead," he said. "You try it."

Davis laughed. "I don't think so."

"Really," said Richter. "Give it a try."

"Okay," said Matt. "Here goes." He took a hard swing, and the ball dribbled to the lip of the trap and fell back in. "See," he said. "I told you I couldn't do it."

"Let me show you how to do it *right*."

Matt stepped back, giving his newfound mentor plenty of room.

"It's really simple," said Father Pete. "Just swing nice and easy." He lined up the shot and, again launched a rocket out of the trap.

Matt was awed. "But what's the secret?" he asked.

"You see, the left hand does all the work," he explained. "Most people mistakenly try to overpower the club with their right hand. Just like you."

Matt listened intently.

Father Pete continued, "There's an old saying in golf. ' The left hand does all the work. The right hand just goes along for the ride.'"

Matt thought a minute, then replied, "Yeah, except in your case, since you're a lefty, it's your right hand does all the work—"

"Exactly!" replied the priest.

Father Richter's tips helped Matt quite a bit as they continued playing. Occasionally, he would stop and show the detective a little trick or help him adjust his stance ever so slightly. Each hole brought a little improvement in Davis's game. Before long, the two players had reached the seventh hole. This was the so-called "signature" hole, a par three that measured 215 yards from an elevated tee to a shallow green below. The toughest pin placement was the one currently in use, with the hole located at the far right-hand side of the green.

Matt watched as Richter lofted a two iron that landed just short of the green. He wondered out loud, "What the heck club do I use *here*?"

"Try your five-wood," offered Father Pete. "You never know."

"Hmmm," said Matt. After a brief hesitation, he reached in his bag and extracted the recommended club. "Oh, what the hell. Oops, I mean, what the heck," he laughed. He teed the ball up; careful to leave half the sphere above the face of the club as Father Pete had shown him. He set himself squarely; knees flexed, left shoulder toward the target, and started his back swing.

"Wait!" interrupted Richter. "Don't forget what I told you. The left hand does all the work. The right hand just goes along for the ride."

"Right," said Matt. He steadied himself over the ball again, and then took his best swing of the day. The ball flew high into the air toward the target. Matt admired the shot as it landed on the green, then frowned as the ball ran past the hole and off the backside of the putting surface.

"That," said Father Pete, "was a *great* shot."

"It was?"

"You better believe it. With that pin placement, only a pro could make a better shot."

Matt beamed. Of course, when they reached the green, he chipped back and forth across the putting surface twice, before landing the ball safely. Richter chipped to within three feet, and made his putt for a par.   Matt ended up with a respectable five – his best hole of the afternoon.

They concluded the front nine by four p.m.   Matt had shot a disappointing 59, while Father Richter had carded, what was for him, a mediocre forty.   Nevertheless, Matt was envious. He'd have given his left nut to shoot a 40.   Matt waited until Father Pete had driven his ball from the tenth tee before he exited the parking lot and headed for home.

CHAPTER 54

It was nearly dark when Richter arrived back at St. Jude. He parked the Cadillac in the garage across the street from the rectory, and removed his clubs from the spacious trunk. The service of God surely had its advantages, he thought, as he crossed the street to the rectory. It had been a lovely day.

Father Anthony, dressed in blue jeans and a tee shirt, was in the kitchen, gnawing upon the remains of a chicken leg, while alternately stuffing spoonfuls of delicatessen potato salad and sliced tomatoes into his mouth. The young priest looked up from his impromptu feast, and waved a silent hello to Richter, who motioned for him to keep on with his meal.

Father Anthony never took his eyes off the Monsignor, following him around the kitchen, first as he washed his hands, and then as he rummaged through the refrigerator for something to nibble on. Father Pete sensed the younger man's attention, and turned to face him.

"Is there something I can help you with, Father Anthony?"

Embarrassed at being detected, the young priest lowered his eyes to his plate and mumbled, "No, no, Father. It's nothing."

"Are you sure?"

Father Anthony hesitated, unsure of how to broach the delicate subject that had occupied his thoughts since the murder of Linda Vogel. Father Pete stood waiting; his eyes fixed on the top of Father Anthony's head. Finally, when he could endure the silence no longer, he asked again.

"Are you sure there's nothing you want to talk to me about?"

That did it.   With a shrug of his shoulders, Father Anthony looked up into his superior's eyes and spoke.

"Monsignor," he said. "There's something that has been bothering me ever since the day we met with that detective."

"Yes? What is it, Father?"

"Well, do you remember how we went through that whole business of twenty questions about Ms. McKenzie's confession?"

"Yes. What about it?"

"Well, there was quite a bit I didn't tell the detective *or* you about her confession that Friday."

"Such as what?" asked Richter.

The young priest swallowed hard, an audible gulp from his throat escaping his mouth. "I know who killed her. I mean I—"

"You what?" said Father Pete, incredulously.   He couldn't believe what he was hearing.

Father Anthony continued, "I don't know exactly who the person *was*, but I know who he was—*sort* of."

Richter's eyes darted nervously around the room.   He was speechless.

"Remember I said she was cheating?" said the younger cleric.

"Yes, but you assumed she was speaking in generalities."

"Oh no. She was very specific. It's been bothering me ever since I heard of her death."

Richter felt the room swimming around. He leaned on the back of Father Anthony's chair for support. He closed his eyes, then opened them, this time staring hard at the young priest. He struggled to regain his composure.

"Why didn't you tell me sooner?" he finally managed to ask.

"I wanted to, but—"

"But what?" shouted Richter. "A woman is dead!"

"I was afraid – I was afraid of violating her trust."

Father Pete felt his hands shaking, and fought to control himself, but Father Anthony could see that Richter was visibly shaken.

"Father Richter," he said, "What's wrong? Why are you so upset?"

The older priest wiped his hand across his forehead. He was sweating. "It's just that if you had brought this to my attention sooner. Perhaps we could have—"

"Could have what?" Now it was the young priest's turn to be upset. "Do you think we might have saved her life?"

"I'm not sure," answered Father Richter. "Who knows. Perhaps."

A mournful look crossed Father Anthony's face. It appeared as if he might cry at any moment.

"Father Anthony," said Richter, "Did Cindy McKenzie tell you *whom* it was that she was cheating with?"

"Not exactly," said Father Anthony. "She had been spending a lot of time on the Internet and she had met someone – someone very special. She had become very intimate with him in a chatroom, and had decided to meet him. She was afraid she wouldn't be able to control her desires, and she wanted to confess the weakness of her spirit."

"But you said you knew—"

"I meant I knew more than the fact that she was just cheating."

"I see."

"But now that's she gone," said Father Anthony. "Don't you think we should tell the police?"

Richter paused to think. Father Anthony watched him intently, and felt sure he had done the right thing in telling his superior. Perhaps now he would stop dreaming of the poor woman.

Father Pete spoke. "Father Anthony," he said. "I'm glad you told me—"

"Yes, perhaps now we can call that detective—"

"But," continued the Monsignor, "it must go no further."

"But, I thought—"

"It would serve no purpose to drag that poor woman's reputation through the gutter. It's probably just a coincidence, anyway. Don't you think so?"

"I'm not sure. I *guess* it could be a coincidence, but what if—"

"That's it then," continued Richter. "It's simply a coincidence. We must protect her reputation at all cost. She has made her peace with her Maker. That is what's important."

Relieved to have his conscience clear, Father Anthony acquiesced. He nodded his head in agreement. He picked up the remains of the chicken leg and began eating again. Father Pete opened the cupboard and removed a teacup. He withdrew a teabag from a China canister, placed it in the cup, and filled the cup three-quarters full of water. Then he placed the cup in the microwave oven over the range and set the timer. In less than two minutes, he was sipping the hot brew and watching the evening news in his study.

Around eleven, after Father Anthony had retired to his room, Father Richter turned on his computer. He double-clicked on the AOL icon, and waited until the familiar home page appeared. Then, he stopped, got up from his chair, and walked over to the door and locked it. He returned to his chair and sat down again, confident that no one would enter unannounced. However, this time he loosened his belt a couple of notches.

After his little "session," Father Pete looked down at the computer, and then at the picture of Sister Francis, hanging on the wall. He lowered his head and crossed himself. He had to stop, he thought. If anyone ever caught him, they'd never understand. In the beginning it had just been the newness of it all. The very idea that he could flirt openly with women he didn't even know – without any fear of revealing his identity – was like an aphrodisiac. And, it certainly was exciting – at least at first. Now it was more of a habit, a kind of addiction. He exited AOL, and quickly closed down the computer. He buckled his belt, got up, and walked out of the study, through the kitchen, and into his bedroom.

His usual ritual consisted of undressing, hanging his clothes in the closet, and donning his robe and slippers, before using the bathroom. Then he would say his evening prayers, and retire for the night. As usual, he knelt at the side of his bed, closed his eyes, and began to pray.

"Father," he intoned, "Forgive me for my weakness. Help me to resist the temptation that constantly tests my resolve. Show me other ways to be happy. Help me to resist the ways of the flesh. All this I pray, in Jesus' name, amen."

In less than five minutes, Father Richter was fast asleep.

He awoke in the morning, shaky and disoriented. He was surprised to find his undershirt drenched in perspiration. He sat up and placed his feet on the floor, and noted that the bottom sheet had worked itself nearly free of the mattress. He made a mental not to remind Mrs. Flynn to use the fitted sheets on the bottom, from now on. Oddly, he had no memory of the disturbing dream that caused him to awake with his bedcovers in such disarray. It was just as well.

CHAPTER 55

8 a.m. Thursday, May 18

"Freitag!" shouted Davis, "Get in here. We're gonna take a little ride."

Freitag popped his head through Davis's office doorway. "What's up, boss?" he asked.

"I think you and me will take a trip to Pennsylvania. Let's see if we can find out more about this John Curran character."

"You think it's worth it?" asked Freitag. "I mean, it's only been – what? – Over forty years?"

"You got any other suggestions?" Davis asked.

"No, but—"

"Well, then we'll start with him," said Matt. "Besides, we don't have anybody else who looks good. Now, why don't you—"

"I know, get directions to Lewisburg and pick you up in a few minutes. I'm already on my way," said Chris.

"Good," said Davis, in an "I told you so" tone of voice.

Twenty minutes later, armed with directions and a map from the computer program, the two detectives were heading through the Lincoln Tunnel.

The drive took a little over three hours. They passed the racetrack at Hazleton, where Mario Andretti had cut his teeth before making it big at Indianapolis, and Bloomsburg, home of a nice little college by the same name. This was blue-collar country – working class America – characterized by numerous decaying factories that littered the landscape like children's toys in a sandbox.

It was around eleven-thirty, when Freitag steered the Impala onto Franklin Avenue in Lewisburg. The university was situated on a rise overlooking the small Pennsylvania mining town. It consisted of a cluster of brick classroom buildings, surrounded by a cadre of dormitories. At the far end of the campus was a student union building, with a small pond, guarding the entrance. The administration building was located immediately to the left of the student union.

The two detectives were shown into the office of the Dean of Students. She was a woman in her forties, dressed in a conservative navy blue suit. Her graying hair was impeccably coifed, and her nails bore the look of professional care. She stood immediately, and offered a manicured hand to the detectives.

"How do you do? I'm Ann Palmer. We spoke on the phone."

"My name is Detective Davis; this is Detective Freitag." Each officer displayed his gold NYPD Detective's shield.

"It's a pleasure to meet you," she said. "Won't you have a seat?"

Davis and Freitag nodded, and pulled up chairs on each side of the large, wooden desk.

"You mentioned on the phone that you were looking for information regarding a former student. I hope I can help you," she said.

"Well, we certainly appreciate your seeing us on such short notice," said Matt. "Actually, we turned up this fellow Curran's fingerprints at a crime scene, but all we know is that he attended the university around nineteen-sixty-two."

"I see," said the dean. "But, I still don't see how we can help."

"Well," continued Davis. "Apparently, he was arrested on an assault charge; beat up his girlfriend. Anyway, he was released on probation, and appears to have kept his nose clean since. What we're hoping to find out is whether he went on to graduate school – maybe pick up his trail from there. Or, if he didn't, maybe there's a record of what happened to him when he graduated – *if* he graduated."

"Well, we can certainly check that out," offered the dean. "We have records dating back to 1927 of *all* our graduating classes. And, we *do* have an alumni organization. But, since we don't have fraternities or sororities, I'm afraid there's not *too* much to tie our graduates to BFU once they're gone."

"I know just what you mean," said Matt. "All I remember about City College is that that's where I went nights, when I wasn't working."

"Dean Palmer," asked Freitag, "Would it be possible for us to see those graduation records?" He was getting impatient, and figured it time to move on.

"Certainly," replied the dean. "I'll have Janice take you to the records room. Everything up until five years ago is on microfiche."

Dean Palmer introduced the detectives to her young female aide. She was a blonde, who appeared to be dressed as if in opposition to the dean's conservative attire. Her jeans were tight enough to reveal no trace of a panty line, and the man's work shirt that she wore suggested that no bra was in evidence. Janice's hips swayed seductively as she led the two men toward the records office, located on the second floor of the building.

"What year did you say you were looking for?" she asked. She stared at Freitag in that open way that only a young girl can—suggesting everything, yet revealing nothing.

"We didn't," replied Davis. "But, we know the individual we're looking for was a student here in 1962. Whether he was a freshman, sophomore, or what, is anybody's guess."

The girl scanned the labels on the metal filing cabinets, until she came to one marked "Graduation Records." She opened the drawer, and extracted a roll of microfiche.

"You can start here," she suggested. "This is the class of 1962. If you don't find what you're looking for, you can try going backward or forwards."

"Thank you," said Matt, accepting the roll of film.

"The machine is over here. Do you know how to operate it?" asked the young woman.

Both detectives smiled. "Oh, yeah," said Freitag. "Just lead us to it; we'll do the rest."

The girl turned and started to walk away, then stopped.

"You know, we have a school newspaper," she offered. "There might be something in one of the old issues that might help."

"Thanks," replied Davis. "If we can't find anything in the graduation records, we'll take a look at the newspapers." The girl smiled and left the room.

Freitag made sure she was gone before speaking to his partner.

"I think I was born too late," he said. "Did you get a look at the body on her? Man, what I wouldn't give to—"

"Never mind," scolded Matt. "Let's just find what we came for, and get the hell out of here."

It took a while, but they eventually located John Curran's name among those listed with the class of 1964. Unfortunately, no mention was made of any graduate school he might have attended, or career plans he might have made. There was a class picture, but Curran's image was missing. The two detectives thanked the young aide, and left the building.

"Shit," said Chris. "I was hoping there would be more information than that."

"Well, I hoped so too," said Matt. "But, deep down inside I think I knew that we'd have to do more digging."

They hunted down the female aide, who seemed pleased at having her advice taken. She pointed them in the direction of the cabinet that held the rolls of microfiche containing the copies of the old newspapers.

"Lots of times there are stories about the really good students," she said. "You know, like what awards they get, or where they're going – stuff like that."

Chris began rifling through the canisters until he found the one for 1964. "Here it is," he said, holding the metal container up like a trophy.

Together, they spooled the film through the projector's sprockets, and Davis began turning the handle. He moved hurriedly through the first four or five months' issues, then slowed as he approached the June edition. Suddenly, he stopped.

"Here it is!" exclaimed Matt.

"What've you got?" asked Chris.

Davis was moving his lips as he used his finger to follow the lines in the article. "Wait, wait – here – I'll be a son of a bitch!"

"What?" said Chris.

"You won't believe this—"

"What won't I believe?" asked Freitag, his voice bordering on a shout.

"The guy went to a seminary," said Matt.

"You mean he's a—"

"He's a priest!" exclaimed Davis.

"No shit," said Freitag, quietly. He was stunned.

"It makes perfect sense." Davis shook his head slowly back and forth. He copied down the pertinent information in his notebook, including the name and location of the seminary. Returning the canister to the file cabinet, he stood up and turned to face his partner. "Okay," he said. "Let's head over to the local precinct house and see what we can find out there."

"Well, we know most of the details about the incident in sixty-two," said Freitag. "But, maybe we can get a hold of the arrest report. Hopefully they took his portrait. It's a long shot, but if they did, we can have our resident Van Gogh work a little computer magic. Then, if we're lucky, we'll have some idea what he might look like today."

A dingy, stucco building that looked more like a park ranger station than a headquarters, housed the Lewisburg Police Station. It was situated at the end of a gravel road on the outskirts of town. The only suggestion as to the building's function was the bright, new police cruiser parked in the rear. Small town police work did have its privileges.

"Let me see," said the bespectacled policeman. He was rummaging through a rusty file cabinet, situated alongside an ancient water cooler that periodically burped as if to make its presence known. At last, the uniformed officer located what he had been searching for. "Here it is: Curran, J: Probation Records." In his hand, he held a dust covered accordion file, which he offered to Davis.

Matt scanned the enclosed documents until he found one that interested him. It was a data sheet listing all of Curran's personal information, including the fact that he was an orphan from the Holy Angels Foster Home in Baltimore, Maryland. Then, Davis found what he was really after: a mug shot. It was black and white and a bit faded, but the images were of a clean cut young man, facing the camera full on and in profile. The faced looked familiar to Matt, but he just couldn't place it.

"Can I get a copy of this?" he asked.

"No problem," replied the officer. "Wait here. I'll be right back."

Davis paced back and forth. It was all starting to fit.

"If this guy was a priest, he'd have plenty of access to women," he thought aloud. "He could hear their confessions— Hell, he could even visit them at their homes. That would explain how he gets in—"

"Yeah," said Chris. "And even if he's not in our precinct, he could be getting a line on his victims from another priest—"

"Who wouldn't even know," said Matt.

Just then, the officer returned with the photocopy.

"Thanks very much for your time," said Davis.

"No problem," answered the policeman.

It was growing dark as Davis piloted the Impala east, along Interstate 80, back toward New York City. His mind raced feverishly, trying to put the pieces together. Meanwhile, Freitag snoozed quietly in the passenger seat, his head resting against the glass of the police cruiser. It was a time-tested arrangement; Freitag drove to, Davis from whenever they made one of these out-of-state excursions. It suited Matt fine. This way he could sort out all the information they had gathered, hopefully tying up the loose ends. Of course, there were more questions unanswered than answered at this point.

Why would Curran's tracks have suddenly disappeared almost forty years ago? If he was a priest, where was he located? In Manhattan? In one of the outer boroughs? Why would he be so careless as to leave his fingerprints? And *the New Testaments*? What about *them*?

Well, he thought, at least they had some direction now. First thing tomorrow, he would get in touch with the seminary. It was located upstate New York, near Elmira. Hopefully, they would be able to enlighten the police as to Curran's whereabouts.

The next day an army of plainclothes detectives began checking the personnel records of all the Manhattan parishes, in an effort to locate the mystery priest, named John Curran. In addition, every John Curran, who had a driver's license, and who was of approximately the right age, was checked out with Motor Vehicles. After three days though, and, to no one's surprise, they still didn't have a flesh and blood suspect. There *was* one priest located at a small church in Far Rockaway, whose name was *James* Curran, but it turned out that he was nearly eighty years of age, and confined to a wheelchair.

CHAPTER 56

R ita had been true to her vow, and had not been in a chatroom ever since the incident with Callahan. However, this evening she was feeling particularly lonely. She had tried calling Chris earlier in the evening, but after numerous rings without an answer, she remembered that he and Matt were out of town and hung up the phone. She tried watching TV, but nothing there really captured her interest. Finally, after hemming and hawing, she decided to log on to the Internet, but only "to see if good old Carl is there." Although she didn't think there was any future in a relationship with him, it might be nice to just "see" a friendly "face."

After wandering in and out of several of her old haunts without finding Carl, she decided to try one more "place." She located "Friends for Singles," and clicked her way in to the room. There was a heated discussion going on about the possibilities of another terrorist attack, and before long she had joined in the discourse, her promises to refrain chatting long forgotten.

Ever since discovering Rita Valdez's email address and screen name on the back of Detective Freitag's card, Father Pete had been obsessed with thoughts of the voluptuous female cop. Try as he might, he couldn't get her face and body out of his mind. He contemplated calling her, but decided against taking so direct a tact as being too risky. Then, it hit him. If she had a screen name, she just might be one of the many women who occupied those immoral chatrooms. He decided to do one of those "Who's Chatting?' searches, to see if Detective Valdez was online. If he couldn't have a relationship with her in the real world, he might at least be able to foster one founded upon fantasy.

His first attempt at finding Valdez was a failure. All of his usual "contacts" were there, but no Rita. Undaunted, he tried again, and on the second attempt, managed to locate her "Sexy39" screen name in an innocuous room called "Friends for Singles." He was using his "GolfNut1" screen name, and at first he was quite content to sit there in the dark and just watch. It appeared as if Rita Valdez was really just there to socialize, and not particularly interested in pursuing anything other than friendship. The few individuals who occupied the chatroom were discussing politics or some other inane topic, not particularly suited to Father Pete's interests. After watching Valdez for a while, Richter decided to test her "intentions."

Slowly, and more deliberately than usual, Father Pete typed his first words to the woman who had monopolized his thoughts, both sleeping and awake, in recent days.

GolfNut1: Excuse me. I just want to say hi to Sexy39
Sexy39: *And who are you?*
GolfNut1: Oh, just an admirer...that's all
Sexy39: *Do I know you?*
GolfNut1: No. At least, not yet...But, I'd love to...lol.
Sexy39: *What makes you think I'd like to know you?*
GolfNut1: Well...because most of the others usually do...until...well, never mind...they just do.
Sexy39: *Have we ever met?*
GolfNut1: I don't know. What do you think?

Valdez looked at the screen, and something inside her policewoman's brain registered a caution. This was the second time now that someone had contacted her like this. First it was Callahan, and now this *GolfNut1* guy. She decided to go with the flow, and see where it led. Ever since the Callahan "thing" had occurred, Rita had been considering whether Ken himself might not be the killer that had been terrorizing their precinct. Only a confession or conclusive DNA match would provide a satisfactory answer. However, in the meantime, with Ken in custody, and no distinct conclusion yet to be drawn, Valdez's thoughts now turned to other possibilities.

Surely, the Internet, with its myriad of chatrooms, represented a virtual smorgasbord of candidates for a killer like the one presently at large. Who knew, maybe *this* guy was the one they sought? Rita decided to throw up a trial balloon.

Sexy39: *Sorry, I was thinking about something....*

GolfNut1: So, what do you think about meeting people in person?

Sexy39: *What? Like you?*

GolfNut1: Yeah. Would you ever consider meeting someone from a chatroom?

Sexy39: *What did you have in mind?*

Richter had all he could do to contain himself. She was actually encouraging him. Maybe she really *was* a slut like all the others. But, how would she feel when she finally saw him, and realized who and what he was? Well, he'd deal with that then, he thought. *No use putting the cart before the horse.* He felt himself becoming aroused. It was all getting to be too much for him. Any pretense of self-control had long since been abandoned. He pictured the dark-haired beauty, and a shudder went through his body.

GolfNut1: What about meeting somewhere for a drink?

Here we go again, thought Rita. *This is what got me into trouble in the first place.* Then, she pictured those poor women, and her resolve strengthened. Maybe she could end this nightmare. Who knew if this was even the guy? *But, he could be.* She pondered the possibilities. It was a million-to-one long shot. But, what if her intuition was right?

GolfNut1: Is that a no?

Rita's mind raced frantically. *And, if it* isn't *the guy, then what?* What was the big deal? She decided to throw caution to the wind. *Damn Chris, why couldn't you be home?*

Sexy39: *I'm thinking...*

Another tease, thought Richter. *She's no different than all the rest.* Now, he was even more determined than ever to convince her to meet with him.

GolfNut1: Look...I'll even let you pick the place...someplace you're comfortable with. I won't bite...promise!

Rita looked at the latest sentence on the screen, and shook her head. She knew she shouldn't go any further, but just couldn't resist. *Oh well, here goes nothing.*

Sexy39: *And if we don't hit it off, we'll just say thank you very much, and that's it, okay?*

GolfNut1: Sure. Why not? Neither one of us wants to spend time with somebody who doesn't want to be there, right?

Sexy39: *Right! Okay, do you know where Manny's is?*

GolfNut1: I think so. Is that the place over on First Avenue?

Sexy39: *Yep, that's the one. It's on the corner of 20th. When do you want to do this?*

GolfNut1: Do you really want to know?

Sexy39: *Yeah, I know...tonight, right?*

GolfNut1: How'd you guess? But, seriously, how about Friday night?

Sexy39: *What time?*

GolfNut1: 7 o'clock alright?

Sexy39: *Better make it 7:30. You know how we women are...lol.*

GolfNut1: Great! See you then!

Rita started to type a response, but hesitated. *That's funny*, she thought, *how does he know what I look like?* Maybe this wasn't such a good idea after all? The whole situation was giving her the creeps.

GolfNut1: What's wrong?

Sexy39: *Oh, nothing...I was just thinking...*

GolfNut1: About what?

Sexy39: *What's your name?*

    Richter stared at the screen. It was really going to happen, he thought. But, he couldn't stop now, could he? Of course not. It was too late to turn back. He typed the words that would seal his fate.

GolfNut1: It's Pete

Sexy39: *How will we know each other?*

GolfNut1: Why don't we wear something special?

Sexy39: *Like what?*

GolfNut1: How about a hat?

Sexy39: *I have a Yankees hat...is that okay?*

GolfNut1: Well, I'm a Boston fan, but I guess it'll be okay...Only kidding! Actually, I'm a Yankee fan, too. Yankee hats are fine.

Sexy39: *Good! I'll see you at 7:30...Oh, what do you look like?*

GolfNut1: Never mind that...let's just say you'll be pleasantly surprised....

Sexy39: *Yeah, I'll bet...lol.*

GolfNut1: See you Friday...

Sexy39: *7:30 sharp! See you then...*

    They both logged off at the same time. Rita felt a quiver of anxiety go through her, and wondered whether she was making the right decision. *Oh, well, too late now.*

CHAPTER 57

8:45 a.m., Friday, May 19

T he phone rang four times before a soft-spoken male voice answered, "Glen Ellyn Seminary. This is Brother Timothy. How may I help you?"

"Brother Timothy, this is Detective Davis, Tenth Precinct, New York City, Homicide Division—"

"Oh my," said the gentle voice of the clergyman. "Is this about those religious murders?"

Matt was shocked into momentary silence.

"Hello? Are you still there?" asked Brother Timothy.

"Yes, I'm still here," replied Davis. "I'm—it's just..." he grappled for the right words. "Well, actually, you kind of took me by surprise. I mean, what would make you ask me that?"

"Well, I don't know," answered the brother. "I suppose because it's been all over the newspapers. Why else would you be calling here?"

"Well, you're right," said Matt. "I guess I just didn't expect you to be so up to date with the news and all—"

"Well," laughed the cleric, "We aren't monks, you know. We read the papers, watch television, and even use the Internet."

"Yes, yes, I'm sure," replied Matt. "Well, I guess the cat's out of the proverbial bag."

Both men laughed awkwardly.

"Yes, Brother," said Matt. "You're right. I *am* calling about those homicides. Unfortunately, we found fingerprints at each of the crime scenes that belong to an individual who appears to be a priest."

It was the clergyman's turn to be silenced.

"A priest that may have come from your seminary," added Matt.

"Well, what—"

"The problem," said Matt, "is that the individual in question has not been seen or heard from by anyone in the neighborhood in nearly forty years. We believe he may have attended your institution, but we don't know for sure."

"What makes you think so?" asked the brother.

"Well," said Matt. "We traced him back to his undergraduate school in Pennsylvania, and found a story about him in the school paper. An article about him reported that he intended to attend Glen Ellyn."

"I see," said Brother Timothy. "Well, it would be easy enough to check our records—"

"I was hoping you'd say that," said Davis. "His name is John Curran, and he would have been a first-year student in fall of 1965, and—"

"But," interrupted the brother. "I'm afraid it might take some time. You see, all of our records are on paper, and we don't have much of a staff—"

"Would it be too much to ask for us to come up and check the records ourselves?" asked Matt. "I promise we won't cause a commotion."

"Well, I suppose not" answered the clergyman. "Assuming, of course, that you had the proper identification and all. No, that would be fine. When would you like to come?"

"Well," said Matt, "If it wouldn't be too much of an imposition, we'd like to come right up. I figure it's, what, three-and-a-half, maybe four hours? We could be there by one, the latest. Would that be okay?"

"Certainly," replied Brother Timothy. "I'll make sure someone is available to help you."

"Thank you," said Matt. "We'll see you in a little while."

"Freitag!"

CHAPTER 58

12:56 p.m., Friday, May 19

C ontrary to their regular routine—Freitag driving to, and Davis from their appointed destination— Matt assumed the driving chore on the leg up to Glen Ellyn. He was wide-awake when he picked up Chris, and figured the driving would put his energy level to good use. The trip took about four hours, including a stop along the way for a quick breakfast at the Roscoe Diner.

With Matt at the wheel, Chris sat quietly, thinking back to when he and Davis were first assigned as each other's partner, while still in uniform. At first, they were a bit uncomfortable with one another. Davis was somewhat refined, a college man with esoteric hobbies: fly fishing and golf. Freitag, on the other hand, had only graduated high school. His interests revolved around basketball, bowling, and the occasional barbecue, complete with "a couple of cold ones." The only fishing he did was for bass—with worms—and he kept everything he caught. His new partner was into "catch and release," whatever the hell that was.

It wasn't until the two had been "partnered up" on foot patrol for nearly six months that the defining moment in their relationship had occurred. It would forever cement their friendship.

One evening, while "on the knobs" (running a security check of neighborhood businesses), Davis had noticed an alleyway door ajar to a local liquor store in their sector. Without thinking, Matt had left Freitag outside, and pushed open the door, surprising a burglar in the act of robbing the cash register.   The shocked thief had turned, and pulled a gun, catching Davis off guard, his own weapon still holstered at his side. The two stood at a stalemate, but it was obvious to Matt that he was in deep trouble. The thief motioned with his gun for Davis to enter a walk-in refrigerator, and followed behind him, with his gun jammed into the patrolman's back. Suddenly, Freitag entered through the open doorway, surprising the intruder, who turned and fired once, nicking Chris in the shoulder. Instinctively, Chris returned fire, a bullet striking the thief in the chest, killing him almost instantly.   Matt immediately rushed to his partner's side, pressed a handkerchief to the wound, and radioed for an ambulance.

Police procedure dictates an investigation by the Internal Affairs Division anytime a weapon is discharged by an officer. Davis and Freitag both knew that Matt's lack of proper procedure in entering the premises without his partner, and without having his weapon drawn, would probably result not only in a reprimand, but probably a suspension for Davis. Freitag, too, would probably be disciplined for allowing his partner to go into the building alone. So, before the ambulance arrived, Chris had worked out a plausible story to explain the shooting—and to clear his partner—insisting that both men stick to it with conviction when questioned by Internal Affairs. Not only had Freitag taken a bullet for Matt, but by solidifying their alibi, he had earned commendations for both, putting each on a fast track to their detective shields. Later on, when Matt divorced, it was Chris who helped him through the rough times. And, when Matt met Valerie, and announced that he was to be married for the second time, it was Freitag he asked to be his best man. That had been the lynch pin that forever solidified their friendship.

Now, as Chris reflected back upon that pivotal day in their friendship, he smiled broadly as he visualized how beautiful Valerie had looked, and how proud his partner had been of his new bride.   Suddenly, Chris's reverie was interrupted by the sound of his partner's voice.

"Finally," proclaimed Matt with a sigh. He had just spotted the sign indicating the approach to Elmira's city limits. Elmira is just north of the Pennsylvania-New York border, and is perhaps best know now for its parachute jumping. It was part of an industrial triangle—including Ithaca and Binghamton—that provided jobs for an area deeply in need of them. Today, work is scarce, and welfare is the prevailing source of income.

Glen Ellyn Seminary's elegant appearance belies its purpose, that being the education and religious preparation of its students to become Roman Catholic priests. The campus itself occupies approximately ten acres, with several granite buildings and a modest chapel sitting atop a hill overlooking the city of Elmira.   A high wrought-iron fence surrounds the property, interrupted only by a set of gates, held by two granite pillars. Today, the gates were open, and Davis guided the cruiser up a long, winding drive to a parking area adjacent to one of the buildings. He pulled the Impala into one of the spaces marked "Visitors," and nudged Freitag.

Chris yawned, and stretched his arms wide, punching Matt in the shoulder. "Good job," he joked.

"Yeah, yeah," said Davis. "You couldn't have done it better yourself, right?"

"R-i-g-h-t," said Chris.

An elderly man, dressed in street clothes, opened the door to the administration building, and showed the two men into the Spartan-like waiting room.   "Please have a seat, gentlemen," he said.   "I'll tell Brother Timothy that you're here."

The barren confines reminded Davis of his days as an altar boy in his own Parish, at St. Edward's, in Brooklyn. He fidgeted   uncomfortably   awaiting   Brother   Timothy's appearance, as he might have done in his youth, expecting a reprimand for talking during services. He had just closed his eyes when the gentle voice of the brother brought him to attention.

"Ah," said Brother Timothy, "so you are Detective Davis."

Matt popped to his feet. "Pleased to meet you, Brother," he answered.

"Likewise," offered Chris.

"This is Detective Freitag," said Matt.

"My pleasure," responded the cleric. He was a little man, probably under five feet-six, with close-cropped gray hair, and a slender body, encased by a cassock. Davis thought he looked a bit effeminate.

All three men stood there in awkward silence, until Brother Timothy finally broke the quiet. "Well, I guess you'd like to see those records," he said, his words more of a statement, than a question.

"Actually, yes," said Matt. "The sooner we get started, the better our chances of finding what we need."

"By the way, brother," said Matt. "How long does it take to get through seminary?"

"Well, it's hard to say," replied the cleric. "There's no real set timetable. Most generally finish in two years, but some take as long as three or four."

"Well," replied Matt. "We know he started in the fall of '65, or at least we think that's when he got here. I guess that's as good a place to start as any."

The two detectives were shown to a dimly lit room, containing row after row of dusty, metal filing cabinets. "Let me turn on some more lights," offered Brother Timothy. He flipped a couple of switches, and the room brightened considerably. "Everything is clearly marked, but if you need anything, Mr. Jefferson, our housekeeper, will be just outside. Please tell him what you want, and he'll be happy to assist you."

"Thank you very much, Brother," said Matt.

"Well, I certainly hope you find your man," said the clergyman. Then, almost as an afterthought, he added, "Even if he *is* one of ours. I read about those murders. Shocking – absolutely shocking."

It took over an hour to find John Curran's records. Everything was filed according to month and year, not alphabetically. Matt finally found the document that recorded the young man's attendance. Curran indeed did attend Glen Ellyn. As it turned out, John had finished his studies at the seminary in the summer of 1968. Certainly no big surprise there. And, he was ordained as a priest – as expected. Matt continued to read, and then stopped.

"Oh, my God!" he exclaimed.

"What is it?" asked Freitag.

Matt stared down at the document as if it were a poisonous snake, holding it at arm's length. "It's – it's – Richter," he stammered.

"Wha—"

"It's Father Pete," said Matt, so softly that Chris had to strain to hear the words.

"But—"

"He changed his name." Matt dropped the paper to the floor. Freitag stooped down, retrieved the document, and began to read. His partner stood by him in silence. There in black and white was the information they had been hoping for. It just wasn't what they had expected.

"I don't believe it," said Matt. "I don't fucking believe it."

Freitag looked at the piece of paper in his hand and shook his head. "Well, we always said it had something to do with religion."

"Yeah, but Father Pete?" said Davis.

"Hey, you know what?" said Chris. "I've been on the job long enough, nothing surprises me anymore—not even this shit."

"Look," said Davis. "We need to think this out carefully. I don't want to blow this."

"Yeah," said Chris. "I know what you mean. All we need is the Archbishop coming down on our ass when we arrest one of his boys."

"Never mind the Archbishop. It's the PC that worries me. Don't say a word about this when we get back," said Matt. "Especially to that jerk, Cohen, from the *Post*." Chris nodded in the affirmative.

"First thing we need to do is canvas all the neighbors. Show them a picture of Richter. Then, I'll reach out to a judge for a warrant," said Davis. "We're going to need a DNA sample, fingerprints, the works."

As usual, Freitag changed the subject to one of more immediate concern. "What do you say we get some dinner before we head back?" he said, his voice hopeful.

Davis stared at him, then smiled. "It's kind of early, isn't it?"

"Well, we didn't have any lunch yet," whined Chris, almost like a child trying for an extra helping of dessert. "And, I know you. If we wait 'til we get back to the city, we probably won't get anything—"

"Okay, okay," said Matt, in mock surrender. "You win. Besides, it's a good idea. I'm starving." Freitag's face brightened at the prospect.

Davis considered where they were, then quipped, "McDonald's or Burger King?"

"Fuck that fast food shit," laughed Chris. "If this is all I'm gonna get, I want to eat at a good diner."

CHAPTER 59

June 11, 1968

*P*eter Richter's first assignment as a priest had turned out to be his only assignment – St. Jude Roman Catholic Church in the Chelsea District of Manhattan. At the time, it was unusual for a first-year cleric to be sent to a parish as large and busy as St. Jude. However, the newly ordained priest had requested the posting when he learned of the vacancy from a fellow student whose parents lived in Queens. Since he had been such an outstanding theological student, it was generally accepted that Richter would fit in, regardless of where he was sent.

When he arrived at St. Jude, one of the first things he did was to hang the picture of his beloved Sister Francis in his room. Later, when he became the Monsignor at St. Jude, the picture was moved to the wall behind his desk, in the study at the rectory. No one ever questioned the identity of the woman in the picture, but it was generally accepted that it was a photograph of the priest's mother.

Almost from the start, Father "Pete" became known as a priest to whom the women of the parish could relate. It was a marked departure from his earlier relationships with women. Indeed, it could almost be said that Father Pete had become somewhat of a lady's man.

The metamorphosis was complete.

CHAPTER 60

It was nearly three-thirty by the time Matt and Chris finished eating. The ride back to Manhattan seemed to take forever. With Freitag at the wheel, however, Matt was free to explore every detail of the bizarre case. His mind churned away like a computer; moving files here and there, sifting through bits of information, saving some, and discarding others. He hated to admit it, but everything fit. Father Pete had the access. He certainly had the means, in fact, his athletic ability would easily have enabled him to overpower and strangle the victims. He thought back to their golf game. *Hell! He's even left-handed.* So, what was wrong? Why didn't he feel confident that they had the right man? The answer was simple: what was missing was motive. Why would a man in Father Pete's position want to murder five women right in his own parish? And, why would he be so careless as to leave his fingerprints *and* the bibles?

It just didn't make sense.

CHAPTER 61

7:10 p.m., Friday, May 19

R ita wolfed down the remains of her *Diet Gourmet* chicken dinner. A glance at the kitchen clock told her to get moving. She tossed the empty plastic plate in the trash, and quickly washed her utensils and glass, placing them carefully alongside the sink to dry.

What goes with a Yankee hat? Rita asked herself. She pulled open the bi-fold doors to her wardrobe closet, and began rummaging through its contents. Keep it simple, she thought. A blouse and jeans, maybe some running shoes. *Yeah,* she thought, *the old athletic look. Wait a minute,* she thought. *What am I, nuts? This guy could be a killer.* All she wanted to do was smoke him out – not turn him on.

She pulled a blue, short-sleeved blouse from the top rack. It was a relatively new one, a Patagonia brand, with pockets on the front. She removed the sweatshirt she was wearing, and slipped into the blouse. Rita smiled when she noticed how the two flapped pockets accentuated her more than ample breasts. What the hell, she thought, might as well give the guy a thrill – *before I bust his ass!* She unbuttoned the top two buttons, allowing a full view of her spectacular cleavage, then thought better about it, and closed one of the mother-of-pearl fasteners.

Lying down on her unmade bed, Rita shimmied into a pair of skin tight jeans that were worn thin across the buttocks, both by design and from use. She laced up her white and powder blue *Reeboks,* and retreated to the bathroom. A quick glance in the mirror assured her that her make up was still intact, her hair decent, and both earrings were in place. Valdez brushed her teeth, then rifled through the drawer of the small vanity, and found her *White Diamonds* perfume. *Nah. Oh, what the hell.* She dabbed a drop behind each ear, and dragged the glass stopper across her throat.

Rita grabbed up her purse and keys and started for the door. "Shit," she muttered aloud. "I almost forgot the damn Yankee hat. Wouldn't that be great? Walk in like an asshole, with no hat!"

She tucked her long hair up on top of her head and fastened it in place with a barrette from her purse. The Yankees hat was on top of the refrigerator, and she jumped up and grabbed it and slapped it onto her head all in one motion. She opened the door, exited, and locked it behind her, hurrying down the stairs to meet the night.

A light spring breeze threatened to lift the Yankees cap from Rita's head as she stepped down off the Number 23 bus at the corner of Seventh Avenue. With her free right hand, she pressed the hat close to her head; her purse secured in her left. She scurried down the three short blocks along the avenue to West 20th; waiting impatiently at each intersection for the crossing sign to show a little green "pedestrian." It seemed odd, meeting someone here, so close to the precinct headquarters. She smiled to herself as she passed the ancient building. Perhaps, someday, she thought, she could think of it as just a place where others worked.

Manny's Mexican Restaurant was one of the many indistinct eateries that decorated the lower Manhattan landscape like culinary shrubs, each one forgettable in its own right. In fact, the best thing that could be said about Manny's was that it was convenient to the job, and Bob, the bartender made a wicked frozen Margarita.

A flourish of trumpets, emanating from a small mariachi band—complete with towering sombreros—greeted Rita as she entered the restaurant. The lighting in Manny's was one step above movie-theater dark, and she had to squint in order to see. Gradually, she maneuvered her way to the rear of the restaurant, and was pleased to find an empty seat near the end of the bar. The mariachi band stopped playing; apparently it was break time. The bartender finished wiping the glass he was holding, and meandered over to Rita.

"What can I get you?" he asked.

"Hey, Bob, it's me, Rita," she laughed. Then, to further identify herself, she doffed the hat. "See?"

The portly bartender smiled when he realized who it was. "What are you doin'? Working undercover tonight, Rita?"

"Nah. I'm meeting a guy I met on the Internet," said Valdez. "We're both supposed to wear Yankee hats so we'll know who we are. Have you seen anybody else with a baseball hat on?"

"I dunno," replied the bartender. "I just came on a few minutes ago." He smiled and looked down at his hands. "I've been cutting limes for the last ten minutes. Here, smell." He held a large hand out for Rita to inspect.

Rita backed away instinctively. "Thanks," she said. "I think I'll pass."

Just then, the back door opened. "Looks like your date just came in," said Bob, nodding toward the rear of the bar.

Rita turned and looked at the fellow wearing the Yankees cap making his way toward her. An odd look crossed her face. The bartender noticed and inquired, "Anything wrong, Rita?"

"I'm not sure," she said, somewhat distantly.

The stranger approached the two, slid onto the stool adjacent to Rita's, and removed his cap. Reflexively, Rita removed her own, and stared in disbelief, with her mouth agape. *I know him.*

The man stared back at her. Then he smiled. "Is that *you*, Miss Valdez," he asked. *"You're* 'Sexy39'?"

The bartender looked at the couple, each one staring at the other as if they'd seen a ghost, and then walked away shaking his head.

CHAPTER 62

7:20 p.m.

D avis picked up the telephone then put it down. He hesitated, then picked it up again, and dialed. He needed to get a picture of Richter, and Archbishop Romero could probably provide one without alerting the suspect priest. Matt dreaded this conversation, and began rehearsing it in his head as he waited for an answer. *Archbishop Romero, this is Detective Davis, 10th Precinct. No, no,* he thought, *too cold.* He tried another tack. *Hello Archbishop, this is Matt Davis down at the Tenth Precinct.* Who was he kidding? *That's way too familiar.*

The archbishop picked up on the fourth ring. "Hello?"

"Archbishop Romero, this is Detective Davis, Tenth Precinct," said Matt, falling back on precedent. The cleric hesitated, unsure as to why the policeman would be calling at this hour of the day.

"Archbishop, are you there?" said Matt.

"Uh, yes, Detective. I'm here. What is it?" inquired Romero, a bit more abruptly than he intended.

"I'm sorry to bother you at this hour, sir, but something has come up and—"

"No, no, it's me who's sorry," the cleric apologized . "I didn't mean to be so unfriendly. It's just that you caught me a bit by surprise. It's no bother at all, I assure you. But, what's wrong?"

"Well, sir, I'm afraid I've got some bad news," said Matt.

"Not another murder?"

"No sir, thank God, not that. But, well, sir, I'm sorry to say that we believe we have a suspect." Davis breathed a sigh of relief.

"So, that's good news, right?" asked the archbishop.

"I'm afraid not, your holiness—"

"But, you said you had a suspect. I'm confused," said Romero.

"Well, sir, we do have a suspect." Davis took a deep breath. "I hate to have to say this – but, we believe it may be Father Richter down at St. Jude, and we—"

"I'm sorry, but did you say Father Richter?" said Romero.

"Yes, sir. I'm afraid I did," said Matt. "It's a long story, but we believe he may be the man we're looking for." There, he thought, the ice was broken. There was no turning back.

"But—"

"Would you possibly have a photograph of him that we could borrow?" asked Matt.

"Well," said the archbishop. "I don't know if—"

"I know it's hard to understand," said Davis. "But, believe me, I wouldn't call if we weren't sure."

There was a prolonged silence. The archbishop was obviously having trouble digesting the news. Matt pressed on. "About that picture," he began.

"Yes, yes, by all means," replied Romero. "I'll see what I can do."

"I'd really like to get it tonight," said Matt. Then, realizing he might be pressing a bit, he added, "That is, if it wouldn't be too much trouble."

"No, no. But, I'll need a little time," said the archbishop.

Matt looked at his watch, which showed seven-twenty. "Would a half hour be okay?" he asked.

"Yes, that would be fine," answered Romero.

"Good," said Matt. "I'll explain everything when I see you."

Davis hung up the phone, and stood up behind his desk. Suddenly he was very tired. He sat back down, and hunched over the wooden surface, his head in his hands. He stayed in that position for several minutes, until Freitag's voice roused him from his reverie.

"Matt? Are you awake?"

Davis rubbed his eyes and sat up erect, stretching his arms above his head. "Yeah, yeah, I'm just a little tired," he answered. "I got in touch with Romero. He'll have a picture for us in half an hour."

"Should I call the others?" asked Chris.

"Nah. Let's not get everybody all excited yet. I want to see what happens when we start showing the picture around."

"Good idea," replied Freitag.

"We better get going," said Matt.

The two men exited the building and headed for the archbishop's office.

The ride over to the archdiocese took about ten minutes. Along the way, Chris could hardly contain his enthusiasm. Davis concentrated on driving, while his partner chattered away.

"The way I see it," said Freitag. "It makes perfectly good sense. You know how screwed up all these priests are." He talked about the subject as off-handedly as if he were discussing a baseball game. Davis maneuvered the car through the cross-town traffic with a skill born of nearly twenty years on the job. He answered his partner with a nod. Freitag continued. "I mean, it would explain the bibles and—"

"Chris," said Matt. "I just played golf with this guy. I know it fits, but I just don't get it."

"Hey," said Chris. "Bundy was a doctor, wasn't he?" Then, unsure of his assertion, quickly added, "Or something like that. The point is—"

"What *is* the point?" asked Davis. He was trying to get a handle on this, and his partner's observations weren't making things any easier for him.

"All I'm saying is that, why couldn't it be him?"

Another nod from his partner told Freitag that Matt wasn't in the mood for this discussion. Chris stopped talking and gazed out the window in silence. Five minutes later they approached the archdiocese. Matt clicked on the flashers, and double-parked alongside a white Cadillac.

"Let's go," he said, hurrying from the car. "I want to get this over with."

Freitag followed his partner at a distance as the pair hurried toward the ornate entrance to the edifice. The doorbell's ring was answered almost immediately by a white-haired priest who showed the pair to the archbishop's office. Romero wore a grim look on his face as he greeted the two detectives. "Detective Davis," he acknowledged.

"Archbishop," replied Matt.

Davis wasted no time in getting right to the point. "I know it's late, sir, and we don't want to take up much of your time. So, do you have the picture?" asked Matt.

"Please, detective, first things first," said Romero. He raised his right hand like a crossing guard. "You promised to explain."

With a flourish of his other hand, he motioned the two detectives to a small table with several chairs around it. "Please, gentlemen, sit down."

Freitag did as he was requested, and seated himself. Davis remained erect.

"I know this is hard to believe," began Matt, "but, it all makes perfect sense."

"Please, detective," insisted Romero, "please sit down."

Reluctantly, Matt seated himself, and continued. "You see, at each of the murder scenes, we found many sets of fingerprints." The archbishop sat quietly, listening in stony silence.

"And," he went on, "each time, all of the prints were accounted for – except for one set at each scene – those that we traced back to a Jack Curran."

Romero looked puzzled. "But, what does that have to do with Father Richter?"

"Curran *is* Richter," said Davis. "He changed his name when he became a priest."

"And you think—"

"Yes, Father, we think that Monsignor Richter had the opportunity and the means to—"

This time it was the archbishop's turn to interrupt. "To what? To murder?"

"Yes," answered Matt.

"But why?" asked Romero.

"That's the only thing we haven't figured out yet," answered Davis. "We know he was orphaned as a very young boy. We also know he got into some trouble in college. In fact, that's how we found him."

"What do you mean?" asked Romero.

"Well, when we ran a trace on the fingerprints, it turns out that he had beaten up his girlfriend back when he was a student at a college in Pennsylvania. There was a pre-trial intervention, and the records should have been expunged—"

"Then how—"

"But, there was some kind of screw up and—" Matt stopped, realized his mistake in using the vernacular, and corrected himself. "Excuse me, Father," he smiled. "There was a *foul* up, and somehow the records remained on file. Otherwise we probably never would have found out."

"I see," said the archbishop, the sad facts finally sinking home.

"Anyway, everything fits," said Matt. "Even the fact that Father Richter is left-handed."

"That's right," interrupted Freitag. "Forensics says the killer is a lefty. Richter's the one, alright."

Davis gave his partner a look that said *knock it off.*

"What I mean," said Chris, "is that it certainly looks that way. That's all."

Romero stood and walked over to his desk. "Here," he said, sadly. "Here's the picture. I'm afraid it's not exactly the most flattering of pictures. I think it was taken about ten years ago. Do you think it will be sufficient?"

Matt looked at the picture. Although it showed Richter a bit younger than he currently appeared, it would probably do. "It's fine, Father," said Matt, accepting the photograph from Romero's outstretched hand. "I wish I were wrong on this one. I actually enjoyed his company."

"There are many mysteries to His way," said the archbishop. "We shall see what we shall see."

Davis patted the archbishop tenderly on the shoulder. "Thank you, sir," he said. "I wish it were someone else. I really do."

Freitag lowered his eyes as he mumbled a quick goodbye to the archbishop. Together, he and Davis exited the office, leaving the forlorn archbishop standing silently in the middle of the room.

CHAPTER 63

8:07 p.m.

R ita stared at the man in the light tan jacket. The lighting barely illuminated his face, so she moved slightly closer to get a better look. Suddenly, it dawned on her. It was Father Pete.

"Oh, my God – *Father Pete*," a look of astonishment crossing her face, "is that *you*?"

"I'm afraid it is," he answered sheepishly, "and I'm *more* than a little embarrassed."

Valdez shook her head back and forth. "No, no," she said. "*I'm* the one who should be embarrassed. I thought you were – well – never mind."

"I won't tell, if you won't tell," quipped Richter. "But, seriously – you won't say anything to anyone, will you?"

"I won't tell a soul," replied Rita. "Get it? A *soul*?" Richter frowned. "Okay – my bad," she said. "So, now what?"

"Well, I don't know about you, Miss Valdez, but *I* could really use a drink."

Rita reflected on Father Pete's offer. *Why not?* After all, he *was* only a man – and not a bad looking one at that. Take away the title, remove the collar, and beneath the clerical facade beat the heart of a red-blooded male – cloistered, perhaps, but a man nevertheless. She had always wondered what religious types did after dark, and now she knew – or, at least she knew what this one did. Rita decided to go wherever the evening took her. Besides, she reasoned, this man *certainly* wasn't a killer – a little *horny* perhaps, but no threat to her.

Richter shuffled uncomfortably on the stool. Then, as if suddenly remembering why they were there, he blurted out, "So, how about a frozen Margarita?"

"I think I could really use one," admitted Rita. She smiled warmly, and Father Pete relaxed a bit. *God, she's gorgeous*, he thought.

"So, you've really got that computer thing going, huh, Miss Valdez?" He was obviously uncomfortable with what to call her.

"Father Pete," she said. "Why don't you just call me Rita. Never mind that Miss Valdez stuff. Okay?"

There was an uncomfortable silence. This was probably the most awkward situation in which Rita had ever found herself.

"Look," said Richter, "this is probably a big mistake. Why don't we just have that Margarita, and then I'll see you home?"

They both turned toward the bartender, who, as if possessing a talent for reading peoples' minds, moved toward them, ready to take their drink order. "Two frozen Margaritas," said Father Pete.

"So, Rita, have you done this before?" he asked.

"You mean, meet with a stranger for a drink?"

Richter nodded.

"Well, to tell you the truth, no," she replied. "At least, not for a very long time."

The drinks arrived, and Richter took one and handed it to Rita. "So, what shall we toast to?" he asked, raising his glass.

"To silly blind dates!" said Rita.

"Better yet," added Richter, "to the Internet!"

The mariachi band was starting to play again; it was a slow, sensuous melody that begged to be danced to. The couple sat quietly. Richter broke the awkward silence. "How about just *one* dance?" he asked.

Why not?   The poor bastard probably hasn't danced since high school.   She stood, and extended her hand. "Okay, but just one," she said.   Richter took her hand in his, and gently guided Rita to the dance floor; she noticed his hands were sweating. "Don't worry," she said with a smile, "I won't bite. You *can* dance, can't you?"

"Well, it *has* been a long time," replied Richter.

Soon, they were dancing, the earlier awkwardness replaced by a growing familiarity. Bob, the bartender, watched them move around the dance floor, and thought they made a nice couple.

CHAPTER 64

7:41 p.m.

D avis held the photograph of the suspect loosely at
his side, as he and Chris made their way to the
car.   Once inside, Chris tapped his fingers
impatiently on the dashboard, waiting for his partner to speak.

"I *doubt* that we're going to get an ID," said Davis. "The
only one who saw *anything* was that old lady next door to the
Caruso apartment, and I really doubt that she's credible. I say
we pick up Richter now, and worry about the ID's tomorrow."
Freitag knew his partner had good instincts.   Besides the
obvious evidence of the fingerprints, there was no doubting that
Richter certainly had opportunity. After all, who wouldn't let
their neighborhood priest in?

"Oh, what the hell," said Davis, glancing at his watch,
"let's show her the picture."

"You got it!" said Chris.

In the first two minutes of the interview, the detectives
learned the following: Mrs. Milam was a widow; had four
children, and thirteen grandchildren; enjoyed Mahjong once a
week; had recently lost twenty seven pounds; and hoped that
she could help them "find that terrible man."

Finally, Freitag had had enough. He placed his hand
firmly on her somewhat flabby upper arm, and thrust the
photograph in front of her face. "So, what do you think? Does
this look like the man?" he asked.

The woman studied the picture carefully, all the while opening and closing her free hand nervously at her side. She frowned.

"What's wrong?" asked Davis.

"Well, I'm not sure," she said. "It could be him, but—"

Realizing that he was showing her a picture of a much younger Richter, Chris explained that the picture had been taken about ten years ago. "If you could, try picturing him older, you know, with gray hair and—"

The woman shook her head. "I don't know," she said. "I just don't know."

"So, it's not him?" said Chris.

"Oh, it could be," said the woman. "It's just that I'm not quite sure. I mean, I'd hate to make a mistake."

It was obvious to the two detectives that the woman hadn't seen a thing. Like many widows who lived alone, she enjoyed the attention – even if it involved a murder case. For her, this was like a Friday night date. They thanked her politely, and left her standing in the dim light of the hallway.

The police radio chattered incessantly, as the two detectives sat quietly in the front seat of the unmarked car; the white noise of the radio masking that of the passing weekend traffic.

Something was bothering Davis. "You know," he said to his partner. "I'm starting to have second thoughts about this whole thing."

"What do you mean?" asked Freitag.

"Maybe I'm too close—" said Matt.

"Shit, you know we can get a warrant," said Chris. "The prints alone—"

"Yeah, I know we can get a warrant, but—"

"So, let's get the warrant, and let's go get the cock sucker."

Davis scratched his head, considering his options. They could just get the warrant and go talk to the priest. Or, they could get the warrant, and make the arrest. Deep down inside he didn't want to believe the man was guilty. But, he'd seen other cases like this one before: an innocent- looking wife, ultimately found guilty of bashing her husband's head in with a clock; retired spinster school teacher poisoning her overbearing mother.

"Maybe you're right," said Matt. "Tell you what. Let's run it by Foster. If he likes Richter, we'll go with it."

"Sounds good to me," replied Chris. "If we go the warrant route, we ought to bring Martini, Wolinski, and Valdez along."

"Give the three of 'em a call when we get back to the station," said Matt. "I'll see if I can track down Foster."

In a few minutes, they arrived at the precinct. Freitag headed for his office to phone the other members of the squad, while Matt hurried upstairs to Foster's office. The lights were out, and he turned to head back down to his own office, when Davis heard Foster's unmistakable baritone voice.

"Davis, is that you?" he called.

"Yeah, boss, I thought you were gone."

"Nah," said the Captain, "I'm just catching a few Z's. I'm on a four to midnight."

"Yeah," said Matt. "Well, I'm glad you're here."

"Something happen?" asked his boss.

"I think we like somebody for the stranglings," said Matt matter-of-factly.

Foster sat up straight in his chair, all evidence of sleepiness gone. He flipped on the light.

"Come again?" he said. He and Davis blinked their eyes, trying to adjust to the light.

"It's weird," said Davis. "You know I've been working with that priest down at St. Jude, right?"

"Yeah," replied Foster. "He steer you to somebody?"

"I wish," said Matt.

"What do you mean?"

"It's *him* we like," said Matt, quietly.

"Him, who?"

"The priest."

"The priest? You've got to be kidding me!"

"I wish I was. You remember all those fingerprints belonging to a John Curran?"

Foster nodded in the affirmative.

"Well, for a while we hit a dead end. But we finally traced them all the way back to an assault and battery case in the sixties in Pennsylvania. That's where Freitag and I went last week."

"Okay, so what's the connection?"

Davis spent the next ten minutes detailing the unraveling of the mystery concerning Richter, before Foster finally stopped him.

"Okay, okay, I get the picture," he said. "Let's get a warrant and pick the guy up."

"Tonight?" asked Matt. He was still in denial.

"No time like the present," said Foster. "I'm not giving this guy another chance. Get the rest of your people, and I'll reach out to Judge Marcus in Manhattan South for a warrant. He owes me one."

Davis grabbed the portable phone on his desk, and dialed his home number. Valerie looked at the caller ID on the phone, and answered on the first ring. "Hello, who is this?"

"You picked that phone up pretty quick, lady. Expecting somebody?" quipped Matt.

"Yeah, my secret lover boy."

"Well, I hate to disappoint you," he said. "But I'm afraid he's going to be late." Matt had promised to be home early, and it was already going on ten.

"How come?" asked Valerie, disappointment showing in the tone of her voice.

"He had a better offer," said Matt, with a laugh.

Valerie was not amused.   "Seriously, honey, you promised to come home early tonight.   Can't whatever it is wait?"

"I'm afraid not, Val. We had a real break in the case. You'll never believe what happened."

Valerie wanted to be as excited as Matt appeared to be, she really did. But all she felt now was disappointment. She took a deep breath, blowing the air out slowly between her pursed lips.

"Val?"

"Yeah, yeah, I'm here," she said. Trying hard to sound excited, she said, "Okay, I'll bite. What happened?"

"Remember what you said about it probably being some horny old priest?"

"Uh huh," she replied.

"Well, you were right!"

Valerie sat up straight. Now she really was interested. "You're kidding! Really?"

"Nope," said Matt. "And you'll never believe who we like."

"Who?"

"Father Pete."

"Father Pete? I don't believe it!   What made you suspect *him*?"

"We didn't. You know how we went up to Glen Ellyn? Well, when we finally found Curran's records, they showed that he had changed his name when he took his vows. Curran is Richter."

"That's incredible. So, what are you going to do, arrest him?"

"Yep," said Matt. "Foster's getting the warrant right now. Then we're going over to St. Jude to make the collar."

Valerie giggled. "That's funny," she said.

"What's funny?" asked Matt.

"Oh, nothing. It's silly—really. I just had this stupid thought – a little gallows humor."

"Tell me," he said.

"Well, it's just that, you know, you're going to make the collar—on the *collar*."

"V-e-r-y funny."

"Who would've ever thought it," said Val. "I'm sorry it turned out to be him," she said. "I know you kind of liked him and all." Then, not wanting to dwell on the subject, she added, "I guess you'll be late, huh?

"Yep."

"Any idea what time?"

"No clue. Even if everything goes perfect, it'll be after midnight, maybe later."

"Well, we'll leave the light on for ya." It was her standard line whenever Matt worked overtime.

"Thanks, honey," he said. "But, seriously, don't wait up, okay?"

"We'll see." Davis knew what that meant. No matter how late he came home, Val would always be waiting to greet him.

"I love you, Val," he said.

"Love you, too, honey. Be careful."

"I will," said Matt. He hung up the phone just as Foster appeared in the open doorway.

"Okay, Matt," he said. "We're all set. Marcus came through for us. He'll fax over the warrant in a couple of minutes."

"Good. I'll get the rest of my guys, and as soon as you've got the warrant we'll go." Davis buzzed Freitag. "Get a hold of Martini, Wolinski, and Valdez. Tell 'em we'll pick 'em up on the way over to St. Jude."

CHAPTER 65

8:45 p.m.

R ita and Father Pete shuffled lazily around the miniature dance floor, barely noticing that the mariachi band had stopped playing. The effects of just one drink on Rita were noticeable, and she leaned heavily against the priest, who had a high tolerance for alcohol. What Rita didn't realize was that while she was visiting the Ladies Room, Richter had slipped a dose of Rohypnol into her second drink. He had never used drugs before – but, tonight was different. Realizing that he couldn't take any chances, he talked a local junkie into getting the drug for him, in exchange for salvation – *and* two crisp twenty-dollar bills. Now, the "date rape" drug was taking full effect, and he knew he had to move fast.

"I really think we should be getting you home, don't you think?" said Richter, his heart pounding in anticipation.

"My place or yours?" giggled Rita. Her tongue was thick with the effects of the Rohypnol, and the words came out slurred.

"Well, actually, I thought I'd just see you home – what with my – uh – *situation* and all," said Richter.

"Let's just have one more eensie – weensie drink," slurred Rita. "I promise I won't tell." Richter had all he could do to contain himself. He ordered two more Margaritas, paid the tab when they arrived, and left Bob a hefty tip. He downed his drink in one swallow, and waited patiently while Rita slowly sipped hers. *Can't rush*, he thought. *God, I wish she'd hurry up.*

Five minutes later he helped her out the front door. Anyone watching the couple would have thought they had known each other for years. The sky was clear, and the temperature had dropped appreciably. Rita snuggled against Richter, in an effort to get warm, and he waived at several passing taxis, before successfully stopping one with an illuminated vacant sign. He gave the Middle Eastern driver Rita's address, and relaxed back into the seat alongside Valdez, who was nearly asleep.

In a little while, the cab pulled to the curb in front of Rita's apartment building. Richter shook Valdez gently, "Hey, Rita, we're home."

"Wha—?" Cobwebs filled her head from the brief sleep in the taxi, along with the effects of the Rohypnol and the alcohol from the Margaritas. Richter paid the driver, and helped Rita from the vehicle. Together, they wobbled up the stairs to her apartment. He waited while Rita fumbled in her purse for her house keys.

"Oh, shit," she said. "I forgot my hat."

Oh great, thought Richter. He could imagine what would happen if they went back to the bar now. She'd sober up, and probably change her mind. It was early, and he still had big plans for the rest of the evening.

"So, get it tomorrow." His mind was racing madly. "Tell you what," he offered. "I'll pick it up tomorrow, and drop it off to you."

"You promise?"

"Yes, yes. I promise. You have my word as a gentleman." He couldn't resist giggling at the absurdity of it all. "If I don't get it, I'll give you mine."

"I don't want yours," she pouted. "I want mine."

"I promise, I'll get it."

"Okay. But, if you don't—"

"Hey, what is this? Our first fight?" he laughed. *Just like all the rest,* he thought. *Why do they always have to make it so hard?*

"I'm sorry," she said, her voice barely a whisper. "I didn't mean to be a ball buster," she sighed. The drug was working rapidly.

There was no time to waste, thought Richter. He laughed nervously to himself. He wasn't sure how to act. He had never done it like this before. It had never been planned; it had just happened. Women made him so damned uncomfortable. *Christ, now what do I do?*

Rita unlocked the door, and stumbled through the opening. The light was blinking on her answering machine, but she didn't bother checking her messages. "I'll just make us some coffee," she offered. Those drinks had really been strong, she thought. *I've just got to wake up.*

Richter was shocked – no, elated would best describe what he felt – at how well things were progressing. It was too good to be true. He squeezed his eyes shut tight, then opened them again. Everything was still just like it was a second ago. Rita was just standing there, looking fantastic, waiting for him to close the door. So he did. And when he did, his hand brushed across her breast, causing her to stiffen. *Oh God, now I've done it.* He hesitated, then feeling a need to do something – anything – he kissed her hard on the mouth. She gasped for breath, and broke free.

"Hey," she said, "That's not supposed to happen. You were just going to see me home, and—"

"And do what – just be a good boy and go home?" said Richter, a hint of angry sarcasm in his voice. He grabbed Rita, and kissed her again – hard enough to cut her lip.

"Hey!" she shouted. "What the hell are you doing?"

Rita turned on the light.

Oh shit, said a voice in Richter's head, *now I really screwed it up.* And then, another voice sounded from deep within the recesses of his mind – a much louder one this time. *You're already screwed* – Jack – *you might as well enjoy it!*

"Yes, yes, I know it," he whispered back. "I will. I promise."

Rita looked at him with a puzzled expression. "What did you say?" she asked.

You don't owe her any explanations, Jack, said the voice in Richter's head. *She's just a cunt – like all the rest. Tell her nothing!*

"Look, Father, I think you better leave – before this gets really out of hand." Rita turned on the light, caught the wild look in his eyes, and realized it was already too late. Suddenly, she was more frightened than she had ever been in her life.

"You're just like all the others!" shouted Richter. Without warning, he slammed his fist into Rita's face, knocking her to the floor; she tasted blood inside her mouth. A second punch, an uppercut, caught her under her chin, and knocked out a tooth. She felt as if she might lose consciousness; her head was swimming. Richter stood over her, his hands at his sides. Rita's service revolver was inside her purse on the table by the door. If she could only reach it, she might have a chance. But, before she could make a move, Richter reached down and yanked her to her feet by her hair. He was incredibly strong, and she knew that her only chance was to convince him that she wasn't a threat.

She never got the chance.

CHAPTER 66

Freitag reached Martini on the second ring. He told him to be outside his apartment in five minutes. Wolinski sounded tired, but also agreed to be ready.

When he called Valdez, the phone rang unanswered for five rings before the answering machine picked up. *Boy, will she be pissed when she finds out we went without her,* he thought. *Oh well, that's the way it goes.* He started to hang up, and then changed his mind and decided to leave a message. "Hey, Rita," he said. "It's Chris. We're heading over to St. Jude to pick up Father Richter. We'll tell you all about it when we see you." He hated talking to a machine. He hesitated, then added, "Hey, if you get this message, meet us over there as soon as you can." Then, he hung up and headed out the door.

Foster sat alongside Matt in the seat usually reserved for Freitag, who sat crunched up in the backseat. Chris's long legs nearly rested against his chest, but he knew better than to protest. Davis drove quickly toward Martini's place; the magnetic police light affixed to the car's roof flashed brightly against the dark of the night. They had agreed not to use the siren; no point in alerting Richter, who probably wasn't even aware he was a suspect.

Martini was standing in front of his apartment building, wearing a puzzled expression when Davis pulled the cruiser to the curb.

"Just get in!" shouted Freitag, as he swung open the back door, and slid over to permit Martini to enter, all in one

practiced move.   Martini plopped down next to Chris, and
slammed the door barely in time, as Davis wasted no time in
powering the car out into traffic, tires screeching in protest. A
few minutes later, they picked up Wolinski.

"So, what's the story?" asked Martini. Freitag filled
him on the details. Like everyone else, Martini expressed his
disbelief, not bothering to spare the expletives.

"Holy shit! You gotta be fuckin' kiddin'," exclaimed
Wolinski.

"Nope," said Chris.   "Richter's the guy alright.   I
couldn't believe it either, but it all fits."

It was eight-thirty when Foster, armed with the faxed
copy of the search warrant in his left hand, rang the doorbell of
the rectory with the other.   Davis, Freitag, Wolinski, and
Martini stood in a row behind the Captain. In a moment, the
darkness   inside   and   outside   the   building   were   erased
simultaneously, as a light within the foyer was turned on, along
with one outside the front door.   Davis and Foster stood side-
by-side as the white-haired housekeeper answered the door.

"New York Police Department," said Foster, flashing his
shield. "We need to see Father Richter immediately."

The woman began to respond, but before she could speak,
a voice rang out behind her, "Who is it, Mrs. Flynn?" It was
Father Anthony.

Davis and Freitag looked past the woman at the young
priest. "Father Anthony, we're looking for Father Richter. Do
you know where he is?" asked Matt.

The priest appeared confused.

"Sir, it's imperative that we speak with Father Richter."

"But, why?" asked the priest, his voice filled with
confusion.

"I'm afraid we're not at liberty to answer that," replied
Freitag.

"But, I don't understand," said Father Anthony.

"That's not important," said Matt. "Right now, what's important is that we find Father Richter. Now, can you please tell me where he is?"

The young priest's face turned red.

"You *do* know where he is, don't you?" asked Freitag.

"Y-y-es, yes," stammered Father Anthony, "well, not exactly." He leaned close, and whispered into Matt's ear. "I think he has a – well – a date. My God, this is all so – embarrassing.

He turned to the elderly housekeeper. "Mrs. Flynn, could you excuse us for a moment?"

The housekeeper started to leave, shaking her head and mumbling under her breath.

"What did you say?" asked Matt.

"Oh, nothing," she said. "It's just that I knew this was going to happen some day."

"What do you mean by that?" asked Matt.

"Well, it's all about that Internet stuff, isn't it?"

"What do you mean?" asked Freitag.

Mrs. Flynn looked furtively left and right, then, apparently satisfied that there were no hidden cameras, leaned close to Matt and whispered in his ear. "He goes in those—you know—chat rooms. He doesn't know that I know, but one time he fell asleep and I saw—"

"Where does he have his computer?" asked Davis.

"Why it's in his study," replied Father Anthony, "but—"

"Don't worry," said Matt. "We have a search warrant permitting us to search the premises. I give you my word that he won't know a thing."

"Well, I hope not. I wouldn't want him to think—"

"We just want to look around a bit. Chris, go to Richter's study and get his computer. Look for any floppy disks or CD's, or anything that might have to do with the Internet." He turned back to Father Anthony. "Do you have any idea with whom – or where?"

Father Anthony shook his head. "I'm sorry. I would never have known, but I happened to be looking for something in his study, and saw—"

"Matt, you better get in here!" It was Freitag, calling out from Richter's study.

Davis started for the study, then turned to Father Anthony. "You do understand, Father. It's very important."

Father Anthony nodded his permission.

"Thank you."

When Matt entered the study, Freitag was holding the business card, with Rita's Internet information on the back, in his hand. "I'm afraid it's my fault," he said, handing the card to Matt. "I'd have never given it to him if I realized it was this one," he said. "Take a look at this." He pointed to a slip of paper resting on Richter's desk. On it were scrawled the words: "Rita – Friday night – Manny's – Don't forget to wear Yankee hat!"

"Son of a bitch!" said Matt. "Do you think she has any idea who she's dealing with?" He was already starting out of the study, on his way out of St. Jude. Freitag followed behind.

"You know," said Freitag. "She's a lot smarter than any of us gives her credit for. Maybe she already had a hunch, and smoked him out on the 'net'."

"Let's get over to Manny's," said Matt. "You know where it is, right?"

"Yeah," said Chris. "It's over on First Avenue, by 20th."

"I just hope we're not too late," said Matt.

Foster, Martini, and Wolinski were standing in the foyer, when Matt and Chris exited the study. "He's meeting Rita at Manny's – over on First Avenue," said Matt to Foster. "You, me, and Chris'll ride together." Foster nodded. "Martini – you and Wolinski gather up the computer and anything that looks important: discs, papers – notes – whatever. Take 'em back to headquarters, then meet us at Manny's."

CHAPTER 67

Driving over to the Eastside bar, Freitag pictured Rita with Richter, and cursed himself for not keeping her more in 'the loop.' "If that son-of-a-bitch touches a hair on her head," he said, "I swear I'll—"

"Just calm down," said Foster. "I doubt he'd do anything stupid. Remember, he doesn't even know we're on to him yet."

"Yeah," said Matt, "we'll just walk in nice and quiet like. Pretend we're just there for drinks."

Freitag glided the car up to the curb, and immediately jumped out, his hand instinctively reaching for his gun.

"You wait here," said Foster. "Matt and I'll go inside. If he makes a break, grab him."

"Remember, nice and easy does it," said Matt. "We don't want anybody getting hurt – least of all, Rita."

Foster nodded his approval. "Let's get inside," he said.

The first thing Matt noticed upon entering the front door was the absence of patrons. For a Friday night, things were unusually quiet. He scanned the interior quickly, then approached the bartender, who was busy polishing glasses. He flashed his badge, and spoke quietly to the man across the bar. "I was just wondering – have you seen a guy and a gal wearing a Yankees hat tonight? He'd be on the tall side – sixty-ish?"

"Oh, you mean Rita." he replied. "Yeah, sure. They were *both* wearing them – in fact, she left *hers* here," replied the Bartender. "She said it was a blind date – some guy she met on the Internet. The hats were probably some kind of a sign so they'd know each other. *Rita's* a regular here. *Him* I don't know."

"Did they leave already?" asked Foster.

"Yeah, about twenty minutes ago," replied the bartender. "Anything wrong?"

"Don't know," said Matt. "Do you know where they were headed?"

"No, not really," said the bartender. "Sorry, but I wasn't paying much attention. One minute they were here, dancing; next thing I know they're gone."

Matt had already started for the door.

"My guess, they went to *his* place – or *hers!*" shouted the bartender, with a laugh.

Matt broke into a trot. Foster had to run to keep up. "Where are we going?" he shouted at Matt's back.

"Rita's apartment!" shouted Matt. "Richter might be nuts, but he's *not* crazy. Guaranteed he's headed for her place."

Freitag stood by the car, a worried look on his face. When he saw Foster and Davis come running out the front door of Manny's, he immediately jumped behind the wheel and waited for his partner's instructions.

"Head over to Rita's apartment – and call for back-up," said Matt. He flipped open his cell phone, and dialed Valdez's phone number. After five or six rings, he heard Rita's familiar voice on the answering machine. He waited for the beep and then left a message. "Rita," he said. "It's Matt. I've got something really important to tell you. Be very careful tonight. I'll be in touch ASAP." He didn't want to be too specific, just in case Richter was there with her; he prayed he wasn't.

CHAPTER 68

9:15 p.m.

R ichter stiffened as the shrill ring of the phone located next to the bed, jolted him back to reality. He stared wild-eyed at the instrument as it rang five times, then stopped. "Nobody's home!" he shouted. He turned his attention back to Rita, who was moaning softly beneath him. Suddenly, he heard the recorded voice of his prisoner coming from the answering machine in the other room, as it instructed the caller to leave a message. Richter waited to hear whether or not there would be one, and then, to his horror heard Davis's familiar voice begin to speak. He listened intently until Matt had finished, and then screamed a reply of his own: "Fuck you, you son of a bitch! I'll show you what I can really do!"

In a fit of rage, Richter reached over and yanked the phone wire from the wall. Rita tried to speak, but the weight of his body kneeling on her chest limited her ability to breathe, or to cry out; any movement was entirely out of the question. The sound of the phone had brought with it a faint measure of hope, but it was fading quickly. If anything, the call had only served to push Richter further beyond the brink of self control, and he lashed out angrily in response to the intrusion by striking her hard in the face with his open hand. "Son of a bitch!" he screamed again at his captive. He withdrew a small penknife from his pocket, and used his teeth to extract the blade from the body of the weapon.

Oh my God thought Rita, as she finally realized the horrible truth: *it's him!* She tried to struggle, but in response,

Richter brought the shiny blade to her face. "If you make one move I'll kill you," he said. He was looking around the room for something to tie Rita to the bed with.

Valdez knew she had very little time if she was to have any hope of surviving. Her mind raced wildly; she had to act fast. She knew she was taking a chance, but it was the only one she had. She had to try to convince Richter it was over. If he had *any* connection left to reality, *maybe* he'd stop. If not, she thought, it wouldn't matter. *I'll never see Chris again.* Tears began to stream down her face; her mascara formed dark streaks on her cheeks.

"Father Pete," she pleaded. "It's not too late. You need help. You're sick. The church will help. You *don't* have to do this."

A crazed look flashed across Richter's face. "No, *you're* the one who needs the help. You made a big mistake!" he screamed. "You thought you could just play your little game – and watch Jack suffer. Did you think Jack would just put up with it? I tried to convince him you were different, but *he* knew – you're just like all the rest of them. You're no fucking good!" He dropped the knife, and began punching the helpless woman with both fists, using her head like a punching bag. Then, just as suddenly as he had started, he stopped and looked down. Valdez was unconscious.

"You cunt," he whispered in her unhearing ear, "now *Jack's* gonna give you just what you deserve." He jumped off the bed, and began flinging open the drawers of her dresser, throwing garments in every direction. He needed something to tie her up with. At last, he located what he was looking for – some loose stockings. He grabbed a pair, and quickly bound each of Rita's arms to the bedposts. He pulled off her Reeboks, and then yanked her jeans roughly down across her hips, and past her feet.

He needed something to tie her feet with. Retrieving the knife from her chest, he cut the elastic waistband of her panties, and yanked the garment from her body, scraping the flesh above her navel in the process. Angry red welts sprang up on the soft flesh. "Fuck you!" he shouted, and he flung the knife against the wall, from where it clattered to the floor. Then, he used the panties to tie her left leg securely to the post at the foot of the bed. With both hands, he grabbed the front of Rita's blouse, and pulled with all his might – buttons flew in every direction – as he ripped open the material.

Without hesitating, he grabbed the collar of the blouse, and yanked it over her shoulders, pulling the garment free. In a moment, he had secured her other leg to the right post at the foot of the bed. He removed one of her abbreviated socks and jammed it roughly into her mouth, breaking the soft skin of her lower lip, which began to bleed almost immediately.

"Okay, bitch," he said. "Now we'll just see who's in control."

He had very little doubt that it was he.

CHAPTER 69

9:22 p.m.

"Still no answer," said Matt. "I'll try again in a few minutes."

Freitag's fingers beat a nervous tattoo on the steering wheel, as he raced toward Rita's apartment. Foster was on the police radio, calling for back-up.

Matt opened his cell phone again, quickly dialing his home number. Val answered on the second ring. "Matt, what's happening?" she asked. "I tried reaching you at headquarters, but Hard-on – well, it seemed like he knew something, but didn't want to tell me. Is everything okay?"

"I wish I could say 'yes,'" said Matt, "but, it's not. Richter's got Rita."

"Rita?" said Val. "What do you mean?" Negative thoughts of Matt's evening out with the female detective filled her head. "I don't get it. What's *she* doing with *him*?"

"I can't explain now," said Matt. "But, don't wait up. It could be a long night."

"But, Matt, what if—"

"I'll call you when I can. I gotta go." Matt closed his cell phone just as the big Impala pulled up in front of Rita's apartment building on East 23rd Street.

"Jesus," said Foster. "You'd think she could find a better place to live than this dump. I guess she's still waiting for that knight in shining armor on a white horse." He immediately regretted his remarks as neither Matt nor Freitag said a word, underscoring the gravity of the situation.

"Why don't you two wait here," said Matt. "I'll go up and see what's—"

"No way!" said Chris. "I'm coming with you."

Foster nodded. "I'll stay here until back-up arrives. Don't take any unnecessary chances. We'll have plenty of manpower in a couple of minutes. I don't need any dead heroes."

The two partners started up the stairs, Matt in front, Chris not far behind. It appeared few residents were at home, due the beginning of the weekend. Davis and Freitag arrived at the second floor, and Matt reached out and rang the bell to Rita's apartment. No answer. They waited a few seconds longer, then heard a loud crash within the apartment. Chris knocked frantically on the door, calling, "Rita, are you okay?"

CHAPTER 70

R ichter pressed his erect penis hard against Rita's vulva, trying to force the engorged organ between the dry outer lips of her vagina. The female detective had regained consciousness, and squeezed her thighs together as tightly as she could, denying him access to her genitals. She squirmed with all her might, but it was no use. Seconds later she felt Richter enter her. She closed her eyes, willing herself not to feel anything. Richter began thrusting deeper and deeper, grunting and straining toward his inevitable climax.

What if he has AIDS? What difference does it make? When she heard the doorbell ring, she thought, *Fuck you, you son of a bitch. I'm not making it easy for you.* With every ounce of strength she possessed, Rita bucked her hips hard against her intruder. He momentarily lost his balance, and as he swung his arms out to the side to right himself, he knocked the lamp to the floor. It made a loud crash, and the room was plunged into darkness. Now, she heard the unmistakable sound of her partner's voice calling her name. *In here, Chris. I'm in here.*

Through the haze surrounding her senses, Rita heard Chris's voice call out again. *He must have heard the lamp*, she thought. *Oh God, Chris, please—please help me!* She had always said she didn't believe in mental telepathy, yet here she was desperately trying to communicate by the very method she had previously decried. *I'm in here, Chris,* her mind screamed – but to no avail. *Help me! Help me!*

Matt drew his revolver from beneath his jacket. He stepped back from the entryway, and with one efficient kick of his right leg, separated the cheap wooden door from its hinges. The apartment was pitch black. He called out into the darkness, "Rita? Are you alright?"

Valdez heard his voice. *In here, Matt. I'm in the bedroom,* she screamed inside her head. Richter rolled off Rita's body, his erection shrinking immediately. He pulled his pants up from around his knees, and buckled his belt. He needed to find the knife, he thought. But it was dark. Desperately, he groped for the lamp on the table. He lost his balance, and stumbled forward making contact with the piece of furniture. "Shit!" he yelled, pain radiating throughout his lower leg. Using his left hand to steady himself, he leaned his chest on the top of the nightstand, and carefully reached down to the floor below. Feeling around with his right hand, he finally located the little knife.

"Stay here," whispered Matt to Freitag, "in case he gets past me." He crouched low, feeling his way along the perimeter of the apartment's living room, one hand tracing the cool surface of the wall, as he made his way toward the noise coming from the bedroom. He didn't want to risk turning on a light in case Richter had a gun. Holding his breath, Matt sensed, rather than felt the opening to the bedroom. He could hear Rita moaning, and decided he had to make a move. Slipping his hand inside the doorway, he found the wall switch for the ceiling light, and flipped it on, dropping immediately to his knees as the room erupted in light.

Richter turned around, saw the detective crouched on the floor, and swung his right foot hard, separating the revolver from Matt's hand. As Davis tried to get back to his feet, the priest slashed wildly with his left hand, and caught Matt firmly on the neck with the blade of the knife. The pain was incredible, and as Matt reached up to his neck in response, Richter tried to get past him the bedroom door.

"Watch it, Chris!" shouted Matt. "He's got a knife!" At the same time, he felt warm blood begin to spurt from the cut on his neck. "Shit!" he yelled. He was losing blood fast, and could already feel himself growing lightheaded. He reached out and grabbed one of Richter's legs, pulling him to the floor. The two men struggled briefly, but Matt was losing blood rapidly, and with one final effort, Richter managed to free himself. With his head swimming wildly, Matt reached down to his ankle holster for his gun. As he did, Richter rose from the floor and rushed out of the bedroom, towards the living room. Sitting in a pool of his own blood, Davis raised his weapon and fired blindly at the retreating figure. He continued to fire, until he was out of bullets. Then, everything went black, and he collapsed into unconsciousness.

When Freitag heard the shots, he crouched low, and leveled his service revolver toward the bedroom. Richter came charging out, catching him by surprise, and knocked him to the floor. In the blink of an eye Richter was out the door. Knowing Foster was covering the downstairs entrance, Chris got up and rushed into the bedroom, nearly tripping over Matt's unconscious form. He saw Rita on the bed, and thought, *Oh my god, she's dead.* He turned back to his partner on the floor. Blood spurted freely from a huge gash along the side of Matt's neck. Freitag kneeled down, yanked a handkerchief from his pocket, and pressed it against his partner's neck. With his free hand, he felt for a pulse. A faint, rapid beating told him that his partner was still alive, but barely. He reached for his radio. "Officers down. Need medical assistance immediately. 225 East Twenty Third. Make it fast!"

Valdez lay on the bed, just clinging to life. All Chris could do was pray.

Outside, Foster heard the unmistakable sound of gunfire. He immediately reached for the two-way radio on his belt. He scanned the front of the building for its address. "225 East Twenty Third Street! Shots fired!" he shouted into the mouthpiece. "Officers need assistance!" He jumped out of the car, and started up the stairs, revolver drawn. Halfway up the stairs, he saw a man race out of the apartment, a knife held in his left hand. Foster aimed and fired once. The bullet slammed into the wall, just inches from the man's head. The man whirled and started up the stairs toward the rooftop.

Foster hesitated at the top of the landing, then made a right, and rushed into the open apartment. He felt along the wall by the door and found the light switch. He flipped it on, and was surprised to find no one there. Fearing the worst, he shouted, "Freitag? Davis? Valdez?"

"In here!" shouted Chris. "It's Matt. He's hurt bad!" Foster hurried through the apartment, and into the bedroom. Freitag continued applying pressure against the wound on his partner's neck. Blood was everywhere.

"It's really bad," said Chris, when he saw Foster. "If we don't get him to the hospital fast, I don't think he's gonna make it. I already called the paramedics."

Foster untied Valdez's hands and feet from the bed, then gently removed the sock from her mouth. "Are you okay?" he asked the semi-conscious woman.

Rita's eyes filled with tears, and she nodded her head up and down weakly in response. Her voice was barely audible as she asked, "Did you get him?"

"He's on the roof," said Foster. "Chris'll stay here with you and Matt until the paramedics get here. I'm going after Richter."

"Be careful," whispered Rita.

On the rooftop, Richter ran wildly about, searching in vain for a way out. A low concrete wall about three feet high encircled the perimeter of the rooftop. He was trapped. *What should I do, Jack?* He looked up at the sky for guidance. There was none. He opened his mouth and howled like a wounded animal in the jungle.

Foster heard the noise just as he was opening the steel door to the rooftop. He stopped dead in his tracks, and cocked his gun. Then, slowly, his revolver held tightly in his hand, he slipped through the doorway, and peered into the blackness. As his eyes adjusted to the darkness, he saw the figure of the man with his back to him, silhouetted against the night sky. Foster took a step forward, his feet crunching on the gravel and tar roof. Richter turned toward the noise, and spotted the detective.

"Give it up, Father," said Foster, in a voice as cold as ice. "It's all over."

Richter saw Foster, and raised his hands, dropping the knife. "Don't shoot me, please," he said timidly.

Foster kept his gun leveled at the suspect's chest, approaching him cautiously. "Down on the ground!" he shouted. "Down on the ground! Now! Arms where I can see them!"

Richter did as he was told. Foster reached behind his back for his handcuffs, all the while keeping his revolver aimed at the suspect. "Okay," he said. "Put your hands behind your back, nice and slow." Richter obeyed, and Foster quickly secured the handcuffs to his wrists. "Okay. On your feet," he commanded.

Foster yanked hard on the man's left arm in an effort to force him to stand, and as Richter stood, the detective relaxed his grip for just an instant. Instantly, Richter swiveled around and drove his shoulder into Foster's midsection, knocking him off his feet. The police captain landed hard on the rooftop, losing his grip on his gun, which fell to the ground, landing between the suspect and him. Realizing that the weapon was useless to him with his hands cuffed behind his back, Richter kicked hard, and sent the gun tumbling across the rooftop. Foster turned, and when he did, the priest sprinted into the darkness, disappearing behind a maze of chimneys and vent pipes. Foster cursed to himself, and strained his eyes in an effort to adjust his sight to the blackness of the night – but, he couldn't see a thing. His heart pounded a steady stream of blood against his eardrums, the noise all but drowning out any sound that might have revealed Richter's location. Then, a scraping sound to his right caught Foster's attention. Was it a shoe brushing the rooftop gravel? Or, perhaps just a rat? He crouched even lower, and crept slowly toward the sound, feeling with his hand along the roof's surface for his gun, while never taking his eyes off his invisible target.

There was a gap between the building he was on and the adjacent tenement. It was only about ten feet wide, but he figured that if a man took a good running leap he could probably make it across. Just as Foster's hand found the revolver, and his fingers closed around its grip, he heard a sound to his right that caused him to turn. Richter came flying past him from out of the darkness, actually brushing his arm as he ran by. Foster raised his gun and fired at the receding shadow, but apparently missed. The man continued running, sprinting toward the low wall. Foster stood up, and charged after him, shouting, "Halt!" as he struggled to aim his gun.

With a loud scream, Richter pushed hard off the surface of the rooftop, and vaulted through the night air like an Olympic broad jumper – his legs pumping furiously in an effort to assist his improbable journey to the other side. At that moment, Foster slipped on the gravel surface, and his gun discharged with a loud roar and a flash of light as he tumbled to the ground. He felt the flesh on the palms of his hands tear, and his face smashed into the rough surface of the tar and gravel roof. He swore to himself and retrieved his gun, before scrambling to his feet. He stared into the darkness, across to the other rooftop, hoping to see the man. There was no one there. Maybe he'd hit him? He couldn't be sure. Foster hurried over to the edge of the rooftop and looked down. Below him was Richter's body, impaled, face up, on a wrought-iron fence, several sharp pieces of metal protruding through his chest as he lay staring up at the detective with unseeing eyes.

A shudder coursed through Foster's body. He knelt down on the asphalt surface and vomited. A crunching noise behind him made him turn. It was one of the responding uniformed officers. Wiping his mouth with one hand, and motioning toward the edge of the roof with the other, Foster said, "He's down there."

"Are you okay?" asked the cop.

"Yeah, just great," said Foster. "How's Davis?"

"They're taking the Lieutenant to the ER. It doesn't look good."

"Did they leave yet?"

"No, but, if you want to go with them, you better hurry."

Foster pulled a handkerchief from his pocket and wiped his mouth, raising himself to his feet. "How's the woman?" he asked.

"She's banged up pretty bad; it's probably fifty-fifty that she makes it."

Foster hurried across the rooftop and down the stairs to the street to find the paramedics carefully placing the stretcher with Davis's unconscious body on it, into the ambulance. "I'll ride with Matt," he told Chris.

Another ambulance pulled up, and two paramedics carefully loaded Valdez aboard. Several uniformed officers were busy placing yellow crime-scene tape around the perimeter of the building. Freitag glanced down the alleyway and saw Richter's lifeless form still suspended in mid-air atop the fence in the alley between the two apartment buildings. No one seemed to be paying much attention to it. That suited Chris just fine.

"Come on, let's get a move on!" shouted Freitag to the EMT inside the ambulance. "I'll ride with her." He clambered aboard the ambulance, and seated himself alongside Rita's semi-conscious body. The other paramedic got in, and slammed the door behind them.   Instantly, the ambulance lurched forward, lights flashing, and sirens blaring, headed toward the hospital.

CHAPTER 71

A long with opening a four-inch wound on Matt's neck, Richter's knife had nicked the carotid artery, the main blood supply to the brain; the detective was sinking into a deep coma. One technician maintained steady pressure on Davis's neck, just managing to stem the flow of blood, as the other EMT struggled to insert an intravenous drip in order to provide much-needed saline to the detective's body tissue. He checked Matt's blood type on the medical card he found inside the detective's wallet, then called ahead to the hospital.

"We've got an ALOC; our ETA is ten minutes!" he called into the two-way radio in contact with the ER at Cornell. "We're going to need at least three, maybe four units of O Neg. BP is eighty over fifty; pulse is rapid and weak – probably a hundred and twenty."
Foster sat alongside Davis, holding his hand and watching helplessly, while the two EMTs struggled to keep him alive. Matt's skin was cold and clammy, and Foster feared the worst. "Can't this thing go any faster?" he asked the nearest technician. The young man just stared straight ahead, lips tight.

"Sorry," said Foster. "Just hurry up, okay?"
Less than five minutes later, the ambulance slammed to a stop outside the Emergency Room entrance. Instantly, the doors to the rear compartment were yanked open, and several orderlies took hold of the stretcher and lowered it to the ground. Foster ran alongside the gurney, as it was wheeled into the building.

The news that an injured detective was being transported to Cornell had been picked up on police radios throughout the borough, and several uniformed officers were waiting when the ambulance arrived. One of the patrolmen asked Foster, "Is he going to make it?"

"How the fuck do I know!" shouted the police captain. "He's lost a lot blood." Then, he stopped and turned toward the cop. "Look, he's a good cop, and it doesn't look good. Just say a prayer."

The procession of medical personnel, Davis on the stretcher, EMTs and Foster rushed past the admitting office window, until they reached the double doors leading to the Trauma Unit. A young doctor, dressed in green scrubs met them, and raised his hand like a crossing guard.

"I'm sorry sir, but you'll have to wait out here," he said. "We'll let you know how he's doing as soon as we get him stabilized." Foster watched helplessly as Matt was wheeled inside, the doors closing with a "whoosh."

Fighting exhaustion, Foster went to a pay phone and tried to call Valerie, but the line was busy. He guessed she already knew, but he kept trying until, at last, the line was free.

"Val, it's Ed – Foster. Matt's been—"

"I just heard," she said. "Chris called me. I'm leaving for the hospital now."

"I'll be in the waiting room—," but Valerie had already hung up the phone.

Foster settled into a red, molded plastic chair, and absently picked up a medical journal. He took one look at the periodical, closed his eyes, and let the magazine drop onto his lap. He was asleep in less than a minute.

Thirty minutes later, Foster awoke with a start. A hand was resting firmly on his shoulder. He looked up and saw Valerie Davis standing alongside him, a drawn look on her face.

Foster was too afraid to ask the only question on his mind; his eyes asked for him.

"It's too soon to tell," said Val. "It took over 75 stitches to close the wound. Thank God, his carotid artery was only nicked. It's a miracle he's still alive. He's lost a lot blood." Val was doing her best to appear brave, but Foster could tell she was barely holding on. He put his arm around her shoulder. "Is he awake?" he asked.

Valerie shook her head. "He's in a coma—a deep one. The doctors say if he makes it through the night, there's a good chance, but—"

"But what?"

"He may have some loss of function—short term memory, that kind of thing."

Foster put his head in his hands, and started to cry quietly. Val patted him on the shoulder. It's not your fault, Ed," she said. "I heard what happened. There was nothing you could have done differently that would have made a difference."

"I swear, Val. If I thought there was any chance, I would have never let them go up there alone. We thought—"

"I know what you thought. Matt told me about Richter, but nobody expected this. Look, Ed, there's no point in you staying here all night. Go home and get some rest. You must be exhausted."

Foster stood up, leaned over, and gave Valerie a long hug. "I'll be back tomorrow. If there's any change, call me right away. Please."

"I promise."

As Foster slipped through the automatic doors to the outside, he turned back to see Valerie disappearing down the hallway toward the ICU. He took a deep breath, and opened the door of a blue and white that was waiting to take him to the precinct. He had a lot of loose ends to tie up.

CHAPTER 72

It was a little past one in the afternoon, the next day, when Freitag returned to the hospital. He had stayed with Rita until he was certain she was out of danger. He had barely slept at all. He walked into the ER waiting room, looking for Valerie, but saw no sign of his partner's wife.

"Excuse me," said Chris, flashing his detective's shield. "My partner was brought in last night with a stab wound. I'm looking for his wife, Mrs. Davis?"

"I believe she's upstairs with her husband," answered the volunteer at the visitor's desk.

"Can you tell me his condition?"

The woman fingered the computer keyboard, her long nails making a clicking sound as she tapped in the information. At last, she found what she wanted. "Still critical I'm afraid. He's still in ICU."

"May I go up?"

"Well, it's supposed to be 'family only,' but if you're his partner—"

"Thanks," said Freitag, who was already halfway down the hallway.

"He's in room 312 in Intensive Care – third floor."

"I know, I know," said Chris, as he sprinted to the elevator.

The elevator doors slid open, and Chris was immediately aware of the unique characteristics of the ICU. The first thing he noticed was the lighting; it was bright and efficient, with little thought to appearance. Nurses and technicians manned remote monitors, measuring everything from blood gases, and blood pressure, to heart function and brain activity. Outsiders observing the ICU command center might liken it to the bridge of an ocean liner.

Chris followed the arrows and numerals painted on the walls, and easily found Davis's room. Inside, Valerie was sitting quietly beside her husband, who lay in a coma, attached by a two-pronged tube in his nose to a supply of oxygen, hidden in the wall. An intravenous connection taped to his arm fed Matt nourishment; while numerous leads attached to his body collected and transmitted vital information to the command center.

Valerie's eyes were closed, so Chris cleared his throat to alert her to his presence. She stirred and opened her eyes, which immediately traveled in the direction of her husband's bed.

"Val," whispered Freitag. "It's me."

Valerie turned, and seeing Chris, smiled. "Hey. How are you doing?"

"I'm fine, Val. Any change?"

"Nothing yet. He's still in a coma."

Chris stood quietly, staring down at his partner.

Val reached out and rubbed Freitag's arm. "Did you get any sleep?"

Chris nodded yes. "You?" he asked.

"A little."

"Why don't you go get yourself something to eat? I want to talk to my partner."

Valerie smiled at the euphemism, stretched her arms over head, and stood up. "Maybe that's not a bad idea. Do you want me to bring you back some coffee?"

"Sure. Light with—"

"I know—two sugars." Valerie knew Chris almost as well as her husband. She bent over and gave Matt a kiss on the cheek, then left the room. When he was sure she was gone, Freitag sat down, taking Val's place alongside Matt's bed.

"Well, partner," he began. "We sure screwed this one up, didn't we?"

Davis remained motionless; his eyes closed tightly, breathing easily with the aid of the supplemental oxygen. Chris thought his friend could just as well have been asleep, if it weren't for the heavy bandages covering the side of his neck, which served as a reminder of his true condition.

Now, as Chris sat quietly by his partner's hospital bed, all the memories of their partnership washed over him in a tide of emotion. He said a silent prayer, then began to speak quietly aloud, as if by some miracle Matt could hear his every word.

"I guess you know it really *was* Richter," said Chris. He was fighting back tears.

"We got the DNA back on that Callahan character. Definitely not a match with the stuff we got at those crime scenes. Richter's the guy, alright. I guess it won't matter much now, but I'll lay odds that Richter's will be a dead match."

Chris laughed quietly at the irony of what he had just said. "Dead match. Get it? Richter's dead, but the DNA matches." He squeezed Matt's hand tightly. "Seems this Callahan had a history of mental problems, way back to the early 70s. He was in and out of the VA hospital. He had this thing about burn scars on his face from 'Nam. Get this – the guy didn't have fingerprints either – got burned off by Napalm or something. Poor bastard never went out, never had anything to do with women in person—except for Valdez. He already knew *her* from his job – delivering groceries for Atchison's. She was one of his customers. At night, he hung out on the Internet; bopped around the chat rooms. Hell, he's the one hooked up Rita's computer. Ain't *that* a bitch—"

Suddenly, Freitag was overcome with emotion, and began to sob quietly. "Matt, I'm so sorry. I should've never let you go in there alone." He cried openly now, his hands shaking uncontrollably.

With great effort, he managed to continue. "And, poor Rita. If it wasn't for me, that horny bastard never would've got a hold of her either. It's all my fault; giving that son of a bitch that card. What the hell was I thinking?

"Of course, if Rita hadn't been such a smart ass, trying to catch that prick by herself, maybe she wouldn't be upstairs with a busted jaw." Then, with tears streaming down his face, Chris added a disclaimer. "Who am I kidding? Nobody in their right mind could have ever figured that priest for those murders."

Freitag looked down at his partner almost as if he half expected him to respond to his remarks. Then, Chris took a deep breath, and continued. "All those other women—well, it looks like he got to all of them on the Internet, too. We checked their computers, and found his screen name on their Buddy Lists."

Freitag stopped talking for a minute, and concentrated on Matt's face, straining to catch a glimpse of anything—anything at all— that would indicate that his partner might be hearing him. But, all he saw was Davis's calm countenance, eyes closed, deeply asleep, unable to wake.

"Too bad Rita had to take a beating to make the damn collar. She's in pretty bad shape, but they say she'll make it. Probably put in her papers, though. Can't say that I blame her. Funny thing was," he continued. "There really wasn't *any* religious connection at all, *except* that the other women were all members of Richter's church. The old 'Catholic Guilt' thing got the best of them, and they called Richter for counseling about their 'so-called' cheating. He underlined the passages in the bibles when he went to see them, but who the hell would have ever thought to get *his* prints for comparison?"

Chris stood up and stretched his arms over his head. "Of course, I guess if we had, we might have figured him for Curran a lot sooner. Funny thing is, if it hadn't have been for Rita we might never have caught the prick.

"Apparently the Good Father spent a lot of time in those chat rooms. We talked to his housekeeper, and she admitted that she found his computer left on once – tuned to some porno site – some pretty nasty stuff."

Here, Freitag lowered his voice in a mock whisper, "My guess is he was into cyber sex. Probably liked to whip his 'Willie' while he talked to the ladies. Guy was a fuckin' *'perv,'* if you ask me."

Chris was so deep into his one-sided conversation with his partner that he failed to notice that Valerie had returned. She stood quietly in the doorway, holding a container of coffee. She waited a few seconds before moving closer. "Chris," she whispered quietly, "here's your coffee."

Freitag turned around. "Yeah, thanks. I was just telling Matt how it all went down."

"Well, I think that's great. At least there won't be any more women wearing unwanted hearts on their bodies." They both smiled uneasily. Chris sensed that Valerie wanted to be alone with her husband, so he got up, took the coffee from her outstretched hand, and started for the door.

"You're leaving?" asked Val.

"Yeah," said Chris. "Thanks for the coffee. But, I think it's better that I leave you two alone. I want to go check in on Rita. Call me when he wakes up, okay?"

"I will."

CHAPTER 73

Matt had been in a deep coma for over six days. Occasionally, there would be faint signs that maybe he would come out of it. But, the doctors cautioned Valerie that it could be quite a while – or *maybe* not at all. That was her worst fear.

…As usual, Matt was the guest of honor at a retirement dinner at the Waldorf Astoria. He and Valerie danced the night away, he in a finely tailored tuxedo, she in an exquisite gown. The Chief of Police got up and toasted Matt's many years on the force, and, of course, paid tribute to his solving of some particularly heinous murder.

Following the affair, they spent the night at the Plaza Hotel—courtesy of the NYPD—and the next morning boarded a jet for a flight to New Brunswick, Canada. Once there, they were met by a professional salmon-fishing guide, who escorted the two of them to a remote camp on the Miramichi River. A red-jacketed butler showed them to their room, remarking off-handedly, that "the fishing has been quite good lately."

The following morning, after an elaborate breakfast, it was time for fishing. Back at their room, all the necessary gear had been arranged on a trunk at the foot of the bed, and Matt dressed carefully, while Valerie read her book. There was a knock on the door, and their guide announced that they "better hurry," as the fish were "jumping all over the pool."

They stopped at the kitchen, where the cook gave Valerie a wicker basket, containing their lunch, along with a thermos of hot coffee. Then the threesome walked a short distance to the river, where Matt proceeded to catch fish after fish.

It was nearly noon. Matt stood knee deep in the cool water, the passing river forming an eddy behind him. His rod was bent with the weight of a large salmon that was hooked securely in the corner of its mouth by the hand-tied fly that Matt had presented to it just moments ago. With an eye out for the fish, Matt glanced at Valerie, seated on a blanket on the shore. She was deeply absorbed in her romance novel. Suddenly, she lifted her eyes and turned them toward the water, and smiled when she noticed Matt gazing lovingly at her.

"Sweetheart," she said. "Why don't you stop fishing and come join me for lunch?" He pointed downstream at the jumping fish, and said, "As soon as I land this salmon." The guide removed the net hanging from behind his vest and moved into position just downstream from the salmon. "I'll net him for you, sir. That way you and the Mrs. can have your lunch..."

Val sat quietly alongside her husband's hospital bed staring absently at the wall, her thoughts focused on Matt. *What will I do without him?* Then, she thought she heard a noise. She turned her head toward the bed and saw a sight that made her heart jump. *Oh my god.* Tears cascaded down her cheeks. But, now the tears were for joy. Matt's eyes were open – and he was smiling. At long last, Valerie could smile, too.

AFTERWORD

I once was lost, but now am found..." *(Lyric from Amazing Grace, a traditional hymn)*
          A number of years ago Al Gore (so we are told) invented the Internet, and its introduction to civilization changed the world forever. It has brought positive change to some; to others it has brought chaos and moral decay. As The Twig Is Bent explores the dark side of this modern force – the ancillary world of chat rooms. These ersatz "meeting halls" are the ultimate playgrounds for those who eschew personal contact in the real world, opting instead for anonymous "connectivity." Many have wandered in, and have been swallowed up by the Internet and its chat rooms, where they remain as prisoners of their own device. Others have merely passed through the shadowy world, ultimately seeing the light, and exiting scarred but wiser for the experience. I am one of the fortunate ones.

ACKNOWLEDGEMENTS

I began this book nearly fifteen years ago, and some of those who helped me along the way are doubtless not with us anymore. Some names have been lost or misplaced, but they know who they are, and to those individuals I would express my profound thanks. In particular, I am indebted to NYPD detective Bob Fiston, whose official rank I am unable to recall, and for that I apologize. He gave generously of his time in answering my every question, no matter how inane, and helped me lend authenticity to my novel..

My thanks to my friend, the "real" Chris Freitag, a retired police captain, who graciously permitted me to use his name for one of my characters, and whose advice and expertise were particularly useful, and to his wife, Susan, a nurse, who helped with technical medical information. I would like to thank two very special friends: Rick Dawley, who took my first draft to Mexico, and spent precious hours in the sun reading it, and "Bobcat" Walker, who never refused to read and re-read the various chapters, revisions, etc., that I thrust upon him, while always offering to read more. Thank you to my son, David, who, after reading the original draft, pronounced it "pretty good!" (strong praise, if you knew him).

Also, I would like to acknowledge the unwavering support and encouragement of my high school friend and "unofficial agent," Tom Connor, whose words of praise for my work kept me writing and hoping all these years. Thanks to Jane Cavolina for her editing skill. A big "I love you!" to my wife's uncle, Vahan Gregory, noted author and playwright, who motivated me to publish online.

A special thanks to my brother, Gene, who helped me find lots of "little" mistakes, and one big one that really made a difference.

And, lastly, a wink and a nod to Victorian novelist, Edward Bulwer-Lytton, 1st Baron Lytton, who wrote in the beginning of his 1830 novel Paul Clifford, *the now famous words "It was a dark and stormy night," which allowed me to finally make a start.*

RAVE REVIEWS FOR

ESCAPING INNOCENCE

A Story of Awakening
by
Joe Perrone Jr.

3507961